PROJECT ARMA

NYSSA KATHRYN

Cover by Dar Albert at Wicked Smart Designs
Edited by Missy Borucki

Created with Vellum

The heart doesn't forget...

The memory of that day still haunts Shylah Kemp. Eden had asked her to wait for him, to remain at the safe house while he went on a mission. But when she learned he was being setup, she didn't have a choice. She had to do something.

It was a risk...and Shylah paid dearly.

Eden Cole is not the man he once was. Not since returning from his mission to find his whole world changed. Being betrayed by his own government would change any man. Betrayal by the woman he loved—that nearly broke him.

When his woman suddenly shows up in Marble Falls fourteen months later, Eden is determined to learn why Shylah had disappeared without a trace...and put an end to the danger that's followed in her wake.

ACKNOWLEDGMENTS

As always, thank you to my editor, Missy Borucki, for being my right hand throughout the process of each book I release. I would be lost without you.

Thank you to my sister Jana for beta reading my books even when I give you ridiculous deadlines.

Thank you also to my wonderful husband, for your never-ending love and support.

1

Fourteen Months Ago

Shylah Kemp pressed her foot down harder on the accelerator.

Her eyes darted to the clock on the dash.

Twelve noon.

She had sixty minutes. Sixty minutes to achieve the impossible.

There were so many times in her life that she'd squandered sixty minutes. Gardening, watching a movie, reading a book.

If she could pull all those minutes back and add them to the sixty she had now, maybe she wouldn't be so nervous about being too late.

No. Shylah pushed that idea to the back of her mind. She would not be late. She couldn't be.

Because that would mean she would lose him, and if she lost him, that would destroy her.

Swerving to miss a cyclist, Shylah cursed. Swallowing a sob, she fixed her eyes to the road again. She had to hold it together.

She loved him so much. Too damn much. In such a short

time, Eden had burrowed his way into her heart. Now she couldn't picture a life without him. It would feel empty.

Her heart beat a million miles an hour, and the sweat built on her brow, but she pushed it all down. She could freak out once she'd saved him.

It had only been yesterday that Shylah had watched Eden through her rear-view mirror as she'd driven to his safe house. He should have been safe.

What a load of shit. She should have known he wouldn't be safe. Not with the people they were fighting against.

Shylah's hands clenched the wheel harder as the frustration ate at her.

Pulling into the spot closest to the door, Shylah sat for a moment and took a breath. If she entered the building looking like she was about to have a panic attack, someone would notice that she was somewhere she shouldn't be.

As calmly as possible, Shylah stepped out of her car and walked to the entrance of the building that housed Project Arma. She had the plan worked out in her head. Whether she could pull it off was another thing.

After stepping into the building, Shylah's feet froze. The hall was empty. Silence greeted her where normally there were people, voices, footsteps. There should be the hustle of people getting things done.

As she took a couple of hesitant steps, an eerie quiet filled the space. Each step echoed through the halls, like giant stones hitting the water.

Where was everyone? They couldn't have found out about the raid, could they?

Shylah's heart felt like it would beat through her chest.

Today was the day the government was raiding the facility. Every last soul who had something to do with Project Arma was to be arrested.

It would be hard to arrest people in an empty building.

Then another thought hit Shylah. Would the computer still be here?

Before she could think twice about what she was doing, her legs started running. Speeding down the hall, Shylah didn't care about the threats she might run into.

It was the same hall she'd walked down every day for the last few months on her way to medical, but this time it felt ten times longer.

Arriving at the door, she pushed through and her breath caught.

All the cabinets were empty. The room was trashed. Someone had made to get all the evidence out and out quick.

Turning her head, she breathed a sigh of relief.

A small reprieve. The computer still sat in its usual spot in the corner.

Moving over to it, she powered it up, clenching her hands to stop the nervous tapping.

When the screen lit up, Shylah entered the password. Her fingers trembled so badly it was surprising she could press the right keys.

Clicking into the email browser, she entered the commander's details. She'd seen him use them a couple of times when he'd come into medical, and Shylah had memorized the login in case she ever needed it. That she would ever use it had seemed absurd to Shylah.

At this moment, she couldn't be more grateful she had.

Diverting her eyes to check the time again, her heart stuttered.

Thirty minutes.

She had thirty minutes, or he'd be dead.

Swallowing some of the fear, Shylah breathed a sigh of relief when the email browser finally loaded. Opening a new message, she addressed it to all eight members of Eden's team.

SEAL TEAM 6 — ABORT MISSION. RETURN TO MISSION BASE IMMEDIATELY. COMMANDER HYLAR.

Clicking send, Shylah pulled her fingers from the keyboard as if it would burn her if she kept them there a moment longer. Shoving her hands between her thighs, she tried to control the shaking.

Eyes remaining glued to the screen, Shylah waited for a response. Willing the screen to show one. Leaving this room without confirmation that Eden was safe was something she couldn't bear.

Just when Shylah thought the nerves would consume her, a response came in. It was Mason.

AFFIRMATIVE. HEADING TO BASE NOW. EAGLE.

Releasing a shaky breath, Shylah scrunched her eyes closed.

Oh god. She'd done it. He wouldn't die today.

As the adrenaline eased from her body, Shylah leaned over the desk and dropped her head into her hands.

Eden was safe.

Standing on shaky legs, Shylah turned toward the door but stopped in her tracks. Blocking her exit stood Commander Hylar and Doctor Hoskin.

Oh crap. This was not good.

She worked with Doctor Hoskin every day. He was a key player in the corruption of Project Arma.

Then there was Commander Hylar. Eden's commander. She'd never had proof, but always suspected the man was just as corrupt.

All blood drained from Shylah's face. She hadn't even heard them walk in.

Eyes lowering, she stared at the gun held in the commander's hand. Pointed right at her chest.

Gazing back up to their eyes, pure evil stared back at her. She'd hoped for Eden's sake that she'd been wrong about the commander. Eden had seen him as a father figure.

"Shylah Kemp, how nice of you to join us. I see you've come in on your day off."

Trying to focus on the commander's words, and not at the loaded gun pointed straight at her, she straightened her spine.

"Just shoot her and let's get out of here," the doctor said in a hurry, fear clouding his eyes.

"I guess we have you to thank for all this?" the commander continued, ignoring the doctor's words.

It took a couple of attempts to make her voice work. "All of what?"

Eyes narrowing, the commander's body visibly tensed. "Don't play dumb, Shylah. We know you sent the information."

They knew?

"How . . . how did you find out?"

"About the raid?" Both of the commander's brows raised like it was a ridiculous question. "We have a far reach here. So much further than you could imagine. They won't shut us down. We'll relocate. Continue our work. What we've achieved is too valuable. Soon, everyone will want this."

Shylah's heart broke for Eden. So definitely not innocent. "Eden saw you as a father figure. How could you do this to him and the team?"

"Do what? Give them a chance to become unstoppable? Shylah, do you know what they are capable of now? They are faster and stronger than just about any other species in the world. They can see in any conditions, recover from injury in a split second. They can hear noises from ridiculous distances. They are the ultimate weapons. I gave them that!"

"Shoot her, they'll be here any moment," the doctor pleaded, desperation leaking from his voice. His eyes darted to the hall.

"You didn't know this version of the drug would work, or the effects of the next."

Shaking his head, the commander almost looked bored. "Exactly. Imagine if they became even stronger, faster. Sometimes these things are worth the risk."

These "things" being Eden's life and his teammates.

There was no reasoning with this man. He was power hungry and saw no problem in risking people's lives if the end justified the means.

"Is that why you tried to have him and his team killed on their mission today?"

The commander visibly flinched. "What are you talking about?"

"The government officials got in contact with me this morning to tell me they intercepted information that their mission was a suicide mission. That's why I'm here. To save them."

The fury in the commander's eyes sent fear into Shylah. Then his body turned to the doctor and pointed the gun at his chest.

"You tried to kill my team?" The commander's voice was hard. Deadly.

Sweat dripped down the doctor's head as his eyes widened. "It wasn't me. It was them. They didn't want any evidence."

The sound of the gun going off echoed through the room, causing Shylah to cry out.

As she watched the doctor fall to the ground, blood flowed from his chest.

Bile rose in Shylah's throat. He was so still. His eyes stared at the ceiling, lifeless.

"That was a mistake on their part. I appreciate your help on that matter," the commander said before he paused as footsteps sounded from the hall. "That's my cue to go."

A scream left Shylah's chest as another gunshot sounded. Rather than hit her, the bullet hit the computer.

Shylah watched as the machine went up in flames. Then the gun swung back to Shylah. She saw his fingers tighten just before he pulled the trigger.

Diving behind the bed, Shylah's body hit the cabinet. Searing pain from her left shoulder pulled her attention. Turning her head, she noticed thick blood running down her body.

She'd been shot.

Breaths coming out faster, Shylah heard the commander's footsteps as he moved closer to her. At the same time, the boots in the hall became louder. Closer.

Would they get here in time to save me?

She watched as the commander immediately changed direction and headed for the window. Jumping onto the frame, he was almost out when he turned.

Shylah's breath shuddered as the gun again aimed at her. Before she could move, a bullet hit her in the lower abdomen.

This time she didn't feel the pain. Her body felt numb. Cold.

Vaguely aware that the commander had now left the room, her hands went to the bullet wound in her stomach. She almost felt like she was in someone else's body.

Her fingers moved through the warm liquid as the door to the room banged open.

When hands pushed her back onto the ground and covered the wounds, Shylah's eyes slid closed. Eden entered her mind.

She'd saved him. Even if she died, Eden would live, and Shylah was okay with that.

2

Present Day

"I don't need a damn doctor."

What Eden needed was a cold beer and for everyone to leave him the hell alone. Mason was lucky Eden wasn't kicking his ass for dragging him into the hospital.

"Stop being an ass, Hunter. You put your hand through a fucking window. You're seeing a doctor."

Eden knew he could fight Mason on it, but his friends and teammates would be on him within the hour, dragging his ass back.

Eden was good, but not good enough to take on seven former Navy SEALs who had been through Project Arma.

As they walked up to the desk, the girl behind the counter did a double-take before her eyes widened.

This was the normal reaction. Eden knew he was big at six and a half feet. Mason could hold his own too.

Whenever they went anywhere, they knew they made an intimidating sight.

The permanent scowl etched on Eden's face probably did nothing to help the matter.

"Hey, darlin', we need to see a doctor. My pinhead friend here put his hand through some glass."

Mason took hold of Eden's left arm and pulled it up so the girl could see.

The guys had done a good job of wrapping it, but the blood was seeping through the bandage.

Eden would have just left it if Mason and Wyatt hadn't heard the glass shatter and come looking for the source.

The receptionist's eyes softened at Mason's smile.

"You came in at the right time. We don't have much of a wait now. You can go straight through to room five just to the left."

The nurse's eyes remained glued to Mason like he was a damn hero. Eden's scowl deepened.

When the nurse turned her head back to Eden, she visibly drew back.

Before she could say anything, Mason retook hold of Eden's arm.

"Thanks, darlin'."

Walking down the hall with Mason's hand still on his arm, Eden went with his friend to avoid a fight.

Jesus, he didn't have the energy for any of this shit. He just wanted to be back in his own space. People did nothing but irritate him.

As they walked into room five, a bed sat in the middle of the space surrounded by the normal beeping of machines and the smell of disinfectant.

Eden hated hospitals. They reminded him of medical at Project Arma. And that reminded him of her. Eden spent most of his energy trying to push memories of her to the back of his mind.

Not that it ever worked.

Letting go of Eden's arm, Mason pointed to the bed. "Sit your

dumb ass on that bed and don't even think about getting up until the doctor arrives."

"You're almost as much of an ass as me today, Eagle."

Sitting on the bed, Eden watched his friend prowl the room.

"We've got shit to take care of, Hunter." Eden winced at the frustration in Mason's voice. "We have people to find. We need you on your game. You spend your whole life in the back room punching the shit out of a bag."

Closing his eyes, Eden leaned his head back on the pillow. "I know," he muttered. "I'm sorry. I need to get my shit together."

He needed to get his shit together months ago.

"I know losing Shylah was a blow." Eden flinched at the sound of her name. "That's just one reason we're working so hard to get these people. To find everyone from Project Arma who we trusted when we shouldn't have. Get the answers we deserve."

"I want to find them too, Eagle. All of them."

Including her.

"Let's do it then." Mason's eyes pleaded with Eden.

Jeez, he felt like a jerk. He'd been the worst friend and teammate for over a year, and he knew it.

"Okay."

The look on Mason's face was anything but trusting. Before he could argue, the doctor entered the room with a nurse behind him.

Not giving either a good look, Eden turned back to his hand and began unwrapping the bandage. It wasn't until he heard the curse from Mason that Eden's head popped up to look at his friend.

Mason's expression was somewhere between shock and disbelief.

Turning his head back to the door, Eden noticed nothing amiss about the doctor. Then his gaze fell to the nurse.

Eden's entire body froze.

As he looked into those familiar hazel eyes, they took him back in time.

She hadn't changed a bit. Same freckles splattered across the nose, same long brown hair. Same Shylah.

The shock faded quickly, only to be replaced by searing anger. Eyes narrowing, rage pulsed through his veins.

Shylah's eyes widened as her gaze met his. Her body went deathly still.

The look on Shylah's face told Eden she was somewhere between fleeing the room and having a panic attack right where she stood.

"Eden Cole, good to meet you." Eden only vaguely registered the doctor's voice, unable to focus on anything but her. "I'm Doctor O'Neil, and this is Shylah Kemp, your nurse. We'll be looking over your hand today."

Eyes glued to Shylah, he wondered if she'd thought about him for a second over the last year.

There wasn't a single day that had passed where he hadn't thought about her. Some days he was sure that he had built up their connection to be more than it was.

His fingers itched to touch her, run his hand down her cheek.

What the hell was wrong with him?

This was Shylah. The woman who promised she loved him only to disappear off the face of the planet.

"Nurse, can you please clean the wound while I get some information from the patient?"

Shylah remained where she stood. Her eyes wide. Eden could hear her pulse thundering.

Was that fear he saw in her eyes?

The anger inside Eden intensified. A person only showed

fear if they had a reason. Hers could only be that she'd wronged him and now had to face the music.

"Shylah?"

Shylah's eyes suddenly pulled away from Eden's. Pain shot through Eden's chest at the loss.

Moving toward the cabinet, Shylah's body was rigid, her steps stilted.

For the first time in his life, Eden was at a loss of what to do. He wanted to get up and grab her. Drag her to the nearest private room and force the answers to her absence from her.

He also wanted to know what her plan was. Did she just intend to pretend they didn't know each other?

Turning back toward Eden, medical supplies in hand, Shylah's eyes remained downcast. Eden took the opportunity to inspect the rest of her.

She'd pulled her brown hair back into a high ponytail like she usually wore it, and the dusting of freckles across her nose still gave her the appearance of being younger than she was.

She was still the most stunning woman Eden had ever seen. Even if it killed him to admit.

"While the nurse cleans your hand, can you take me through what happened, Eden?"

Shylah took the lid off the antiseptic bottle and poured some onto a cloth. A slight tremor in her left hand, which was holding the bottle, made Eden stop.

Shylah's hands never shook when she did her job.

Brows pulling together, Eden's gaze lifted back up to Shylah's face.

"Not as steady-handed as you used to be, Shylah."

~

Shylah's gaze swung up to meet the pair of familiar gray eyes. The gray eyes that had haunted her every thought for the last fourteen months.

His voice was the same. A deep timbre that sent shivers ricocheting down Shylah's spine.

If possible, he looked bigger. Broad shoulders stretching the fabric of his shirt. Arms so muscled they would put most bodybuilders to shame.

Although it was possible, she'd just forgotten how big he was.

When Shylah had walked into the room and seen Eden, she had thought her eyes were playing tricks on her. Like she'd dreamed about the guy enough times, maybe she was hallucinating him now.

When her brain had figured out Eden was a living, breathing human right in front of her, she'd wanted to throw herself into his arms. Tell him how much she'd missed him.

Once recovered from the surprise of it being Eden, she'd noticed the look on his face. Shock mixed with anger, mixed with undiluted rage.

The scowl that had followed did nothing to calm her. In fact, it made Shylah want to find the nearest rock to hide behind.

Eden directed his anger entirely at her.

Anger at her disappearing for over a year?

Shylah had done what she had to do. Not that he seemed like he'd be receptive to anything she said right now. He looked like he'd rather throw her on a bed of hot coals than listen to a word she had to say.

Pulling her hands back, she held his gaze. It was tough when the look in his eyes made her hairs stand on end.

"Hi, Eden." Shylah forced the words from her mouth.

"So, you do remember me?" The venom in his tone shocked

Shylah. He'd never spoken to her like that. She hadn't heard him talk to anyone like that before.

The silence that followed was a thick fog that coated the room.

"You two know each other?" the doctor asked after clearing his throat.

"They dated." Noticing the other man in the room for the first time, Shylah recognized him immediately. Mason.

Mason had been part of Eden's SEAL team and was probably Eden's closest friend.

When Mason's eyes clashed with hers, there was anger there too, but also questions.

Did that mean Eden didn't have any questions? Did he already have the answers to what had happened to her?

"Oh . . . well, that makes things slightly awkward. Would you like a different nurse, Eden?" The doctor's words cut through the air.

Did he?

Did she hope that he would say yes or no? She wasn't sure. Confusion took the forefront in Shylah's mind.

"No." Eden's gaze didn't leave Shylah's face. Like razor blades cutting through her thin armor.

Shylah wanted to shrink back. Find a dark corner to hide within.

Holding firm, she straightened her spine. Shylah had nothing to feel bad about. She'd done nothing wrong. If Eden assumed she'd betrayed him, then it was him who was in the wrong.

Trying not to show her emotions, she steadied her injured left hand as much as possible before continuing with her job.

As soon as her skin touched Eden's, a jolt of awareness coursed through her. It took effort not to flinch and pull her hand back.

Still feeling the heat of Eden's eyes on her, Shylah kept herself busy with the job at hand.

"So, ah, Eden, can you take me through what happened to your hand?" the doctor asked in an overly cheery voice.

"I punched my fist through a window," Eden responded immediately, not taking a moment before answering.

"Okay. Would you like to tell me why?"

When Eden didn't respond, just continued to stare daggers into Shylah's skull, Mason answered, "He was angry."

"Have been angry for the last fourteen months."

Flinching at Eden's insinuation, Shylah's left hand dropped the cloth. The tension in the room so thick you could cut it with a knife.

Grabbing a fresh cleaning pad, Shylah attempted to make quick work of the wound.

"Where were you when you hurt your hand, Eden?" Silence followed the doctor's question until Mason spoke for him once again.

"We run Marble Protection here in town. He was in one of the workout rooms."

Shylah tried not to squirm at Eden's intense glare.

"How's it looking, Shylah?" the doctor asked, still overcompensating for the awkward situation they were in.

"Finished."

Thank god.

As she took her hand away from Eden's warm skin, she felt the loss immediately. Like she'd found something that had been missing and now she was losing it again.

"It wasn't too bad—no glass shards in the skin. Maybe next time don't be so quick to react. It might be more than your hand that you damage."

Why the hell had she said that?

Eden's eyes narrowed, understanding the insinuation immediately.

Pulling off her gloves, Shylah turned to leave when Eden's fingers wrapped around her upper arm.

Stopping in her tracks, Shylah turned to face Eden again, unsure what his next move would be.

For a moment, time stood still as Eden and Shylah watched each other. Shylah was transported back fourteen months when there was no distance or anger. Just Shylah and Eden.

Mason bent down and placed a hand on Eden's shoulder. He said something into Eden's ear that Shylah didn't catch before standing upright again.

A moment passed before Eden abruptly released Shylah.

A part of her wished Eden's hand was still on her arm.

Another part of her, a more rational part, wanted to get as far as possible from this man. This man who seemed so different from the one she remembered and loved.

Which was crazy, seeing as how he was the reason she was in this town to begin with.

"You may leave now, Shylah," the doctor blurted the words as if scared to see what Eden might do next.

Pulling her gaze from Eden's, Shylah turned and left the room on shaky legs.

Walking down the hall, she almost felt like she had an out-of-body experience.

Did that really happen? Had she just treated Eden—her Eden? Did he hate her now?

The last question made Shylah's breath catch.

Once she was inside the safety of the staff locker room, Shylah walked into one of the stalls, shutting it with shaky fingers.

When her legs gave out on her, Shylah dropped to the

ground. Placing her head in her hands, she released a breath she hadn't realized she'd been holding.

What the hell had just happened?

It had taken Shylah over a year to get to where she was ready to search out Eden. Over a year of waiting, of recovering, of healing.

She had dreamed of the moment she would see him again.

Never had she pictured it would be like that. That she would get that reaction. Shylah didn't even know what that was. Disgust? Distrust? Hate?

At the memory of how Eden had looked at her, a small part of Shylah's heart broke.

The idea that what they had might be gone forever was too much to comprehend.

Had their relationship been so fragile that it didn't survive their time apart?

Shylah had thought they had something unbreakable. Her faith in what she and Eden felt for each other was so strong that she hadn't ever considered that their reunion wouldn't be what she dreamed it would.

Glancing at her watch, Shylah still had two hours left of her shift. She didn't know how she would survive those two hours, but she would have to.

She needed to hold it together until she could leave, then she could fall apart. Break. Shatter.

3

Eden stormed into Marble Protection.

He knew Mason trailed closely behind, but he had eyes for one person.

When his gaze darted around the sizeable mat area and didn't spot the man he was looking for, he moved to the reception desk.

"Where's Wyatt?" Eden knew that he all but growled the question, but he couldn't control the storm raging inside him.

Lexie visibly flinched at his words. Recovering quickly, she placed her hands on her hips, eyes narrowing.

"I know you're part owner of this company and technically my boss, but don't think that gives you the right to bark orders at me, Eden." Lexie huffed with a stony look on her face.

Feeling Mason's warning grip on his shoulder, Eden took a slight breath before asking again.

"Sorry, it's been a . . . confusing day. Have you seen Wyatt?"

Drawing her brows together, Lexie still appeared unhappy, but some of the anger dissipated. "He's in the workout room at the end of the hall."

Giving a small nod of thanks, Eden moved down the hall of Marble Protection.

This was the company that he and his team had created. Their sanctuary.

The government had given them a payout after what Project Arma had done to them, and they'd poured that money into this.

Wasn't fucking enough for what happened to them. Nothing would be.

Stomping down the hall, Eden heard Mason's steps behind him but didn't pay him any attention.

Reaching the end room, Eden pushed the door open without knocking. Wyatt dropped from the pull-up bar as Eden stormed in.

"Did you know she was in town?" The words were out, loud and angry before Eden could stop himself. Trying to push down the tornado of emotions inside him, Eden ground his jaw.

"Who?"

Moving forward so that his face was an inch from Wyatt's, Eden barely had a hold on himself.

"Shylah. Did you know Shylah was in Marble Falls?"

Holding his ground, Wyatt didn't shift or pull back from Eden's advance.

Brows drawn together, the surprise on Wyatt's face gave Eden his answer before Wyatt did.

"Shylah's here? In Marble Falls?"

Feeling like he needed to hit something, Eden turned and ran his hands through his hair.

He didn't know how to feel. How the hell was he supposed to react to this?

The woman who he'd loved and had betrayed him was within reaching distance. He didn't know whether he wanted to make love to the woman or murder her.

"She's at the hospital. Working," Eden muttered.

Wyatt's brows pulled up as he looked at Mason for confirmation.

"It's true. She just walked right into his hospital room wearing scrubs," Mason said, shoving his hands in his pockets.

"No shit?" Picking up a towel, Wyatt wiped the sweat from his face. Turning back to Eden, Wyatt took a step toward him. "You need one of us to deal with this? We can go talk to her."

"No." The suggestion that anyone would talk to her before him was not an option. Hell, the idea of any man just being around her other than him sent him spiraling. "No one talks to her but me."

Not appearing surprised or fazed, Wyatt shrugged. "Okay."

"Can you get me her address?"

"Now that I know she's in town, it shouldn't be hard."

Turning, Eden stepped right into Mason, who had moved directly behind Eden.

"But don't do anything stupid, Hunter." Mason's voice was hard. Unyielding.

Narrowing his eyes, Eden didn't back down. "Like what?"

Shrugging, Mason didn't take his eyes from Eden. "Fall straight back into bed with her."

Almost laughing at the idea, Eden stepped around Mason. "Don't worry, Eagle. I don't see her through rose-colored glasses anymore. I'll get us the answers, regardless of whether she wants me to know them this time."

Pushing the door to her apartment closed behind her, Shylah shut her eyes as she leaned her back against it.

Today felt like it was eighty hours long.

Seeing Eden had been like dumping a bucket of ice water on her head. Shocking. Not in a million years did she think he would waltz into the hospital before she gained the courage to go look for him.

Guess that made her a bit of a sucker because, in his line of work, it was possible.

How many times had she pictured their reunion in her head over the past fourteen months? Not one of those times had Eden looked at her like she'd run over his puppy then murdered his cat.

That scowl on his face could scare the toughest man to run.

A shiver ran down Shylah's back at the thought of it.

Confusion swirled through Shylah's mind. Did he hate her that much for being gone for so long? Shouldn't there have been even a sliver of excitement in him to see her again?

Throughout the day, she'd gone over Eden's reaction to her in her head a million times, and always came back to the same place. If the guy loved her as much as she loved him, there would be some trust there.

Just thinking about Eden's obvious lack of faith in Shylah left her feeling a bit broken.

The rest of the day had been a mess. Shylah had been so frazzled that she hadn't been able to concentrate on the job.

When you worked as a nurse, and people's lives were on the line, that was unacceptable.

At one point, a doctor had asked her if she needed to go home. It had mortified her.

Not an impressive start to a job she was still fairly new at.

Pushing off the door, Shylah removed her shoes before she walked into the living room of her one-bedroom apartment. It was small, but she didn't need much space.

She had moved to Marble Falls for one reason. Eden.

Dropping her bag on the round table, Shylah turned and let out a scream at the gigantic man leaning against the kitchen wall. Make that familiar gigantic man.

Although the man looking at her right now may as well be a stranger.

As Eden took a step forward, Shylah took a step back. There was an air of danger about him. Any sane person would want to get far away from him as fast as possible.

She must be nuts not to be running full speed toward the door.

Either that or Shylah was just one of the few who knew that no normal human could outrun him.

"Eden." Placing her hand on her chest, Shylah took a breath to calm her thundering heart. "How did you get in?"

Taking another step forward, Eden didn't appear bothered that he was frightening her.

He looked like a predator in every sense of the word, and Shylah appeared to be his prey.

"You know me better than that, Shy. When has there been a door that could keep us apart?" Pausing for a moment, Eden's eyes narrowed slightly. "When I know where you are."

Eyes drifting down his body, it reminded Shylah of how much bigger he seemed.

Either the guy had spent the last fourteen months working out, or her mind was playing tricks on her.

Words seemed to be lost on her. It had been over a year since she'd seen him. Months of missing him. Of wishing every day that he was right there with her.

Now that he was, Shylah was at a loss for words.

"Nothing to say, Shy? How about you tell me where you've been for the last fourteen months? Because you sure as hell weren't at the cabin when I got back. You were conveniently missing when my whole world changed." Eden's voice remained calm as he spoke, but daggers of anger were shot through his eyes.

Another shiver raced down Shylah's spine as he again moved closer, emphasizing their significant size difference even more.

Shylah had a damn good reason for not being at the cabin when he returned. But if she told him that, she'd have to tell him the rest.

The painful memory of what she'd lost was like a dagger to her heart.

Glancing up at Eden's hate-filled eyes, there was no way she was baring her soul to him when he looked at her like that.

"I had to get some space after everything happened, Eden. I'm sorry if that hurt you. I know you probably won't believe this, but I've missed you."

Her voice had a slight tremble in it as she spoke. She felt like she was swimming in uncharted waters.

There was something in Eden's eyes that Shylah couldn't quite identify. Something new and dangerous.

How was he so different?

Shylah had rehearsed in her head so many times what she would say to him once she finally saw him again. But this wasn't the Eden she knew. The man standing in front of her was a stranger.

"Missed me so much you couldn't pick up the phone to call?"

Shrinking back, Shylah's brain struggled to comprehend what was happening. Was this really the man she loved? The man she'd thought about every day, craving to be back at his side? There was so much anger inside of him.

Had Project Arma done this to him? Or had she?

"You're different." The words slipped out.

There was no emotion on Eden's face when he replied, "Well, being lied to and betrayed by the person who's supposed to love you will do that."

Flinching, Shylah focused on one word in that sentence.

Betrayed.

Did he mean that he knew she'd been the one to uncover the truth behind Project Arma? The government personnel she had been in contact with said they would let her tell him. She couldn't have told him while it was happening, that would have gotten him killed.

"I wanted to tell you, Eden. You have no idea how badly I wanted to tell you."

Eden took another step closer while Shylah attempted to take another step back, only to feel the hard edge of the table against her body.

The closer Eden came, the bigger he got. Easily two to three times her size. If the man decided he wanted to hurt her, there was nothing she could do.

Eden wouldn't hurt her.

Well, the old Eden wouldn't. She had no idea what this man would do.

"I can smell the fear on you, Shy."

"I keep telling myself you wouldn't hurt me, but I don't think I really know who you are."

A hint of a smile touched Eden's lips. Only it wasn't the smile she was used to. "I'm exactly who you wanted me to be. Who you made me."

"I don't understand, Eden. Who I made you? What does that mean?"

Eden reached out his hand, and Shylah forced herself to remain still as his knuckles grazed her cheek. His touch was surprisingly gentle. "Tell me something true, Shy. Something real."

That her heart was breaking? That she'd thought she was returning to the man she loved, but he wasn't there? The possibility that the man she knew no longer existed seemed very real. And it was soul-wrenching.

"Not a day has passed during the last fourteen months when I didn't think of you."

Not a single damn day.

Lowering his head, Eden's mouth touched Shylah's neck.

Not moving a muscle, Shylah stood as still as possible. The scent of him being so close was intoxicating. Her mind said run, but the only running she wanted to do was running her hands down his body. Pulling herself closer.

"Because you felt guilty?"

Guilty? For not telling him what she knew?

She didn't tell him to save him. There was no way she felt guilty about saving the man she loved.

"Because I missed you."

Eden's teeth nipped Shylah's neck, a bolt of awareness shooting through her.

Even though he didn't act like the same Eden she once knew, her body still remembered him. She wanted to sink into his warmth.

"The day I got back from my mission, the day they told me what Project Arma did to us, I went for you. When you weren't there, I told myself that you'd just popped out somewhere. There was no way you could be connected to any of that. So, I waited."

Eden's lips remained on Shylah's neck while his arms bracketed her to the table. Leaning his body into her, Shylah felt every inch of the man that touched her.

"I can't remember how long I waited. But I remember the moment I realized you weren't coming back. The moment it all became clear to me what had happened. That was the moment I lost faith in people."

Before Shylah could respond, Eden lowered his hands and lifted her onto the table. In one swift move, he widened her hips, forcing her thighs to part.

Eden's hardness pressed against her, causing a throbbing of need deep in her core. "You, Shylah, are my kryptonite. I should hate you, but here we are."

Shylah couldn't think. It had been too long since she'd felt Eden like this. There'd been so many nights where she'd craved him.

A moan released from Shylah's lips as his hand ran under her shirt against her bare stomach. His mouth moving to the sensitive spot on her neck, hand reaching up to cover her breast.

Shylah surrendered to the sensations. His hand massaging, lips sucking. Throwing her head back, she ground her hips against Eden's.

"So much of it couldn't have been real. This wasn't fake though, was it?" When Shylah remained silent, Eden halted his torment for a moment and went to remove his hand. "Tell me this was real, Shy."

Desperate need filled Shylah as Eden pulled away. "It was real, Eden." The words were torn from Shylah's lips, begging him not to stop. "It was real to me."

Always real.

Lowering his head once again, Eden moved his hand to her other breast. The combination of the sucking on her neck with the massaging of her breast set Shylah's body alight.

There was a burning inside of her where it had been cold for so long.

"Eden . . ." Not recognizing her own voice, Shylah couldn't suppress the urgency.

Moving her hands under his shirt, Shylah scraped her fingers down his chest.

He was all hard. Her nails ran over the ridges of his muscles.

Lowering her right hand, she covered his crotch in a firm grip.

When he didn't pull away, Shylah wrapped her fingers around him over his jeans.

Hardening in her fingers, Eden released a growl of approval.

Eden's hands moved to the waistband of her jeans, undoing the button and zipper. Pulling them down in one swift move, the underwear went with them, leaving Shylah bare from the waist down.

Not feeling an ounce of embarrassment, she moved her own hands to the button and zipper of his pants, undoing both and pushing them down.

Stepping out of his pants, Eden's hands quickly returned to Shylah's body, this time moving to her core.

The feel of his fingers against her took Shylah's breath away. As his thumb rubbed her clit, Shylah's body burned. His touch was firm as he made circular motions.

The throbbing intensified and Shylah's breaths shortened. Then he inserted a finger inside her as his mouth lowered to her breast on top of the shirt.

Shylah cried out when Eden's mouth suctioned her nipple.

"Already ready for me, Shy," Eden drawled as he lifted his head for a moment.

"Yes." Her voice didn't sound like her own. "Please, Eden."

"Tell me what you want, Shy."

Him. All of him. "You. Inside me."

To confirm her words, Shylah placed her hand back on his rock-hard penis, now bare. Tightening her grip, she moved her hand in the way she remembered that he liked.

A guttural growl tore from Eden's lips as he lifted Shylah and turned to press her against the wall. The tip of Eden's penis pressed against her entrance before sliding inside her.

A cry tore from Shylah's lips as her eyes drifted shut.

"No, eyes on me, Shylah."

Snapping her eyes open, she watched Eden as he thrust in

and out of her. On every thrust, Eden pulled himself out so only the tip touched Shylah, then pushed back inside to fill her so completely.

The sound of their bodies connecting and their heavy breathing were the only sounds in the room.

Without breaking eye contact, there was an intensity with the way Eden watched her.

Her fingers latched onto his shoulders. His hands dug in where he held her hips.

As his thrusts got harder, deeper, the throbbing increased to an unbearable level. Shylah's body was close to breaking.

Moving his hand to her nipple, Eden pinched.

Throwing her head back, Shylah's body exploded.

Crying out when her whole body went up in flames.

Eden tightened and let go, experiencing his own orgasm.

Dropping her head onto Eden's shoulder, she felt sated and relaxed. His penis still throbbed inside her, connecting their bodies.

Emotions that she hadn't felt in too long moved their way to the surface.

This was the man she'd fought so hard to keep safe. This was why she'd done what she'd done and fought to make her way back to him.

Being in his arms felt like home.

"So, tell me, Shylah, when were you going to tell me you were part of the Project Arma cover-up?"

For a moment, Shylah's brain couldn't comprehend what Eden had said. When the words filtered through her consciousness, her body stiffened.

Eden thought Shylah was part of the Project Arma cover-up? Shylah had never in a million years considered that Eden's thoughts might go there when she'd disappeared.

Lifting her head, she looked into Eden's eyes, hoping that she'd misinterpreted his words.

Seeing nothing but steel in his hard eyes, a part of Shylah's fragile heart shattered.

"Get the fuck off me, Eden." Shylah's voice was hard.

The feel of Eden touching her, inside her, was suddenly too much to bear.

Placing her hands against his chest, Shylah pushed and was grateful when he let her go, setting her on her feet.

Turning, Shylah went straight over to her jeans to put them on to cover herself.

It took her longer than she'd hoped because of her stupid left hand, which wouldn't stop shaking, but she got there.

Taking a breath, she turned back to Eden, who had also dressed in that time. "You think I was in on what Project Arma did to you?"

"Yes."

One word. That's all it took to break Shylah's heart.

"Tell me it's not true."

Narrowing her eyes, Shylah placed her hands on her hips. "Fuck you, Eden. I don't have to tell you anything. Get out."

The anger felt much better than the devastation that her body wanted to express.

When Eden remained where he was, Shylah repeated the words, but this time with more venom. "I said, GET. THE. FUCK. OUT."

Without any emotion on his face or in his words, Eden spoke before moving, "This isn't over, Shylah. I want the details, and I wanted them yesterday. I'll be back."

Shylah said nothing. She knew her voice would shake, and she refused to show Eden any weakness.

As he turned to leave, Shylah kept her steely gaze on Eden until the door shut behind him. Then she let the tears fall.

Lowering to the floor, Shylah broke. She had risked her life for that man. Almost died. She'd lost a part of herself for him.

Lowering her head to her knees, Shylah gave in to the pain in her chest. Never in her life had she felt so alone. The only thing that had gotten her through the healing process was the knowledge that she would soon be back with him, back with the man she loved.

So far, it seemed that man was gone.

4

Eden's fist hit the bag. Hard.

The sun still hadn't risen. Eden had barely slept, but he didn't need much.

Another perk of the damn project. Can't be a superweapon if you sleep too much.

Hitting the bag again, Eden's mind flicked back to Shylah. The same place it always went.

This time it didn't remember the Shylah from Project Arma. It remembered the Shylah from last night.

He could still feel her damn body around him. Hear her voice in his head.

He shouldn't have done what he did, damn it.

Then he pictured her face after he accused her of being part of the Project Arma cover-up.

Shattered.

Eden didn't know any other way to describe it.

He was such a jerk. He shouldn't have said it then. Could have at least waited until he wasn't inside her. He could kick his own ass.

Those sad hazel eyes were etched into his mind, and he couldn't get them out.

Footsteps sounded outside the door. Eden knew from the sound it was one of the guys. They knew each other that well.

Turning, he watched Wyatt step into the room.

"Lucky you're a fast healer, or that hand would need some more medical attention."

Turning back to the bag, Eden threw another punch. "Yeah, I'm the luckiest son of a bitch to walk the planet, aren't I?"

Crossing his arms, Wyatt leaned against the wall. "You know I didn't peg you as a martyr."

The sound of Eden's fists hitting the bag filled the room. "Didn't you hear, Jobs? You never really know a person until it's too late."

Pushing off the wall, Wyatt pulled his sweatshirt over his head. "Pretty sure I know you. Pigheaded. Overconfident. I got you pegged, Hunter. Now stop hitting the damn bag and hit a person like I know you want to."

"Fuck off," Eden muttered, giving the bag a kick at full force.

About to throw another punch, searing pain to Eden's midsection made him stop. With a turn of his head, his gaze zoomed in on Wyatt. Rather than look guilty, the asshole seemed pleased with himself.

"Hit me."

Clenching his fists, Eden refused to bite. "Get the fuck out of here."

"No." Wyatt went for another hit, but Eden was ready this time. Easily blocking the punch, he clenched his jaw.

"You can't spend the rest of your life in this damn room hitting a bag," Wyatt scolded, walking around Eden, ready to pounce.

"I can do whatever the hell I want."

Raising his brows, Wyatt didn't stop moving. "Whatever the

hell you want? Well, do you *want* to find the assholes who ran Project Arma?"

Another kick came Eden's way, this one so quick that it landed on his leg. His patience was running short.

"What the fuck do you think? You think I want those assholes running free?" Eden growled.

"I think you're too busy feeling sorry for yourself to see things clearly. To do what needs to be done."

When Wyatt threw the next punch, Eden didn't just block it, he turned and raised an elbow, hitting Wyatt in the face.

Pausing, Wyatt wiped the smear of blood from his jaw. "Felt good, didn't it?"

"What else do you think, Jobs? Seeing as you're the fucking genius of the group?"

He was the man the team went to when they needed information. A lethal SEAL, and just as good at digging up information. But right now, he was acting like a fucking therapist.

Wyatt moved around Eden so quickly that a normal man would have missed it. Eden caught every step.

Before Wyatt could wrap his arms around Eden's neck, Eden dropped and cut his legs through the air.

Falling to the ground with a heavy thud, Wyatt wasted no time rolling to the side before Eden could take advantage. Going into a crouch position, Wyatt shrugged.

"I think we've been one man short of a team for the last fourteen months, and we need you to get your shit together."

Fuck this.

Eden didn't have time for Wyatt's opinions.

Lunging at his friend with the speed only his team had, Eden landed one good punch to Wyatt's stomach.

Eden was bigger by a couple of inches, but Wyatt was just as deadly. Moving his fist back again, Wyatt then flipped their bodies so that Eden was on his stomach and Wyatt on top.

"It doesn't matter how strong, fast, or deadly you are, Hunter. If you don't have your head screwed on straight, you will get yourself killed."

Eden tried to move, but Wyatt had him in too tight a hold.

"We need you, and we need you at your best. She's here, Hunter. She's within reaching distance. Find out what happened, where she's been, and why she's back. Then join our damn team again."

Flipping their bodies, Eden threw Wyatt's weight onto his back then jumped to his feet. Wyatt followed suit and stood in front of him, unmoving.

Running his hands over his face, the frustration was like a parasite, eating at Eden. "We had sex yesterday."

Crossing his arms across his chest, Wyatt nodded. "And?"

Of course, Wyatt would know there was more to the story. "And then I accused her of being part of the Project Arma cover-up."

Shit. It sounded even worse coming out of his mouth.

"We read her file on the encrypted Project Arma document someone sent us. It said nothing about her working with them, only that she was a nurse. That leads me to think she's likely innocent. Do you really believe that she was part of it?"

Yes. No. Who the fuck knows? What Eden knew was that he wanted to hate her.

Maybe he'd been telling himself she'd betrayed him all these months so he could channel his emotions into fury.

"Until I know where she's been, I don't think I can make a call on who she is or isn't."

Taking a step closer, Wyatt put his hand on Eden's shoulder. "We're all here to support you, Hunter. Whatever you need."

Looking into his friend's eye, Eden nodded. He didn't deserve Wyatt. Hell, he didn't deserve any of the guys after the way he'd been acting the last few months. But he'd be an idiot not to take their friendship.

The sound of her phone buzzing pulled Shylah from her sleep. Glancing at the time, she noticed it was only just past seven in the morning.

Jeez, did people in Marble Falls not know how to sleep in?

Closing her eyes again, she blindly reached for the phone. She must have gotten all of three hours sleep last night.

Eden wasn't just consuming her thoughts while she was awake, the man had to disturb her sleep too.

Pulling the phone to her ear, Shylah tried to clear the sleep from her voice.

"Hello?"

"Shylah, it's Nurse Bode. We're short-staffed today in the ER, and I'm hoping you'll be able to come in. Can you?"

Holding back a groan, Shylah threw her hand over her face. Working was the last thing she wanted to do today. Sleeping was the first. Feeling sorry for herself with a bucket of ice cream and watching *The Notebook* was a close second.

"Okay."

The word reluctantly came out when what she really wanted to say was "no thanks" and pull the covers over her head.

Damn her and her inability to say no.

Shylah knew it wasn't just that, though. She took her job in the medical world seriously. Not enough nurses in the hospital meant more pressure on those who were there and less care for patients.

"Great! See you as soon as you can get here."

As the phone call ended, Shylah dropped it onto the bed and turned her head into the pillow.

Eventually, she pushed herself into a sitting position only to have her left wrist give out. Dropping back onto the pillow, Shylah snagged her left hand with her right and did some gentle massage.

She needed to get back into her rehab exercises. She wouldn't be much use as a one-handed nurse.

Moving out of bed, Shylah felt a soreness in her core she hadn't felt in a while.

Jesus, even though the guy was a jerk, the sex had been just as good as she remembered. Maybe better.

There had always been a ridiculous physical spark between them. Being held in his arms made her feel like he sheltered her from the world.

Then he had to open his mouth.

Thinking back to his words, Shylah cringed. Spoken just after making her feel on top of the world, Eden thought she was part of Project Arma. He thought she was working with those bastards and covering for them.

Her brain still struggled to comprehend that. Did he really think so little of her?

Removing her clothes, Shylah stepped under the spray of water. Closing her eyes, she felt the heat hit her shoulders.

Growing up, her family had always made her feel like she wasn't enough. Snide comments here and there, combined with the fact she had to work extra hard to get breadcrumbs of affection, meant that she usually felt undeserving.

So, when she'd encountered Eden, her first instinct was to think he was too good for her. But over time, he wormed his way into her heart and gave her the impression that their feelings were mutual. That she was enough for him.

What a load of baloney.

If Eden felt for her even a shred of what she felt for him, he would never have thought she was capable of what he did.

Project Arma was supposed to be a government-sanctioned project which helped soldiers and Navy SEALs train more efficiently and recover quicker.

Shylah had discovered the project had gone rogue and used Eden and his team for an off-the-books, experimental drug trial.

Eden was now faster, stronger, and healed quicker than the normal man, in addition to many other enhanced abilities.

The drugs could have done far worse damage. They had to previous test subjects.

A shiver ran down Shylah's spine. Even if Eden didn't like her, the idea of him no longer being in the world was too much to bear.

That Eden thought she could be part of such evil was like a dagger to the heart. She wanted to cry and scream, but she refused to allow the emotions to take over.

Shylah needed to figure out what she wanted to do. She loved him. Oh god, did she love him.

There was a possibility that she could stay in Marble Falls and nothing improved. Months from now, the man she loved could still hate her.

Shaking her head, Shylah stepped out of the shower. She needed to get ready for work. She could deal with the Eden mess later.

Dressing with speed, Shylah grabbed a coffee and made quick work of the walk to work. Stepping into the hospital, Shylah got changed into her scrubs and started her shift.

Throughout the day, there was a steady flow of patients—most with minor injuries and illnesses.

Spending the majority of the day working with Doctor O'Neil, it went by quickly. She found he was easy to talk to and liked to crack jokes that weren't great but weren't terrible either.

Leaving a patient's room, Shylah looked at the time to realize her shift already ended. On the way to the staff locker room, Doctor O'Neil joined her.

"Good job today, Shylah. Was everything okay yesterday?"

Eyes flickering to him before she looked straight ahead, Shylah nodded. "Yes, I was just a bit off. Sorry, Doctor, I wasn't feeling the best. It won't happen again."

She hoped it didn't happen again.

As they reached the locker room, he placed his hand on her elbow, stopping her near the door. "You can call me Trent, Shylah. And if there's something you need to talk about, I'm happy to listen."

Taken aback, Shylah found herself at a loss for words. "Oh . . . thank you." Not feeling confident about using his first name, Shylah went with not calling him anything. "I'm okay, but I really appreciate it."

Noticing he still had his hand on her elbow, Shylah waited awkwardly for him to remove it.

"I was wondering if you would be interested in going out with me. I could show you around town. Maybe this Friday night?"

Raising her brows, Shylah wouldn't be surprised if the shock was like a postage stamp plastered to her face. "Wow, ah, that's nice of you to ask."

"Before you say no, we can keep things strictly friends." Raising his hands, the doctor finally released Shylah's elbow.

On instinct, she went to say no, then stopped.

Realistically, what else would she be doing this weekend other than watching Netflix and drowning her sorrows in a tub of Ben and Jerry's?

"Just as friends?" The skepticism would be hard to miss from her tone.

"One friend hanging with another. I'll even let you pay for your own meal."

She couldn't believe she was entertaining this, but why the hell not? It wasn't like it would be romantic, and even if it was, she didn't have anyone who had waited around for her for over a year or anything.

"Okay."

The doctor's eyes lit up. "Great! I'll see you during your next shift. We can organize details then. See you soon, Shylah."

Placing his hand on her forearm and squeezing, he then turned and left.

Watching him go, Shylah was still in shock that she'd said yes. Turning, she headed for the locker room to put on her regular clothes.

Why would the doctor want to go out with her, even just as friends? Why had she said yes?

Oh yeah, because she had been ridiculously lonely for the last fourteen months.

He was cute, she guessed. Probably about six feet tall and lean.

He wasn't Eden. No one would be.

When he touched her arm, she didn't feel the warmth shoot through her body like a shotgun.

On the positive, going out with him sure beat locking herself up in her small apartment and thinking about the man she loved who didn't love her back.

5

Eden watched Shylah from the hospital entrance.

His eyes narrowed as the doctor touched her. Eden was moments away from walking up to the man and tearing his damn arm off.

Tuning into their conversion, Eden's blood boiled when he heard Shylah agree to go on a date with the guy.

What the hell?

She comes back into his life then wants to date the town doctor?

As the doctor left, Eden watched Shylah head to the locker room before exiting out the back.

Keeping a slight distance, Eden trailed her for a few blocks. Watching.

Shylah still walked with purpose. Straight back, eyes front. Although every so often, she would glance over her shoulder. That was new.

Not that she would see any threats. She hadn't even noticed him. Watching her for a moment longer, Eden finally made himself known.

"There's a quicker way to get back to your place, you know?"

Shylah spun around, bag dropping from her shoulder in the process. "Good lord, Eden, make some noise or something, you creeper."

Taking a step closer to her, Eden crossed his arms. Being close to her was dangerous, but being far apart caused him physical pain.

Leaning down, Shylah picked up her bag and threw it over her shoulder before turning and stomping forward. "I know there's a quicker way home. Through some dark alleys and tunnels."

Easily keeping pace with her, Eden shoved his hands in his pockets. "You scared of your neighbors here in the little town of Marble Falls?"

Giving a small shrug, Shylah kept her gaze on the path ahead. "You can never be too careful, Eden. You should know that."

What he knew was that his biggest threat was the five-foot-six, hazel-eyed woman standing right next to him.

"I know that you should only be scared if you piss off the wrong people."

Turning her head toward Eden for a moment, something flashed through her eyes before she quickly blinked it away. "I only just got to town. How could I have already pissed people off?"

"Lots of ways. You could have come to a town where you knew people hated you." Shylah flinched. Eden tried to shrug it off like he didn't care, but the hurt in her eyes left an imprint. "Or they could have followed you. Could even be both."

Silent for a moment, Shylah's brows pulled together. "Do you think I came to a town where people hate me?"

Hate? As much as Eden may want to, he didn't think he

would ever be capable of hating Shylah. "I think you came to a town where people want answers."

A sad smile crossed Shylah's face. "You didn't answer the question, Eden."

"You don't seem to answer all mine, Shylah."

"Shylah? Pulling out the full name now." Increasing her pace, Shylah continued, "And why would I? Seems you've already figured it all out."

"Have I already figured it all out?"

Jesus, he hoped he hadn't. Most of his thoughts were maybe's, hopefully not's.

"No. You haven't." There was no pause and no hesitation in Shylah's response.

Eden wanted to believe her.

"Then tell me." The frustration bled from his voice. He'd waited long enough to find the truth.

Scoffing, Shylah visibly tightened her fingers around the strap of her bag. "Would you listen?"

Eden listened to every damn word she spoke. "Only one way to find out."

Not speaking for a moment, Shylah seemed to work her way up to telling him something.

"Remember that day at Project Arma when I ran into you in the hall? I told you I left something in my car, and I didn't want to get in trouble for being late."

Eden remembered that day well. It was the first day she'd started acting differently. The first day he could tell she was hiding something. "I remember."

Swallowing, Shylah continued, "I overheard something that I shouldn't have just before I ran into you."

Slowing his pace, Eden's brows drew together. "What?"

"Doctor Hoskin was threatening someone from the science department." Shylah's knuckles started turning white as she spoke from holding onto the bag strap so tightly. "The guy said he wanted to stop what they were doing. Go with the results they had. Doctor Hoskin was basically threatening the guy to continue with the project. Saying if he pulled out, they'd kill him. They required results and didn't care who died. They wanted a new version of the drug so they could start testing it on you guys in the next couple of months."

Eden's hand shot out and wrapped around Shylah's upper arm, halting her. "You're saying you had no idea what was happening there before that day? Before you heard that conversation?" Shylah nodded. Eden was almost too scared to believe it, but all he could see was honesty in her eyes. "If that's true, why didn't you tell me as soon as you ran into me?"

Eyes widening, Shylah cocked her head to the side. "He threatened to kill the scientist, Eden. I heard him say that everyone was expendable." Pausing, Shylah crossed her arms. "If I had told you, what would you have done?"

"I would have shut the damn project down."

"You would have gotten yourself killed, Eden."

"So, you're saying you found that my team and I were being injected with experimental drugs and rather than tell us, you what? Kept it a secret for a couple of months?" Eden didn't know what would hurt more, that she didn't trust him to protect them both or that she'd found lying to him so easy.

Taking a step forward, Shylah pointed her finger at Eden's chest. "You asked me out, remember? You made me fall in love with you. You think I was just going to hand a ticking time bomb to the man I loved? I knew I could get the program shut down, so I hid the truth from you. To save your dumb ass. I tried to reason with the government officials I was communicating with to stop you from being injected with the drug, but I was told it was safe. You were safe for the moment."

Eyes narrowing, Eden struggled to comprehend the words

she was telling him. "You're saying you're the one who got the program shut down?"

"Yes." Shylah looked at Eden like she was daring him not to believe her. Daring him to disagree.

Eden couldn't pick up any signs of dishonesty in Shylah. Her heart rate remained steady, her gaze firm.

Shit. Had Shylah really been the one to save him and the others?

"How?"

Turning, Shylah continued walking. Eden could have stopped her but chose to follow. "I got the evidence I needed and sent it in."

There were enough holes in that description to sink the Titanic.

"If you weren't part of the project, then how did you get the evidence you needed? They wouldn't have just made it available to you."

Arriving at the door to her apartment building, Shylah stopped and turned to face Eden. "Remember that night when you were waiting for me at my place, but I wasn't there?"

Eden nodded. He remembered it clearly. When he'd called, she'd said she was at the grocery store but then returned empty-handed.

"I broke into the building that night and took the information I needed."

"You broke in? And stole highly classified information after hours after hearing the doctor say everyone was expendable?"

Shylah's expression didn't change. "Yes."

"You're saying you were the anonymous tip that got the project shut down?"

"I asked them not to bring my name into it when they told you guys. It was important to me that I told you myself."

"That was the secret you would tell me when I got back from my mission?"

"Yes."

Something still wasn't adding up. If that were true, then why hadn't she been there? Where the hell had she been all this time?

Voice lowering, Eden watched Shylah closely as he asked the next question. "So where were you then, Shy? When I got back. And where have you been all this time?"

Breaking eye contact, Shylah glanced down at her hands. "I was going to wait for you. That was the plan, but something happened."

"What?" Eden knew he'd all but barked the word. He felt agitated. Angry that so much had happened that he'd had no idea about.

As soon as the word left his mouth, a veil came over Shylah's face. All emotions masked. "I need to go, Eden. It's been a long day. We can finish this conversation another time."

Another time? Like hell, they would. Eden had waited fourteen goddamn months for this.

"You need to tell me, Shylah, and you need to tell me now."

Anger flashed across her features. "Or what, Eden? What are you going to do? Will you look at me like I'm the scum of the earth? How about have sex with me against the wall then accuse me of being part of Project Arma?"

Anger laced her words. But behind the anger was hurt.

Damn it, he didn't want to be affected, but every time she was in pain, it pierced through him.

Taking a step closer, Eden gentled his voice. "I just need some answers, Shy."

Reaching his hand up, Eden stroked her cheek. Shylah moved her head into him just slightly.

"I have a lot to tell you, Eden, but I need us to work our way back to a safe zone first."

"A safe zone?"

"We don't have to be where we were before. But you not hating me would be nice."

"I could never hate you, Shy. I just don't know what to believe anymore."

The hazel eyes that stared back at Eden were filled with sorrow. "There was once a time when you trusted me, Eden."

That was before his reality had been exposed.

"Trust is fragile. Easily broken."

Nibbling her bottom lip, Shylah didn't break eye contact. "I used to think we were unbreakable."

"Me too."

So damn unbreakable. Reality was a bitch.

Shylah's gaze dropped to her feet as her arms wrapped around her middle. It was a protective stance. Eden felt a powerful urge to pull her into his arms.

Just stopping himself, Eden needed the whole truth before he could continue to move forward.

A relationship with secrets could never work.

"Well, I need to go, Eden. A tired nurse is rarely a good nurse." Shylah's head turned toward the door.

"Why are you here, Shylah?"

Turning back to him for a moment, Shylah shrugged. "I thought that would be obvious?"

Obvious to who?

Shoving his hands into his pockets to stop himself from touching her, Eden half turned. "You working tomorrow?"

Frowning, Shylah shook her head. "No, why?"

"No reason." Eden started heading down the steps. As he reached the bottom, he heard the building door shut and turned in time to see Shylah disappear through the building.

Facing the street again, his gaze zoomed in on the pickup truck in the distance. He'd been aware of it following them since the hospital, but when all they'd done was keep their distance, he'd ignored it.

The question was, who was it following—Eden or Shylah?

6

Tipping her head back, Shylah closed her eyes as the warm water fell on her body.

Shylah had allowed herself to sleep in this morning. Not for long, but enough so that for the first time in a week, she woke without feeling like she had a hangover.

That didn't mean that she felt good.

Unless a heavy ball sitting in your stomach could be interpreted that way.

If Shylah thought Eden had consumed her thoughts during their time apart, that was nothing compared to now.

Only it wasn't the sweet boyfriend Eden that she couldn't stop thinking about. It was the new Eden.

Scrunching her eyes closed, she tried to ward off the empty feeling inside of her. Her heart felt like it was fracturing more and more every time she saw him. The idea that she might have lost him was almost too much to bear.

Eden had become an integral part of her life so quickly when they were on base. He'd filled the hole in her life that she hadn't known had existed.

Now it was wide open and gaping. If she and Eden couldn't

repair what was broken, it almost felt like it would have been better to have never felt that type of happiness, because then she wouldn't have known what she lost.

Turning off the water, Shylah stepped onto the mat and quickly dried off. Halting by the mirror, Shylah took a moment to study her reflection.

Ever so slowly, Shylah's fingers hovered over the scars. The one on her shoulder was small. Most wouldn't even recognize it as a bullet wound. Nerve damage that could mostly be hidden with some exercises.

It had taken months to regain the use of her left hand and wrist. The scar didn't even begin to tell the story.

Trailing her fingers down to her stomach, she traced the jagged surgery scars which entwined with the bullet wound. Surgeries that tried to save that part of her. Surgeries that failed.

Every time she saw the markings on her skin, they reminded her of what she would never have. Anger filled Shylah as she thought of what Commander Hylar did to her.

Pushing that thought down, Shylah knew that anger got you nowhere. If it wasn't for the immediate medical attention she'd received, she would be dead right now. That's what Shylah tried to focus on.

Wrapping a robe around her body, Shylah tightened the string. She had done some thinking last night. She would stay in town for a bit longer to figure out if Eden did, in fact, still love her, or if he ever had. Was their relationship salvageable?

If the answer was no, it might destroy her, but she refused to consider that until the time came.

Stepping out into the bedroom, Shylah let out a screech.

Almost falling backward, she barely saved herself with an arm on the doorframe. Scrambling to recover, she cast her angry glare at Eden.

"What the heck, Eden? Will you stop breaking in!"

Eden's eyes heated as they dropped to her body. Very aware that the robe was likely sticking to her still damp skin, she wrapped her arms around her waist self-consciously.

Seemingly unfazed, Eden remained where he stood. "You need better security here. Your apartment's too damn easy to break into."

"I have a feeling the Rolls Royce of security systems wouldn't keep you out." Keeping her gaze fixed on Eden's face, Shylah refused to be affected by his eyes on her body. "Now, can you please get out so I can get dressed."

"Why? There's nothing I haven't seen before."

"Get. Out. Before I karate your ass."

Raising his brows, Eden almost seemed like he wanted to laugh. It probably was quite comical. Eden was a million times bigger and stronger than her, but she was sick of having her privacy invaded. Maybe her rage would give her an edge?

"I'd like to see that."

Shylah pointed in the door's direction, glad when Eden eventually headed toward it. "Don't take long, or I'm coming back in, clothed or not."

Shylah's eyes narrowed at the threat.

As Eden pulled the door shut, Shylah threw on some jeans and a T-shirt quicker than she had possibly ever dressed in her life, not doubting that Eden had meant every word.

Walking out into the living space, Eden stood by the window looking out.

"What are you doing here, Eden?"

Casting his gaze onto Shylah, she noticed Eden took up a lot of the space in the little apartment. If she thought it looked small before, that was nothing compared to having a six and a half foot Eden in the place.

"I talked to the guys, and if you really uncovered the truth behind Project Arma, and are one of the good guys, we'd like you to come to Marble Protection to help us sort out this mess. Find those missing."

If she'd uncovered the truth? Shylah tried not to let the hurt at Eden's obvious lack of trust in her show.

"Will all the guys be there?" A tingle of nervousness ran down Shylah's spine.

Seven deadly former Navy SEALs hating her was not her idea of a good time.

"They will."

Damn. If Eden thought she was one of the bad guys, she could just imagine what they all thought. Probably that she was the blasted ringleader of the whole organization.

Shylah's gaze returned to Eden's. Did she really have a choice? She wanted Eden to trust her, so she had to put her big girl pants on and get down there. "I mean, I want to help—"

"Great, let's go," Eden interrupted and began walking toward the door while Shylah remained rooted to the spot.

Anger started bubbling inside her. Was this their new normal? She just followed the guy and did whatever he asked?

"So, this is us now. We're what? Acquaintances?"

Eyes softening, Eden waited by the door. "We'll go with friends for the time being."

Refusing to let him see that he was slowly shattering what small remnants of her self-esteem she had left, Shylah reached for her bag and followed Eden out of the apartment.

The ride over was quiet, Shylah kept her gaze on the passing trees and her mind off the man who seemingly hated her.

When Eden stopped out in front of what must have been Marble Protection, she glanced up at the building.

From the outside, it didn't look like much. If she'd been walking down the street, she probably would have dismissed it as an empty building.

The windows were dark so you couldn't see inside from the road.

Skeptical of the setup, Shylah climbed out of Eden's truck. Trailing behind, she followed him inside, surprised to see that it was a fully operational business.

A large mat area was to the left where a class appeared to be running, and a hall ran behind it. The setup was similar to what she'd think a martial arts gym would be. Not that she'd ever stepped foot in one of those either.

She recognized Luca and Asher out on the floor, running the class. They looked the same.

Shylah's nerves increased.

Walking up to the desk, two girls smiled at them. One was a tall redhead that looked like she belonged on a runway, and the other, a shorter green-eyed girl who was just as beautiful. Both women were gorgeous and made Shylah feel self-conscious.

At the touch of Eden's hand on her back, Shylah realized she had stopped walking once she'd stepped inside. Forcing her feet to move, she walked up to the front desk.

"Ladies, this is Shylah. She'll be helping the guys and me with something for a bit."

The redhead gave her a smile and stepped forward. "Hi, Shylah, I'm Lexie. I waste most of my life away at this front desk. If you need anything, don't hesitate to ask."

The smaller green-eyed lady remained where she was but also gave Shylah a smile. "I'm Evie," she said in a much softer voice. "I work out here but also do some tech stuff for the company. I'll probably be joining you today."

Shylah nodded. She wondered if by working at the company that they knew about Project Arma. Since neither woman seemed to hold anything against her, she was guessing they didn't, or they at least didn't know about her.

"Hi." Shylah smiled. Unsure what to say because she was

unsure whether they'd heard about her. "I'm looking forward to getting to know you girls. Ladies. I mean, women."

Mentally slapping herself on the forehead, Shylah smiled through the awkwardness. The pressure of Eden's hand on her back pushed her forward as he moved toward the hall.

"Evie, we'll see you soon. Shylah's just going to talk to the guys first."

Swallowing, Shylah wanted to call out that she would stay with the smiling women but simply walked toward what felt like would be her doom.

Stepping into the office, five deadly soldiers scattered around the small space. She remembered them all.

Bodie had brown hair and eyes. She recalled that when he smiled, he had dimples that showed, though he wasn't smiling now.

Kye sat in the corner and had midnight hair and a small scar that ran across his right eyebrow. The scar had always made him appear that bit more dangerous.

Oliver leaned against the wall with his hazel eyes narrowed in her direction, while Wyatt, with his short but wavy sandy-toned hair, sat in front of his laptop.

And then there was Mason. Mason and his piercing blue eyes. Eden's closest friend. He would no doubt be judging her the hardest.

Shylah felt the strong vibe of danger that filled the room. It was like a thick cloud cover, warning people to be cautious.

Straightening her spine, Shylah refused to show any intimidation. She'd done nothing wrong. On the contrary, she'd saved their butts, so they should be thanking her.

"It's good to see you all again." Glancing around the room, she made eye contact with each man. "I'm not sure how much of a help I can be, but I'll definitely try."

"Hunter tells us you're the one who uncovered the truth

behind Project Arma." Mason was the first to speak, just as Shylah had assumed he'd be.

"That's true. I overheard a conversation that made me suspicious. Did some digging and found out the truth. I contacted the authorities about it." Proud that her voice was firm, she gave herself a mental pat on the back.

"Why didn't you tell Hunter?"

Holding Mason's eye contact, Shylah knew that Eden would have told them all this. They wanted to hear it from her directly. With their abilities, they would be able to tell a lie from the truth.

"I was scared he would piss off the wrong people. Get himself killed. I knew those behind Project Arma wouldn't have any problem getting rid of anyone who jeopardized what they were doing."

"Don't you think that was his decision to make? That he had a right to know?" Wyatt piped up.

"In a way that might be true, but Eden and I developed feelings for each other quickly, and I wasn't prepared to take that chance and possibly lose him. If anyone could get the information needed without alerting the wrong people, it was me. So, I did what I had to do."

Wyatt frowned. "Do you think that was your place? To decide for him."

Hell yes.

Shylah knew that if they'd reversed positions, Eden would have done the same. "As his partner, it was my job to keep him safe, just like he would have done for me."

Shaking his head, Mason didn't seem pleased with that answer. "Eden's capable of a lot more than you are when it comes to that type of stuff."

"Exactly, so he would have raised red flags. I didn't. No one suspected anything with me, which is why I could do it."

Knowing they were trying to catch her out, she stood her ground, determined not to let them.

"Where have you been for the last fourteen months?"

Shylah's eyes flew to Oliver and narrowed. There was no way she would tell what happened that day in front of everyone. She needed to tell Eden first, in private.

"I needed to recover from it all before I saw Eden again. I also needed to stay hidden for a bit, in case the people I exposed came after me."

"I could have protected you, Shylah." Pulling her gaze from the group, the hurt in Eden's voice threw her for a moment.

"I just needed some time, Eden," Shylah said softly, eyes only for him.

"You're going to help us by looking over the information we have?" Wyatt questioned from behind the laptop, his fingers already flying over the keys.

"I'll try to help you as best I can, but I know little more than what I told the government officials I was working with."

"Anything will be better than nothing."

Shylah nodded. Wanting to do what she could for them.

As the guys filtered out of the room, Eden placed his hand on the small of her back and gently pushed her toward the laptop. Taking a seat next to Wyatt, she looked up as Evie walked in.

"Ready for me?" she asked as she entered the room and took a seat on the other side of Wyatt.

Eden smiled at Evie. It was a genuine, warm smile. One that she hadn't seen for over a year.

"Just needed you to finish the team, Ace." Eden chuckled.

A pang of jealousy shot through Shylah at Eden's soft words. He hadn't looked at her like that once. It was possible he never would again.

Swallowing the hurt, Shylah turned her gaze to the computer in front of Wyatt and focused on the screen.

"This is information from Project Arma," Wyatt said once everyone was settled. "There are a lot of names of those involved in the project. The roles and responsibilities of a lot of different people are here too. Ace hacked it for us, but it was sent from an anonymous source."

"I sent the file," Shylah said as she sat back and watched the screen.

The room went silent as all three pairs of eyes set on Shylah.

7

Eden's gut clenched. "Explain."

Shylah didn't look perturbed in the least, which only added to Eden's frustration.

"When I snuck in and stole the information on their system, there was a folder that wouldn't open. I figured it was important. I'd brought a second USB drive because I knew I wanted some information I found to go straight to you guys. So, I copied it over onto the spare and sent the encrypted document to the scientist who studied the drug for me to keep safe. I trusted her. I told her that if I didn't contact her within a few months that I would like her to send it to your private email account, Eden. I figured your military account was being monitored. Obviously, that's what happened."

Eden couldn't hold on to his anger any longer. "How fucking dangerous, Shylah. Are you stupid? I should have been the one doing that. I'm the trained SEAL, damn it, you're a *nurse*."

Drawing her brows together, Shylah appeared confused. "I did it for you, Eden."

Taking a step back, Eden's voice raised another notch. "Who asked you to do that? I wasn't your responsibility. Do you know what would have happened if they'd caught you? You wouldn't have saved anyone. You'd be dead!"

Rising from her chair, Shylah's voice raised in return. "Do you know what would have happened if I hadn't done it. *You'd* be dead." Crossing her arms, Shylah stood there like she didn't have a regret in the world. "I took my chances to save you."

Seconds away from strangling the woman, Eden ran his hands through his hair. "What if I'd done something stupid and got myself killed? How would you feel about that?" The flinch from Shylah told Eden what he needed to know. "Don't you ever do something so dangerous for me again. Got it? It's my job to protect you, not the other way around."

Needing some space, Eden spun around and left the room before Shylah could respond. Storming out the back of Marble Protection, Eden took a breath of the cool morning air, hoping that would calm the storm inside him.

Knowing that Shylah put herself into such a dangerous situation for him damn nearly tore him up inside. She could have died for him. The idea was too painful to consider.

"Don't even think about punching another window, Hunter. We're not replacing one every week to cater to your moods," Mason said while he stood by the door, arms crossed.

"Go back inside, Eagle."

"To listen to the glass shatter instead of stopping it? Not gonna happen." Stepping down, Mason watched Eden through narrowed eyes.

"She's so fucking frustrating. Why the hell would she think putting herself at risk like that would be a good decision? We should have been the ones acquiring the information. We're the trained SEALs, damn it." Scrubbing his face with his hands, Eden turned his back on Mason. "It was the wrong decision."

Keeping his voice even, Eden heard his friend take a step down. "Well, we know that, but she thought she was doing the right thing. She must be just as hardheaded as you. Probably why the two of you like each other so damn much."

"And now she won't tell me where she's been for the last fourteen months."

It was like the woman was trying to kill him.

Nodding, Mason seemed unperturbed. "Besides forcing the truth out of her, it seems it will take time for her to open up."

Spinning around, Eden stormed up to Mason so that only a few inches separated them. "Like the last time I gave her time to tell me and then damn near lost her? I'm not fucking doing that again. I refuse to lose her like I did last time."

"But you found each other again."

Shaking his head, a ball of dread formed in Eden's stomach. "It's not the same. We're not the same."

Eden was having doubts about whether they would ever be.

Mason's gaze drifted over the yard. "We always have options, Hunter. If you're done, walk away."

That was like asking a starving man to walk away from food. Even the thought of walking away from Shylah made his heart clench.

"You know I can't do that, Eagle."

"Then we'll keep an eye on her. Wait her out. See what happens."

Clenching his jaw, Eden shared his fears with his friend. "I don't know how I'll deal with it if we don't work out, and that's a genuine possibility, I'm not the same man she started dating over a year ago."

"She's probably not the same woman."

Was that the case? Had they both changed? Could two people who had changed separately, find enough common ground to come back together?

"Come back inside, Hunter. Give her some space to work through the documents. Just take one day at a time."

Looking up at his friend, their gazes held for a few seconds. Mason knew better than anyone what Shylah's disappearance had cost him.

Nodding, Eden started moving back toward the building.

By spending the rest of the day doing paperwork, Eden avoided Shylah. He tried not to listen in to what was said inside the room.

It wasn't until Wyatt came out after lunch that he got some information on what was happening.

Walking over to Eden and Mason in one of the meeting rooms, Wyatt took a seat.

"She confirmed the information she found that she sent to the government. She also identified a couple of people who were part of the project. She doesn't know much. Apart from the fact that she thinks Doctor Hoskin is dead."

Raising his head, Eden frowned. "How would she know that?"

Shrugging, Wyatt leaned back in the chair. "Said something about him getting killed in the raid. She was sketchy on the details. Wouldn't say much. I didn't push. It's been a long day."

Taking a breath, Eden looked at his friend and asked, "You spent the entire day with her, Jobs. Do you trust her?"

Wyatt gave a long exhale. "I trust that she wasn't a part of what was really going on at Project Arma. I trust that she reported what was happening and did what she did to protect you. But I know that there's something she's not telling us."

Nodding, Wyatt didn't say anything that Eden hadn't already been thinking.

"How much longer do they need?"

"Evie's just going through the final details with Shylah. They shouldn't take long."

Standing, Eden already started moving toward the door. "I'll do some work in the back before I take her home. I appreciate your help on the matter, Jobs."

Spending another hour in the back before returning to Shylah, Eden walked in to see both women look up at him.

"Ready to head home?" Eden asked, eyes only for Shylah.

"Sure." Shylah's lips pulled into a half-smile as she moved to stand.

There was a time when Shylah would have beamed at him before moving into his arms when he entered a room.

Pushing that to the back of his mind, he turned to Evie.

Their relationship had come a long way, and she'd been through a lot.

Guilt weighed heavily on Eden for how he'd treated her at the beginning, so he worked hard now to make her feel comfortable around him.

Softening his voice, Eden gave Evie a warm smile and asked, "All good, Evie?"

Returning the smile, Evie glanced up at Eden before replying, "Shylah has been a significant help. We went through so much information. It must have been a bit of a drag for her, but she was a trooper."

Eden maintained his distance from Evie. He made an effort to ensure she felt safe. Evie was still working through a lot of stuff from her past but had come a long way.

"Thank you, Evie." Turning back to face Shylah, he walked closer to her and put his hand on the small of her back. "I'll take you home."

At the car, Eden held the door open for her before moving to his own side.

"How'd it go with Evie and Wyatt today?" Eden asked, not wanting to make the trip in silence.

"It went well. Like Evie mentioned, we worked through a lot

of information." Catching Shylah watching him, Eden waited for her to say whatever was on her mind. "Evie's nice."

Pausing for a moment, Eden gave Shylah a side glance before watching the road again. "Evie's with Luca."

"I know, she told me. I could see how much she loves him by the look in her eyes when she spoke about him."

Eden frowned. "Why do you not sound happy then?"

"I am happy. It's just . . . I mean, the way you speak to her, you're just nice to her, that's all."

Sighing, Eden tried not to let the insecurity in Shylah's voice affect him. "Evie's been through a lot. I try for a gentle approach with her. I didn't always trust her, and I don't feel great about that. I'm working on being a better friend to her."

"A friend?"

"Yes."

Shylah said nothing after that. Silence filled the car for the last bit of the car trip.

Focusing on the road, Eden's eyes went to the rearview mirror. That same gray pickup truck was trailing them. The driver was good at keeping their distance, but not good enough to go unnoticed.

Throwing in a few extra turns, Eden was glad that Shylah seemed too distracted by her own thoughts to notice what he was doing.

Pulling up out front of Shylah's apartment building, he shot a quick text off to Wyatt with the truck's license plate number.

"You don't need to come up," Shylah said as she unbuckled her seatbelt.

Disregarding her words, Eden stepped out of the car and circled to her side.

Shutting the door after her, he ignored her unhappy muttering that threatened some type of bodily harm against him.

Forcing down a smile, Eden walked beside Shylah as they entered her apartment building. It was an old building, and Eden hated how easy it would be for the wrong person to get in.

Once Shylah had the door unlocked, Eden stepped in first, listening for any breathing or movement. When the only sound came from him or Shylah, he moved to the side, letting Shylah enter.

"Well, sure, come right in, Eden." Shylah huffed.

"Sarcasm doesn't suit you, Shylah," Eden murmured, followed closely behind.

"Because you're such an expert on me these days."

"I'm not, but I wish I was."

Walking over to the table, Shylah dropped her bag before turning back and facing him.

"Eden, what's going on with us? I can't figure out where your head's at or what we're doing."

Shylah's voice was tired. Weary. Jesus, he was tired too.

Moving across the room, Eden stood in front of her. "I still feel this draw to you, Shylah."

"But you don't love me?"

The question took Eden by surprise. He didn't know how not to love the woman standing in front of him. What he felt for her bordered on obsession.

Moving his hand to cup her face, Eden searched her eyes for answers. "Where have you been, Shylah?"

There was a moment of pain mixed with uncertainty on her face before Shylah shuttered her emotions. "You didn't answer my question, Eden."

"You didn't answer mine, Shy." Hand still on her cheek, he moved it lower to caress the skin on her neck.

"I just . . . I just want us to get back to where we were."

There was nothing in this world that Eden wanted more

than that. He wished that were possible every damn day. "We might never get back to where we were, Shylah."

Leaning down, Eden placed a kiss on her cheek before moving to the door.

"Lock it after me," he ordered, not turning around again before pulling the door shut.

He'd seen the glimmer of tears in her eyes and couldn't stomach witnessing that sadness on her face again.

8

Shylah glanced up from her menu to see Trent frowning down at his.

So far, he had been twenty minutes late picking her up, taken her to what appeared to be a pretentious Italian restaurant, and had failed to ask her a single question about herself.

Shylah understood that this wasn't a date, but it was also a far cry from a fun night out with a friend.

Stop being a grump, Shylah scolded herself.

She had to shake herself out of the funk she was in. It was nice that he'd asked her to spend time with him, particularly seeing as she was new in town and didn't have anyone else.

If he hadn't, she would likely be knee-deep in a bowl of chocolate malted milk balls and halfway through *The Notebook* feeling sorry for herself.

Putting down her menu, Shylah looked at up at Trent.

"I think I'll try the mushroom risotto," Shylah said in an over cheery tone. "What are you thinking?"

Scrunching his nose, Trent kept his gaze on the menu. "Mushroom risotto? I'm not sure if you've tried it before, but it has a very strong aroma."

Aroma? If he meant that you could smell the mushrooms in the mushroom risotto then, yes, Shylah was aware.

When his eyes eventually lifted to meet hers, Shylah simply nodded.

Slight annoyance tinged his features before he turned back to his menu.

Did he expect her to change what she was ordering?

As the waitress came over, Shylah ordered her risotto, ignoring Trent's eyes boring into her.

"I'll have the sirloin, medium rare, with the red wine jus."

Of course, you will, Shylah thought, only just stopping the eye roll.

As the waitress walked away with their menus, Shylah lifted the glass of wine to her lips. Studying him from over the rim, she had to admit he wasn't all bad.

The dirty blond hair in a neat cut and bright blue eyes gave him a nice guy appearance. Boyfriend material.

He wasn't what anyone would describe as a muscular man, but he wasn't scrawny either. Most girls would probably fall all over themselves trying to get a date with the small-town doctor.

What was her problem then?

Who was she kidding, Shylah knew exactly what her problem was.

We might never get back to where we were, Shylah.

Well, screw him. She'd saved his life, and he couldn't even put a lick of effort into their relationship.

"Shylah?"

Realizing Trent had asked her something that she'd completely missed, Shylah scrambled to catch up.

"I'm sorry, Trent, what were you saying?"

Who was the rude one now?

A flash of irritation showed on his face before he quickly masked it.

"I was asking how long you dated Eden for?"

He was asking about Eden? That wasn't even something she discussed with friends. Not that she had any at this present moment in time.

"Um, not that long. Maybe a few months."

Trent's brows shot up. "Really? It got intense in that room. I assumed you two had been together long term."

It didn't feel long enough to Shylah.

A tinge of sadness hit her. She'd assumed they would be long term. Forever.

"No. Eden and I dated a couple of months, and we haven't seen each other in over a year."

"You still have feelings for him, don't you?" Thrown by the direction the conversation had taken, Shylah wasn't sure how to respond to such an intimate question. "I want to be friends, remember, Shylah? I can tell you need to talk about it. You can say whatever you want to me."

Well, that was kind of sweet. Also, kind of creepy considering she barely knew the guy.

"That's nice of you to say, Trent, but I'm okay. What Eden and I had is in the past. I might have wanted to pick it up again, but I don't think that's what he wants. We'll just see what happens, I guess."

Grateful when the waitress returned with their food, Shylah gave her a smile as she popped the plates in front of them.

Gaze drifting behind the lady, someone at the bar caught her attention.

Almost spilling her wine, she did a double take when she caught Eden's gray eyes watching her intensely.

What the heck? How did he even know she was here?

Taking a gulp of her wine to calm her nerves, Shylah tried to send him daggers with her eyes.

She would kill him. How dare he tell her he doesn't want her then follow her to a restaurant?

"Um, is everything okay with your meal, ma'am?"

Startled by the waitress's voice, Shylah turned back to her, trying for a smile.

"Oh, sorry, yes, it looks and smells fantastic."

The waitress gave Shylah an awkward smile before walking away. Giving Eden one more hard look, she turned her attention back to Trent.

His frown told Shylah he wasn't convinced either. "Are you sure everything's okay? You don't look happy."

Well, a stalker in the form of six-and-a-half feet of muscle would do that to you.

Forcing a smile, Shylah lifted her fork. "Sorry, everything's fine. It was lovely of you to organize tonight."

Looking pleased for the first time in a while, Trent smiled before turning his attention to his meal. "Great. I've been here a couple of times, and the food's always been fantastic."

Placing a spoonful of risotto in her mouth, she barely tasted it. Thoughts of Eden clouded her senses.

At the feel of a warm hand on her knee, Shylah almost jumped out of her skin. Her knee banged the bottom of the table so hard she knew she'd have a bruise.

Eyes darting across to Trent, she only just restrained herself from whacking his hand off her.

"I'm really glad you said yes," Trent murmured, looking way too personal.

Trying not to choke on the food still in her mouth, she forced herself to swallow. "I, um, need to go to the bathroom."

Ignoring the annoyed look on his face, Shylah stood, glad when his hand fell from her leg.

As she passed the coat check, a hand latched on to Shylah's

arm and pulled her inside. The door shut while a big body pressed her back into the wall.

"Eden?" The room was small and full of coats. Even in the dimly lit space, there was no way she wouldn't know that it was Eden's body pressed against hers. Heat bounced off him. "What are you doing here? Are you following me?"

Eden's hand trailed from her arm down to her hip, while his other curved around her waist.

"Maybe I'm protecting you. I thought that's what we do." His fingers stroked from her hip down her thigh, leaving a trail of goosebumps. "What are you doing here with the doctor, Shy?"

"That's none of your business, Eden," Shylah scolded, her voice much less assertive than she'd intended.

Moving his hand to her inner thigh, he continued the slow strokes. "That's where you're wrong. You are my business, and I don't like his hands on you."

Lowering his head, Eden's breath was fiery on her neck. Pulling her closer, he forced her thighs to widen around his hips.

"Too bad." Her voice was too quiet and weak for her words to have any desired effect.

Raising his hand slightly, Eden's fingers started stroking the place between her thighs over the top of her underwear.

Sucking in air, tension built inside her, and a throbbing began in her core.

Shylah knew she should send Eden away. But the words never came.

"We may not be together, Shy, but make no mistake, you're mine, and I don't want others touching you." His fingers moved to the edge of her underwear, slid inside to her clit, and he restarted the stroking.

Gasping, Shylah latched onto Eden's shoulder. Afraid her legs wouldn't hold her. Mouth still above her neck, his lips lowered to touch her skin, slowly sucking, only taking breaks to speak. "Do you understand?"

Did she understand what? That she was his? She understood that long before he started this torture.

"Shylah, do you understand?" His strokes became firmer, faster. Shylah's breaths became shorter.

"Yes." The single word was wrenched from her chest as the pressure in her core built.

"Good."

His lips once again latched onto her neck, and the tortuous stroking continued. Shylah felt herself reaching a breaking point.

Pushing her chest against his, her sensitive nipples rubbed against his shirt while she simultaneously pushed her hips into his hand.

"Eden . . ." Any other words she'd intended were caught in her throat as Eden's mouth slammed onto her lips.

At her gasp, Eden's tongue immediately entered her mouth. The kiss claimed Shylah. His finger again firmed on her clit. His circular motions harder. Faster.

Not able to stop herself if she wanted to, Shylah exploded into a million pieces, her cry muffled by Eden's lips.

Coming down from the high, her limbs were weak. If he hadn't been holding her, Shylah would be a puddle on the ground.

Soaking in his strength, she anchored herself to him until she was steady enough to stand on her own. She pushed against his chest to give herself some space, Eden moved but didn't take his eyes from her.

Doing a quick body scan to ensure her clothes were all in place, she took a breath before glancing back up at Eden.

His eyes were intense. Watching her and her reaction.

Confusion swirled through Shylah's head. What the hell was

going on between them? One minute they were friends. The next, he was pulling her into a coat closet and giving her a mind-blowing orgasm.

"I need to go."

"He doesn't touch you, and he doesn't go into your apartment."

It wasn't a question but a statement.

"If we're not together, Eden, you can't tell me what to do."

A slow smirk curved his lips, only infuriating Shylah further. "If he touches you again, I will throw you over my shoulder and walk all the way home like that. Got it?"

Anger boiled inside her. "You wouldn't."

Shrugging, Eden lounged back, appearing like he didn't have a care in the world. "Call my bluff."

Wishing she were brave enough to do exactly that, Shylah crossed her arms but stayed silent. She knew that Eden would do what he said.

"Your mood swings are giving me whiplash, Eden."

"I'll be watching."

Without another word, Eden left Shylah in the cramped space on her own.

Taking a moment to compose herself, Shylah then moved out of the room, relieved that no one seemed to notice her none too subtle exit from the coat closet.

Quickly using the bathroom, she checked herself in the mirror before leaving. Her cheeks were red, and her eyes too bright.

Knowing there wasn't much she could do about it, Shylah returned to the table.

The annoyance was clear to see on Trent's face.

"I was about to send out a search party." His tone was clipped. Shylah noticed his meal was almost finished, and hers most likely cold.

Yep, she was definitely the worst date around.

The guilt ate at Shylah. "I'm so sorry, Trent." Placing her napkin on her lap, Shylah planned to eat fast so she could get home as quickly as possible. "There was a long line in the bathroom and only one stall."

Always a terrible liar, this time was no exception. Disbelief was written all over Trent's face.

To his credit, he didn't call her on it. He was probably too busy regretting his decision to ask her out.

The rest of the meal passed with awkward small talk. Shylah asked questions and received curt responses. She'd probably bruised the guy's ego.

Once they ate their meals, Trent drove her the short distance back to her place in silence.

"Thanks for tonight, Trent," Shylah remarked when they were almost at her place. "It was nice to get out. I don't know many people in Marble Falls yet."

Pulling into the lot in front of the building, Trent shrugged. "It was a nice night."

Yeah, right, that was possibly the most untrue statement she'd ever heard.

"You don't need to walk me up, I can see myself to the door."

Half expecting him to insist, it surprised Shylah when he agreed so readily. "Okay, well, have a good night, Shylah."

Leaning down, Trent looked like he was about to kiss her on the lips. Realizing his intention just in time, Shylah turned her head so that his lips grazed her cheek.

Giving him an awkward smile, Shylah jumped out of the car before he could react.

He pulled straight out and drove away. Shylah tried not to feel annoyed at his quick getaway.

Jeez, he didn't even wait to check that she got inside her building okay.

Walking up to the building, Shylah made it into her apartment on tired legs. That was the last time she agreed to go to dinner with a man she hardly knew.

Opening her door, she expected to see Eden. Hoped to see him lurking in a corner. She had pushed through the terrible evening, all with the assumption that he would be waiting on her. Checking.

When nothing but darkness greeted Shylah, she tried to suppress the disappointment that boiled inside her.

He hadn't said he'd be there, so she had no reason to expect him to be.

Only she had expected him. She had looked forward to seeing him. He took away some of the loneliness inside her. The loneliness that had steadily built over the last fourteen months.

Taking a breath, Shylah straightened her shoulders. She was being dumb. What she needed was a big glass of wine and a bath.

Deciding that was what she would do, Shylah ran the bath while she got her wine. Moving back to the bathroom, she undressed and sank into the water.

The water was so hot that it scalded her skin. That was the way she always took her baths. The heat was like a cloak of comfort on her body.

As she lay in the water, her fingers absently stroked the scars on her stomach—the constant reminder of what she would never have.

She remembered the moment she'd woken up. Every muscle in her body had felt a bone dead tired that she'd never experienced in her life.

It was like she'd been swimming for miles and only then could open her eyes and rest.

All Shylah had wanted to do at that moment was go back to sleep, but doctors and nurses surrounded her.

First, she'd been told about her significant blood loss. Blood plasma and platelet transfusions were needed to save her life. According to the doctors, Shylah had been close to death many times.

It had all been so much to take in. There were so many unfamiliar people in her room that Shylah remembered feeling crowded. Claustrophobic even. She'd begged for Eden, cried for him. But he hadn't been there.

Then they'd told her the next bit of information. The information that would change her life and suddenly made her question whether Eden would even still want her.

Through closed eyes, a tear escaped and trickled down her cheek. She needed to tell him the truth. Let him decide whether he wanted her.

When he had all the facts, if he didn't want her, she would deal with it, just like she dealt with everything else life had handed her.

9

"There's no light coming from the west side of the building," Eden said quietly into his earpiece as he crouched behind the hedge.

"No light or movement south side either," Kye's voice sounded in Eden's ear.

Turning his back to the building, Eden's gaze scoured the empty landscape. If there was ever a place to have an illegal drug testing facility, this was it.

The government had given the team intel that there had been unusual activity in an old abandoned warehouse in a town only thirty minutes from Marble Falls.

In the same town, there had also been sightings of some Project Arma scientists who had gone into hiding. Surveillance footage had confirmed their identities.

"Just checking back entrance now," Oliver's voice came through.

"We go in when Ax is in position," Bodie said from the front of the building.

They tasked the four of them with the raid while Mason and Wyatt listened from Marble Protection.

Luca had the night off with Evie while Asher was close by for backup if needed.

"Remember, if we find people, we bring them in alive." Eden nodded at Bodie's words, even though his team wouldn't be able to see.

Eden didn't give a rat's ass about the lives of those scumbags. What he cared about was the information they had.

About a month ago, they attacked Evie in the hospital. The former SEALs who had harassed her told them that Project Arma was still very much alive and running.

That information was like a punch to the gut. Did they have new unsuspecting victims they were testing on?

"Clear. Let's go."

As Oliver's confirmation came through, Eden's muscles clenched before he moved forward, ready for any situation they could face.

Silently, he slid the side window open before slipping through. Dropping to the ground, Eden immediately moved behind the first object he saw.

Grateful for his night vision capability, Eden noticed he stood behind a pile of boxes in a room cloaked in darkness.

The team had decided before the raid not to communicate once inside the building. There was a chance others with the same advanced hearing as them would be there, and they didn't want to risk being heard.

Stilling his body, Eden listened for anything out of place. Other than the sound of his team's breathing and heartbeats, there was silence.

Moving to the side slightly, he turned his head toward the room and noticed the mess that filled the warehouse. Flipped tables, empty boxes, and shattered glass scattered the large space.

Damn it. They were too late.

Stepping out from behind the boxes, Eden saw his team do the same.

"Appears clear of any other people," Bodie said, talking to Wyatt and Mason through the earpiece.

"Shit. Check the place thoroughly. See if there's any evidence of what's been going on there," Wyatt muttered in frustration.

"Affirmative," Oliver said before nodding to the guys to begin the search.

Starting with the boxes, Eden noticed they were all empty. No indication of what they used to contain and no logo or writing on the sides.

Moving further into the center of the room, Eden stepped over glass shards that sat on the ground. Bending down, he inspected the glass closer.

"We have what looks like broken test tubes here," Eden said to no one in particular.

"I found some empty syringes," Kye said from the other end of the room.

A pit formed in Eden's stomach. The combination of test tubes and syringes suggested laboratory work. Medicine. Experimental drugs. It was looking more and more likely that their suspicions were correct. They were standing in the warehouse that Project Arma had been operating in.

"Looks like whoever was here cleared out in a rush," Bodie said as he moved around the overturned tables. "Smells like everything was wiped clean with ammonia. Assholes must have known we were coming."

"How the fuck is that possible?" Oliver fumed as he flipped a table over. The sound of the wood splintering on the ground echoed through the otherwise quiet space.

"The fuckers clearly have a far reach," Mason said through the earpiece. "If they left in a rush, there could be some evidence they overlooked. We'll do a thorough sweep for prints and liquids when it's light, for now, look for anything that stands out."

For a warehouse, the space was clean from the outdoors. No rats or dust. Eden couldn't even see a speck of dirt.

Glancing up, he noticed a camera pointed down. "There's a camera on the roof."

Eden's brows drew together. Were they being watched right now? If so, he hoped the sight of his team raiding their facility filled them with fear, because they were sure as hell going to be caught soon.

"Probably disconnected when they left, but we'll check it out. I'll try to hack into it from my end," Wyatt said, likely already on the job.

"Fuck." Kye's tone was grave, filling Eden with dread. "You guys might want to come over here to see this."

Moving toward Kye's voice, Eden saw the metal first. Huge bars occupied the entire left side of the warehouse.

Wrapping a hand around the metal, he discovered they were damn thick—a hell of a lot thicker than your average cell.

"A cage?" Bodie's voice dripped in disbelief.

"A big-ass cage," Eden mumbled. And lots of them. Eden's eyes scanned down the row of cages. He stopped when he noticed some bent metal, seemingly pulled apart, as if someone were trying to escape. "Looks like whoever was in here sure as hell didn't want to be."

Oliver walked over to the bent metal, hand skimming the bar. "They were strong."

Walking to the corner of the cage, Kye bent over. "I think we have blood here."

"We'll be able to get it tested in the morning," Wyatt said, with the sound of keys tapping on a keyboard in the background.

Spinning around, Oliver's fists clenched. "The assholes are

locking people in cages now? Testing drugs on them like damn animals?"

A deadly silence filled the warehouse.

If that was the case, Eden and his team needed to find them and find them now. Who knew what type of drugs they were currently testing and what the effects would be on the victims.

"We'll know more soon, Ax." Bodie's tone was solemn as he headed out of the cage. "Let's split up and see if we can find anything else."

Moving away from the metal structure, Eden pushed down the anger. He needed to focus on finding evidence now and could let the rage consume him later.

These assholes would pay. Eden and his team would see to that.

Moving to the back of the building, a cool breeze filled the space. Glancing up, Eden could see it came from the door that Oliver had entered from.

On instinct, Eden stepped through it and looked over the landscape. Trees and bushes scattered around the area, but other than that, there was nothing.

Yeah, this place was fucking ideal as an underground drug testing facility.

About to turn back, a soft thumping caught Eden's attention. Shooting his gaze back to the trees, his eyes narrowed. Another heartbeat.

Body tensing, Eden prepared for action.

Catching Bodie's eye from the other side of the room, he made a signal with his hand to say that there was company. Bodie would know exactly what the signal meant.

Turning his head slightly not to draw attention, Eden focused in on where the sound was coming from.

East corner. Likely in the small cluster of trees.

When he had his location, Eden sprang forward. Pushing his

body to move faster than the average man, Eden flew past the trees and bushes.

The leaves in the distance rustled just as a body sprang from the tree. The asshole took off, a distant blur of movement in the darkness.

Damn, he was fast.

It meant he wasn't quite human. That's okay, neither was Eden.

Eden pushed his body faster.

Ignoring the rocks and uneven ground, Eden's eyes focused on the body ahead. Eden was gaining on him. He could hear the man's breaths coming out faster and his heart speeding up.

Maybe the man wasn't just like Eden. Certainly not as durable.

Behind Eden, the crash of footsteps colliding with the dirt told him that someone on his team was close. Not pausing or hesitating, Eden continued his pursuit.

Closing the distance, Eden prepared for his next move.

The sound of a car engine broke through the silent night. Realizing there was a road ahead, dread pooled in Eden's stomach.

Picking up the pace, the man was now close enough that Eden could almost leap forward and grab him. Almost.

The trees broke, and the man hurled himself into a truck.

Motherfucker.

Eden just made it to the road in time to see the gray pickup speed away, leaving dirt flying in its tracks.

Frustration erupted in Eden. They got away. Again.

The shuffle of footsteps behind him sounded, telling him he no longer stood alone.

A hand clasped Eden's shoulder. "Did you get the license plate?"

"Didn't need to," Eden ground out. "Wyatt already ran them, and nothing came up."

A moment of silence followed before Bodie asked, "The gray pickup truck again?"

Nodding, Eden fisted his hands. "The very same one."

10

Shylah took a breath as she made her way to the next patient.

It had been a busy day, and her shift wasn't even over yet. The hospital had been inundated with patients. Some were elderly, a few were kids, but mostly it was teens thinking now was the right time to become the next internet sensation.

Even when the dangerous tricks landed them in the hospital, they still seemed to have little remorse.

She'd bandaged three huge graze wounds, two broken arms, and some dislocated knees.

Sighing, Shylah stepped in front of room twenty-three. Skimming over the chart, she noticed the patient needed stitches removed from the back of the head and broken ribs checked.

Opening the door, Shylah almost tripped over her own feet when she saw Evie sitting on the hospital bed with Luca standing beside her.

Damn, she should have looked at the name.

When the couple glanced up, Evie's face lit up into a sweet smile while Luca gave her a nod.

Stepping further into the room, Shylah put down the file, and she slipped rubber gloves onto her hands.

"Hi, Evie and Luca, it's lovely to see you both." Shylah tried not to sound as awkward as she felt.

Luca had his hand on Evie's back in both a protective and comforting gesture.

"Hi, Shylah." Luca's tone was neutral, with no animosity or anger, which Shylah was grateful for.

"Shylah, it's so nice to see you," Evie said softly.

Moving to the spot next to Evie, Shylah returned Evie's smile. "I'll be looking after you today. How are you feeling?"

"I'm feeling really good. I'd say just about all better."

Shylah noticed the narrowing of Luca's eyes and had a feeling he didn't share Evie's optimism.

"Why don't we check the ribs first, and then we'll take the stitches out?" At Evie's nod, Shylah lowered the back of the bed. "Just lie down. I'll feel around for a pain indication. If I notice any excessive pain or extra bruising, I'll get the doctor in here, and he'll likely recommend an X-ray."

Leaning back onto the bed, Evie raised her shirt.

Splashed across her stomach was a mixture of brown and yellow bruises that looked to be about a month old.

Jeez, whatever had happened to Evie, hadn't been good.

Ensuring her expression remained neutral, Shylah used her right hand to feel around and watch Evie's face. Evie's expression didn't change.

"Can you tell me your pain level from one to ten, one being no pain at all and ten being excruciating pain?"

"Two."

"Evie," Luca growled the word in a low tone.

Turning her head, Evie looked at the man who was clearly infatuated with her. "I'm telling the truth, Luca. Honestly, it barely hurts."

Muttering something incoherent under his breath, Luca started rubbing Evie's arm.

"So, a two, barely any pain, is that correct?"

Turning her attention back to Shylah, Evie nodded. "Yes."

"Okay, that's great news, Evie. Speedy recovery. Luca must take excellent care of you." Darting her gaze over to Luca, he was still watching Evie with predatory eyes. She wished Eden looked at her like that. Like she was the only woman in the world who existed. "I'll just note it, and then we'll look at those stitches. You can sit up now."

Turning, Shylah wrote her notes on Evie's chart. When she went back to face Luca and Evie, she saw the way he helped her into a sitting position with such care.

A shot of pain cut through Shylah's chest. That was the way Eden used to treat her. Before.

Pushing that thought to the back of her mind, Shylah pulled out the equipment she needed. "Evie, you have the option of lying on your stomach or sitting for this."

"Sitting, please." Evie said the words quietly but firmly.

Standing at the edge of the bed, Shylah watched Evie sit with a straight back.

"You shouldn't feel anything, but maybe having a conversation with Luca might help distract you in case there's any sensitivity."

Evie and Luca had eyes only for each other. No one spoke for a moment until Luca broke the silence.

"Maybe we should stay home tonight to give you some more time to rest."

Shylah could almost feel Evie's eyes roll as she started removing the stitches.

"Luca, I can't stay in that house any longer. As it is, I only go out when I go to Marble Protection. I'll be fine. You'll be there, and we can go straight home if we need to. Besides, I promised Lexie that I would go."

Luca opened his mouth to respond when Evie cut him off.

"Shylah, are you coming tonight?"

Pausing for a moment, Shylah took a breath before continuing to remove the stitches. "What's tonight?"

"You don't know? Every year in Marble Falls, there's the big party by the lake. Luca told me that everyone in town goes. This will be my first one, and because you're new in town, you need to come too."

Almost finished, Shylah took out the last few stitches. "I don't know, Evie. I don't know many people in town yet."

And drinking by herself at a party didn't sound like a good time.

"You know Lexie and me. You can hang out with us."

Noticing Luca hadn't said anything, Shylah looked up at him while removing her gloves.

"You should come, Shylah."

For a moment, Shylah thought Luca might just be trying to be polite. When she saw nothing but sincerity in his expression, a small weight lifted from Shylah's chest.

Maybe all of Eden's friends didn't hate her like she thought.

"Okay. Sounds fun." Moving her equipment to the sink, Shylah picked up the chart again. "All done, Evie."

"Great and great. Thanks, Shylah."

"No problem." Evie stood up, immediately reaching for Luca's hand. It was like they couldn't bear not to be touching. "Everything looks wonderful. I'll write it all up in your chart, so the doctor knows. I would still take it easy until you're completely healed."

"Sure." Turning to leave, Evie stopped before exiting the room. "Do you have your phone?"

Brows raising, Shylah nodded and pulled it out of her pocket.

"I'll give you my number in case you can't find us," Evie said.

Reciting her cell number, Shylah typed it in and saved it.

"I'm glad you're coming. We'll see you tonight."

Then with a last smile, she was gone.

Leaving the room, Shylah felt lighter as she worked the last couple hours of her shift.

Instead of being at home on a Friday night, thinking about the man who loved her one minute and hated her the next, she would be out of the house and hopefully having fun.

Evie hadn't specifically said that Eden would be there, but Shylah assumed he would. She hadn't seen him since last weekend at the restaurant, and to say she missed him was an understatement. She tried to push down the hurt that he hadn't contacted her.

Signing off for the day, Shylah was about to head into the locker room when she heard her name.

"Shylah." Turning, Trent walked up to her with a smile on his face. "I haven't seen you around much this week."

That was because she'd been doing everything possible to avoid him since their awkward date.

Probably best not to tell him that, Shylah thought with a cringe.

"Yeah, it's been crazy here, hasn't it?" Averting her eyes, Shylah glanced at the door.

"You coming tonight?"

Eyes shooting to Trent's face, her brows shot up. Trent was going? "To the town party? Um, yeah, probably. You?"

"Most definitely." Shylah tried to hide her disappointment. "You should come. It should be a fun night."

Waiting expectantly for her response, Shylah wasn't sure what she could do other than agree. "Okay."

"Perfect, we can have a drink together," Trent said before turning and heading down the hall.

Confused, Shylah pushed into the locker room. Was it just her, or was he pretending that their date from hell didn't happen?

Changing her clothes quickly, Shylah headed out the back.

So, the guy she wanted attention from would probably avoid her while she hid from the bipolar doctor. How fun would this be?

Shylah sat in the car for a moment, working up the courage to get out.

Cars were parked everywhere, and loud music sounded from within the trees. Shylah had a feeling the entire town would be here, although there was only one man she wanted to see.

Smoothing her hands along her black jeans, she'd paired them with a cream knitted sweater. Not the sexiest outfit, but the best she could do for an outdoor party on short notice.

Taking a calming breath, Shylah stepped out of her car and headed toward the noise. The first thing she noticed as she stepped through the trees was the copious amount of people.

Yep, it looked like the whole town was here tonight.

To the side, there were a couple of food and drink trucks with long lines of people, and in the middle sat a big fire pit.

Scanning the area for anyone she knew, Shylah tried not to look out of place. She wasn't the most outgoing of people and stepping into a social setting like this alone was pushing her out of her comfort zone.

Not seeing any familiar faces, Shylah moved to the drink truck. If she didn't find Evie and Lexie after getting a drink, she might send Evie a text.

Standing in line, she'd only stood there a moment when a hand on her shoulder startled her.

"Shylah, you came." Casting her eyes beside her, she didn't know whether to be annoyed that Trent found her so quickly or happy that he saved her from being the sad loner.

"Hey, I just got here. Just getting a drink." Shylah indicated to the line in front of her even though it was obvious what she was doing.

"Great, I'll join you. I could use a beer."

"Sure," Shylah said as Trent stood next to her. He was so close that his shoulder brushed against hers. There was a moment of uncomfortable silence before Shylah could think of something to say. "So, how long have you been here in Marble Falls?"

"Not long, only about eight months, so this is my first Marble Falls Lake Party too. We can be newbies together."

Feeling his hand brush up next to hers, Shylah resisted the urge to jerk away from him.

"Where were you working before this?" Shylah asked, trying to make conversation.

"I worked in medical research a bit. Did some traveling. Loved it. Had some family stuff happen, so I had to move back to the States."

Before Shylah could ask him about it, they were at the front of the line. After deciding to go with a hard apple cider, the bottle chilled her hand.

It was colder than she'd thought it would be tonight, and she regretted not bringing a jacket.

Edging closer to the fire, Trent followed her with a beer in hand.

"Cold?" Trent asked, moving next to her.

Shrugging, Shylah took a sip of her cider, feeling the alcohol warm her from the inside. "A little, but I'm okay."

"Here, let me help." Before Shylah realized what he was doing, Trent had his arm over her shoulder, and her side pressed into him.

Uncomfortable despite the extra warmth he provided, Shylah wasn't sure whether to push him away or deal with the unwanted contact. In the next moment, a figure stood in front of them. Familiar gray eyes stared back, but not at her eyes, rather on the arm hanging over her shoulder.

"Eden, it's good to see you. How's the hand?" Trent's voice was friendly. Clearly, the guy had no survival skills.

"Hand's doing well, Trent, as long as I don't punch anything that is." There was ice in Eden's voice as he spoke.

Releasing a laugh like he'd just heard a hilarious joke, Trent nudged Eden's shoulder with his own. Eden's eyes narrowed to the spot on his shoulder that Trent had just touched.

Deciding she didn't want to see the town doctor become the next emergency patient, Shylah wriggled out from under his arm.

"Excuse me. I'm going to go find a bathroom." She aimed her words at both men, but she avoided all eye contact.

Walking away from the men, Shylah weaved through the crowd. She didn't need the bathroom. She needed to get away from the testosterone.

Plus, Eden was giving her a complex. He didn't want her, but he didn't want anyone else to have her. Wasn't that the storyline for every good romance?

"Shylah!"

Turning her head, Shylah spotted Evie and Lexie by a tree. Breathing a sigh of relief, Shylah moved over to them.

"Hey," Shylah said once she'd finally reached the women.

"Hey, Shylah, you remember Lexie from Marble Protection?" Evie indicated to the gorgeous redhead next to her. Like she could forget.

"I do, hey, Lexie."

"Call me Lex," she said with a smile.

Both women were so genuine that Evie felt relieved not just that she found them here tonight, but that she'd met them at all. Evie and Lexie seemed to want to be friends with her, and friendship was something Shylah would grab with two hands.

"So, give us the scoop, Shylah," Lexie said with a grin. "What's going on with you and Eden?"

Evie swatted her friend's shoulder with a gasp. "Lexie, you can't ask her that!"

"Why not?" Lexie frowned, clearly trying to appear innocent.

"She's only just met us."

"No, it's okay." Taking another sip of her cider, Shylah turned back to Lexie. "We used to date, but then we didn't see each other for a while. Now we're trying to be friends."

That was a nice condensed version of their dysfunctional relationship, wasn't it?

Giving a snort, Lexie made a face to say she knew there were all sorts of holes in that story. "Once you've had sex with someone, there's no going back to friendship."

"There can be . . . sometimes." Evie huffed.

Shrugging, Shylah appreciated Lexie's honesty. "You're probably right. I honestly don't think I'll be able to be friends with him anyway."

Evie's eyes turned sympathetic. Lowering her voice, Evie leaned in closer to Shylah. "For what it's worth, Eden's been different since you got back."

Raising her brows, Shylah leaned closer to Evie in return. "Different how?"

"Less angry," Evie said softly.

"Less of a bully," Lexie muttered before sipping her beer and continuing, "Let's be honest, that man has been an angry beast since I met him. He lives up in the middle of nowhere, so he doesn't have to talk to people and growls at anyone who attempts a conversation with him. Shylah, if you can bring a long-lost smile to that man's face, please, for the love of all that is holy, do so."

Shylah hadn't known it had been so bad. "I don't know if there's much I can do."

"Hang in there. I think he really cares about you," Evie said with a pat on her shoulder. "I can tell by the way his eyes track you. He probably just needs time."

Nodding, Shylah hoped Evie's words were true. She could give Eden time if he needed it. She just prayed that some time didn't turn into forever.

About to respond, her left hand suddenly spasmed, spilling some of her drink before she could switch the bottle to her right hand.

"Are you okay?" Evie asked with a worried look on her face.

"Yeah, I just, ah, think my hand froze up from the cold is all." Dropping her hand to her side, she squeezed her fist a few times to get some blood flow into it. "It happens sometimes."

The worry was still present in Evie and Lexie's eyes as Shylah's phone vibrated. Quickly pulling it out, she noticed it was a number she didn't recognize.

"Excuse me for a second."

Turning around, Shylah spoke into the phone.

The sound of the music and people prevented Shylah from hearing anything on the other end. Needing a quiet area to hear the other person on the line, Shylah moved through the trees. The surrounding noise faded slightly, but not enough.

Noticing a break in the trees ahead, she moved through it and stood next to the edge of the Marble Falls lake.

"Hello, can you hear me?" When she was greeted with silence, Shylah pulled the phone from her ear to check the screen. Still connected.

Shylah put the phone back to her ear. "Hello?"

The line went dead.

A chill crept up Shylah's back. That was strange.

Popping the phone back into her pocket, Shylah was about to return to the party when she noticed a man a few feet from where she stood.

Jolting from the surprise, Shylah took a hurried step back.

Realizing too late that there was no more ground beneath her feet, Shylah fell into the icy water. Her entire body was pulled under the water. Moving her arms to swim to the surface, her left hand refused to function.

Pushing her body as hard as she could with one arm and two legs, her body was cooling, and it was cooling fast.

Vision beginning to fuzz, darkness descended on Shylah before she could break to the surface.

11

Eden's eyes never left Shylah. As she stood talking to the women, his eyes tracked her. Watched her.

He thought having her back here would get her out of his head a bit. If anything, it made it worse.

She was here, but she wasn't his.

Eden had to decide what he was going to do. There was the possibility that she would never trust him enough to tell him the whole truth about what had happened.

Was he willing to lose her for that?

His gaze dropped to her hand as it spasmed. Almost dropping the drink, she quickly switched it to the other hand.

What the hell?

That was the same hand that often shook.

Looking closer, he saw how she was now clenching it to her side. Almost like she was doing pre-learned exercises.

Pulling her phone out of her pocket, Shylah answered before disappearing into the trees.

Placing his beer down, Eden followed.

Moving away from the crowd, the sounds of people and

music quieted, making it easier for Eden to tune into Shylah's movement.

Stopping for a moment, another sound caught his attention. There was a third person out here.

Eyes darting around, Eden's muscles tensed. The heaviness of the steps told Eden it was a man. It could be someone who had drifted from the party, but Eden's instincts told him otherwise.

Speeding up his steps, Eden moved forward to see a man standing, watching Shylah through the trees.

What the fuck?

About to grab the jerk, Eden's attention was drawn to the sound of Shylah's body hitting the water.

Shooting forward, Eden caught sight of Shylah's head as it got dragged under the surface. When she didn't pop back up, Eden's gut clenched.

Knowing he couldn't reach her from the bank, he tore off his jacket and dove into the lake. The chilly water hit him hard, but he disregarded all outside distractions and focused on finding her.

Diving down, he felt her arm first. Latching onto her, he swam to the surface.

She was unmoving, and when they broke through the water, Shylah's eyes didn't open.

Jumping on the bank, Eden lay her flat on the ground. Lips already a blueish purple shade, hypothermia was a real possibility. But that wasn't Eden's primary concern—Shylah wasn't breathing.

Pressing his mouth onto hers, Eden blew air into her body.

Breathe, damn it.

When she remained unresponsive, Eden pressed his hands into her chest. Her body moved to the rhythm of his compressions. Still, she remained unconscious.

Pressing his mouth to hers again, Eden blew more air into her body.

About to start compressions again, Eden halted when water began fountaining from her mouth. Coughs racking her chest.

Acting immediately, Eden turned Shylah onto her side and held her steady.

Once the water stopped flowing from her mouth, Shylah's body shook violently, likely from the combination of shock and cold.

Reaching behind him for his jacket, he started pulling off her clothes.

Shylah's weak fingers latched onto his. "N-No."

"Shylah, stop it, your body's too damn cold. We need to get you warm."

Reaching again for her sweater, Shylah rolled herself onto her stomach and tried to push up, only to fall back down when her hand gave out.

"I-I'll d-do it m-myself."

"No." Eden's voice was firm. God, the woman couldn't even hold her own weight on her forearms.

Pulling her into a sitting position with her back to him, Eden pulled her top over her head and replaced it with his dry jacket. Shylah's trembling fingers quickly pulled it closed.

Standing, he lifted Shylah to her feet. Her legs wobbled so badly she had to lean heavily on Eden to stop from falling.

Keeping his eyes trained on hers, he reached down and undid her jeans. Once the only items covering her body were her underwear and his jacket, Eden picked up her soaked clothes before lifting Shylah to his chest.

"W-What about y-you?"

Eyes straight ahead, Eden strode through the trees at a brusque pace, needing to get her body warm as soon as possible.

"My body can regulate its temperature under most conditions."

"O-Oh yeah. S-Super s-soldier."

Walking around the edge of the party to avoid everyone, Eden headed straight to his truck. He reached into the pocket of the jacket Shylah wore and pulled out his keys to unlock it.

"W-What about m-my car?"

"I'll get one of the guys to bring it to your place."

Nodding, Shylah shut her eyes and burrowed into his chest. Holding her a little tighter, Eden didn't like that her lips were still tinged blue.

Opening the driver's side door, he started the engine and cranked the heater as high as it would go. Walking around to the passenger side, Eden gently sat Shylah in the seat before moving behind the wheel.

Speeding to her place, Eden ignored the road rules, wanting to get Shylah in a warm shower as fast as possible. Her body was still violently shivering, causing Eden to reach over and rub her bare leg with his hand.

Her skin was ice cold.

Once parked outside her apartment building, Eden wasted no time getting up to her place. Heading straight to the bathroom, Eden turned the shower on hot before releasing Shylah to her feet.

Once she was steady, he reached for the jacket, only to have her spin away. The quick jerk caused her to wobble on her feet. Eden caught her body before she hit the tiles.

"Shylah," Eden growled.

"I'll do it."

"You can barely hold yourself up, Shy." Reaching again for the jacket, Shylah held it so tightly that her knuckles turned white.

What the hell was going on? It's not like he hadn't seen her body before.

"Please, Eden." Glancing down at her eyes, they glistened with the threat of tears.

Reluctantly, Eden stood a step back. "Fine, but if I hear the slightest slip, I'm coming back in here. And the door stays unlocked, it will take me longer to get to you if I have to break it down."

At Shylah's nod, Eden left the bathroom, closing the door behind him.

He stood and listened for a moment. It wasn't until he heard her body moving under the stream of water that he headed to the kitchen.

~

The warm water felt like tiny needles pricking Shylah's skin. But after a few minutes, her body warmed, her limbs regained feeling, and she welcomed the heat. Her left hand took a bit longer.

Placing her wrist so that her palm faced upward, she began some gentle wrist turns. After five minutes of wrist rotations, Shylah touched her thumb to her index finger, applying pressure before moving on to the middle, ring, and pinkie fingers.

Damn hand, Shylah thought to herself.

If Eden hadn't been there tonight, she would have drowned. All because the stupid thing refused to function normally.

Once she felt her body was close to a normal temperature and her wrist was semi-functional again, Shylah stepped out of the shower. Looking at herself in the mirror, her gaze went straight to the scarring.

She didn't care about the outward scarring. What was on the outside was a sign of what happened on the inside.

Scrunching her eyes shut, Shylah let reality wash over her. She would never be able to carry her own baby.

Never.

God, that was so final.

If she'd never met Eden, then that probably wouldn't have bothered her as much as it did. But she had met him. She had fallen in love with him. And never being able to create a family together was a painful reality.

She knew she would have to tell Eden soon. He may not even care. But the possibility was always there that he would be okay with it in the short term, only to grow to resent her later.

Quickly wrapping the towel around her body, Shylah stepped into her bedroom, relieved when she didn't find Eden in there.

Making quick work of putting clothes on, she tentatively made her way into the living room.

Stopping short, the scene in front of Shylah made her pause.

Eden sat at the small table with a steaming drink in front of him and another beside him. Even though he dwarfed the small space, he also fit.

It looked so normal. Domestic. This is what she had pictured her life would be post-Project Arma. Not the mess it had become.

"Hey."

Wrapping her arms around her middle, Shylah felt unsure about how to proceed. If he'd been her old Eden, she would have walked right over and planted a kiss on his lips. Sunk into him.

This Eden seemed to wage war with himself over if he liked her, and she never knew which side would win.

Turning toward her, Eden's gray eyes scanned her body. "You look better. I made you a hot chocolate. It should help warm you from the inside. I used half coconut and half almond milk as you used to like. I wasn't sure if you still did that."

Touched that he remembered, Shylah gave a small smile before walking over to the table. "Thank you. I do still like that."

Taking a seat next to Eden, Shylah took a sip of the warm drink. Closing her eyes, the wonderful warmth hit her. She hadn't realized that the cold was still there, but the drink went straight to her chilled extremities.

Opening her eyes, Eden's bore into hers. His gaze was intense.

"What happened tonight, Shy?"

What happened? She was a clumsy fool with a dysfunctional hand.

Deciding to go with a less dramatic response, Shylah shrugged. "I was trying to find a quiet spot to talk to whoever called me. I saw someone in the trees. It scared me, and I fell in the water. I shouldn't have gotten so close. That will teach me for next time."

Taking another sip of hot chocolate, Shylah wanted to groan in pleasure.

"Who was the guy?"

Confused by the question, Shylah's brows pulled together. "What guy?"

Expression hardened, Eden didn't take his eyes from her. "Don't play games with me, Shylah. Who was the guy by the lake with you?"

And just like that, the cocoon of warmth that had surrounded Shylah vanished.

Eden thought she knew the stranger she saw by the lake. Not only that, by his expression, he thought she was trying to hide something from him.

"I don't know, Eden. As I said, I just went out there to try to hear whoever was on the phone."

The distrust was written all over Eden's face. "Okay, who was on the phone then?"

Putting down her drink, Shylah turned to Eden, holding his hard gaze. She already knew he would not believe her, but she said the words anyway, "I don't know that either."

Jaw clenching, Eden's body held very still. "You don't know who called you or who met you by the lake?"

She was so tired of fighting him.

"That's correct, Eden," she said despondently.

Shylah tried to swallow the hurt over him not trusting her. She probably deserved it. She hadn't told him the whole story of what had happened to her, but damn it, she needed the old Eden back to share such painful information.

Eden's face was closed off to all emotions. It was the same mask that had been in place when she'd first seen him at the hospital. It had slowly been chipping away each time she'd seen him over the last couple weeks, but now it was back in full force.

"You know Evie or Jobs can probably track the number, even if the phone is at the bottom of the lake?"

Frustration building, Shylah narrowed her eyes at Eden. "Who is it exactly that you think called me?"

"You know damn well who I'm asking about."

"Just say it, Eden. I mean, you've been saying it for over a year to all your buddies, so how about now? Project Arma. You think I was part of the project. That I knowingly injected people with experimental drugs that could kill them. That I killed tons of soldiers while figuring out the perfect super soldier concoction. Getting close to you was part of my evil plan. Tonight, I must have been meeting my partner to discuss how we were going to trick you this time." Standing, Shylah crossed her arms. "Is that correct? Did I sum up everything you believe about me, Eden?"

Pushing his chair back, Eden stood in front of Shylah, towering over her. For the first time since she arrived in Marble Falls, his size didn't intimidate her. There was nothing this man could do to hurt her that was more painful than his low opinion.

"If you didn't hide things from me, I wouldn't have to guess what the hell was going on."

Done with the conversation, Shylah marched to the door and pulled it open. "Well, you guessed wrong."

Eden remained where he was for a moment, leading Shylah to wonder if he would leave. She knew full well that if Eden didn't want to go, then she wouldn't be able to force him.

Then he started moving toward the door. Shylah didn't know whether to be hurt or happy that he was leaving.

"Did it ever occur to you that the thing I'm hiding is to protect you? To protect us until I'm ready to share?"

Stopping in his tracks, Eden turned his head. Some of the anger had faded, and resignation shined through. "There is no us, Shylah. You've made damn sure of that."

Then he was gone.

Shutting the door behind him, Shylah leaned against it and scrunched her eyes shut. The pain in her chest was crippling. Was that true? Had she damaged them with her secrets to the point of no return?

She had believed that they were strong enough to get through anything. Maybe they'd always been more fragile than she'd thought.

12

The sound of Shylah's car door banging shut echoed through the afternoon quiet.

What a dumb day.

It started with her sleeping through the alarm—after barely sleeping two hours—and was twenty minutes late for work. On the drive to work, she'd remembered her phone was at the bottom of the lake, so she couldn't even call the hospital to let them know. Then while at work, they'd been so busy she'd had to work straight through her lunch break so she couldn't go pick up a new phone. She hadn't eaten a thing all day, and she was about ready to murder someone for food.

To make matter's worse, Eden had been on her mind every damn minute.

Stomping up to her apartment, Shylah planned to eat whatever food she had in her fridge, crawl into bed, and not crawl out until someone forced her.

Popping her key in the lock, she stopped when it wouldn't go in. Trying again, Shylah frowned when again it got about a third of the way in only to stop.

What the heck?

Today was not the day to mess with her. Grabbing onto the nob, she pushed it back and forth with no luck before finally noticing that the keyhole looked different.

Bending down, Shylah looked at it closer, more confused than ever.

Someone had changed her damn lock!

Banging her fist on the door before resting her forehead on it, Shylah needed a moment to compose herself, or she'd start balling from frustration.

Hearing the door next to her open, Shylah turned her head and saw an older lady standing there with a cat at her feet.

"You okay, dear?"

No, she was not okay. She was a second away from murdering someone. "I think they changed my lock and didn't tell me."

The older lady nodded before smiling. "Yes, the boys were here earlier. Lovely young men. So big too. I didn't know that locksmiths took such good care of their bodies. I'm thinking of getting mine changed now. I made them a nice cup of tea."

Giving the older lady her full attention now, a sour taste came into her mouth. "Do you remember what they looked like? Or maybe a name?"

Frowning, the lady picked up the cat by her feet. "Let me see the tallest one had light brown hair and beautiful gray eyes. Maybe Edward."

"Eden? Was the man's name Eden?" Shylah asked.

Eyes widening, the woman nodded with excitement. "Yes, Eden, that's it. Very nice man."

"Nice my ass," Shylah muttered under her breath.

"What was that, dear?"

Turning toward the older lady, Shylah forced a smile. "Thank you for your help. I'm sorry, I didn't get your name."

"Mirtha."

"Mirtha. My name is Shylah. It was nice to meet you."

Giving another brief smile before moving down the hall, Shylah jumped into her car. Pressing her foot to the accelerator, she made the quick drive to Marble Protection, all the while thinking up a hundred ways to cause bodily harm to Eden.

A voice in the back of her mind warned that she should chill out before she went in there, but the louder part of her mind told her to beat the hell out of the man and leave him for dead.

Pushing through the building entrance, Lexie looked up from her place at the front desk as Shylah stormed into Marble.

"Shylah! What a pleasant surprise. Can I help you with anything?"

Forcing herself to stop for a moment, Shylah took a breath.

"Hi, Lexie, is he here?" she asked through gritted teeth.

"Who, Eden? Ah, yeah, he's—"

Before Lexie could finish, Eden walked out into the mat area next to the desk. Not pausing, Shylah marched up to him until she stood less than a foot away.

"What the hell, Eden? You changed my damn lock so I couldn't even get into my apartment?" Shylah was vaguely aware of people around her stopping and looking but was too angry to care. "You hate me so much you want me to sleep on the street?"

"I left a message for you at the hospital," Eden said, not fazed by Shylah's outburst in the least. "I asked them to tell you to pop by here on your way home to get the key."

"Well, Eden, I didn't get that message, did I. You know why? Because we were so busy, I didn't even get time for a lunch break. Wait, you didn't know that? I thought you knew everything." Face warming, she only held on by a thread. Eden's lack of reaction was doing nothing for her.

"Shylah, there was no way for me to know that you didn't get the message."

"Well, actually, there was. You see, people do this thing

where they *ask* the person before entering their home and changing their locks. It's quite common."

Taking a small step closer to Shylah, Eden lowered his voice. "You need to calm down. I was only trying to protect you."

That's it. Shylah was going to have a full-on bitch meltdown.

"Eden, if you don't want me, you don't get to protect me! You don't get to change my locks, and you sure as hell don't get to tell me to calm down. I've had a long day. I'm hungry, I'm tired, and I'm so fucking sick of you telling me we're done then turning around and acting like my boyfriend."

She shouted the words so loudly Shylah was sure everyone in Marble Falls had heard her.

Leaning closer, Eden lowered his voice. "Shylah, calm the hell down, or I will throw you over my shoulder and walk us out of here."

"Oh well, with a threat like that, how could I not do what you asked. I mean, that's what you're used to, isn't it? Everyone doing exactly what Eden-the-bully requests."

Bending over, Eden threw Shylah over his shoulder before she had time to back away.

Once her brain had caught up with what was happening, Shylah started banging her hands on Eden's back. "Put me down, you big brute."

Not able to see where they were going, Shylah tried to wriggle and twist her body around, but it was no use. The sound of a door opening caught her attention before he dropped her onto a soft couch.

Looking up, Shylah saw Eden shut the door before pulling out his phone.

"Bill, it's Eden, can I have a pepperoni and a meat lover's pizza delivered to Marble?" He was ordering pizza? "Great, thanks."

Hanging up, Eden took a seat next to Shylah. When the silence stretched, her frustration built again.

"What are you doing, Eden?"

"Sitting."

Well, thank you, Captain Obvious. "No, why did you just order pizza?"

"You said you were hungry."

Confused for a moment, Shylah's brows knitted together. "Out of everything I said, that's what you focused on?"

"When you're hungry, Shylah, it's like the world is ending. There's no way we could discuss things. Let's eat, then talk."

Crossing her arms, Shylah sat back. "And if I don't want to eat with you?"

Shrugging, Eden didn't seem bothered. "Then you can take the pizza home with you. I assumed you came here to chat."

Eden knew he shouldn't have changed Shylah's locks. But the second he'd walked outside her apartment last night and saw that gray pickup, he couldn't function until he knew she had more protection, even if it was just a lock that worked.

As he watched Shylah next to him, he could hear her heartbeat racing and smell her vanilla scent.

"You change your products?"

"What?" Angry hazel eyes flickered up to meet his.

"You used to smell different."

Rolling her eyes, Shylah turned her head away. "Like you, a lot has changed about me too, Eden."

Eyes scanning her body, she still looked like the same Shylah to him, and he still had the same unbelievable draw to her.

Eden reached inside the desk drawer and pulled out

Shylah's new apartment key. He also took out a phone. Pulling up a chair, Eden sat opposite Shylah as he handed both to her.

"Got your phone out of the lake today and we put your SIM card in this new phone. It's ready to go." Shylah took the phone and keys but remained silent. "You know I can still care about you without dating you."

Shaking her head, Shylah's voice was pained. "I don't want you to treat me like you're with me when you're not. It messes with my head."

Her eyes fixed on the far wall.

Shrugging, Eden asked Shylah to do what he'd been asking all along. "You could just tell me what I want to know, and then we can take it from there?"

If anything, that comment seemed to anger Shylah more. "You want to know something I've been keeping from you? Okay." Shylah's eyes shot daggers into Eden. "I assumed we were rock solid. I thought we were so strong that we could get through anything. Imagine my surprise when I get back to you, expecting my loving boyfriend to welcome me with open arms, and instead, I get a quickie with a side of hostility."

Cringing, Eden felt the sting of regret at his actions. "There was a time where I thought nothing could pull us apart either."

"Actually no, that's where you're wrong, Eden. If you had loved me like you said you did, then it wouldn't matter if I was gone ten years and hiding a hundred secrets. You would have believed me and given me the benefit of the doubt." Standing from her chair, Eden followed suit and rose from his own. "I loved you. I always knew you were too good for me, but you made me believe that it could work. Then you accused me of being part of Project Arma. You may as well have ripped my heart out and fed it to the wolves, Eden."

"Shylah . . ." Reaching for her, Eden dropped his hand when she violently jerked away.

"No. I am done. I am so done with you and this and trying to be enough for you. I deserve to be treated like a decent human being, at the very least. So next time you feel like telling me I broke us, then change my locks the next day, don't. Thanks for absolutely nothing, Eden. Leave me the hell alone."

Storming from the room, Eden watched her go, not attempting to stop her. What would he say? Every damn word that had come out her mouth had been true.

Except the love part. He had loved her. Still loved her. He just had no trust.

"That went well." Looking up, Eden saw Bodie standing in the doorway, holding pizza boxes. "Now that you've thoroughly pushed her away, I get her half, right?"

Not waiting for a response, Bodie walked to the desk and placed the pizzas down. Dropping his big frame into the chair, Bodie started eating.

"Am I being an idiot right now?"

Mouth full of food, Bodie seemed too relaxed under the circumstances. "You've always been an idiot, but if you're asking whether you're being an even bigger idiot when it comes to Shylah, then the answer is yes. You most definitely are."

Taking the seat opposite Bodie, Eden dropped his head into his hands. "I want to give her the benefit of the doubt, but every time I let people in, I get burned."

Finishing his first slice, Bodie leaned forward. "We trusted the wrong people. But we're all still here, and you know we'd always have your back. I think you've been dealt some shit cards, Eden. I know you still struggle with losing your brother when you were a teenager. Maybe when you thought you'd lost Shylah too, you assumed that was it. If people got too close, you'd lose them. You've sure been trying your best to push us away over the last year."

"Yet you assholes don't give up," Eden muttered.

"But Shylah might. If you push her far enough."

Shit. If he lost her a second time that might destroy him.

"I don't even know if we can go back to what we had."

"You can't." Looking up, Bodie shrugged. "You heard her, she's different, and you're sure as hell not the same person. None of us are. What happened to us messed with all our heads. Eventually, we learn to trust again. You need to learn to trust again."

Eden wasn't sure if he could do that. He sure as hell wanted to, though.

"The question is," Bodie continued, "why is Shylah different. It doesn't look like she will tell you until she believes that you trust her."

"And if I can't?"

"You got to be ready to walk away, Hunter." Standing, Bodie moved toward the door but stopped just before leaving. "The man I'm looking at does not look ready to walk away."

13

Shylah was done?

What an absolute load of baloney. She wasn't done with Eden. He was like a tattoo permanently marked on her skin.

Walking down the hospital hall, Shylah was glad her shift was almost over. The extra stress of the past week was making her hand act up and keeping her distracted.

Stopping at the service desk, Shylah started flexing her hand. Jeez, she needed to take better care of herself. Otherwise, she would reverse all the months of physical therapy.

"All okay with the hand, Shylah?" Turning her head, Trent came over and stood by the desk.

"Trent! I mean Doctor O'Neil, hi! Yes, all is good."

"Great." Picking up a folder from the desk, the doctor turned to face Shylah. "You're with me for the rest of the afternoon."

Forcing a smile, Shylah met his gaze. "Who's first?"

Glancing down at the chart in his hand, a smile crossed his face. "We have Gladys Roberts in room ten for what she suspects is a heart attack."

Eyes widening, Shylah followed Trent as he moved down the hall. "Oh my gosh! She shouldn't have been left alone in a room waiting for a doctor."

Shaking his hand in front of Shylah, Trent didn't look concerned. "No need to panic. Mrs. Roberts comes in a few times a week for a suspected heart attack or stroke, sometimes a broken bone. We check that she's taking all her medication, have a chat, and she goes home."

Entering the room, an elderly lady sat on the bed, worry clouding her eyes.

"Hello, Mrs. Roberts, what brings you in today?" Trent asked.

"Doctor O'Neil, I'm so glad to see you. I've told you before, please call me Gladys. I've been having chest pains this morning. They're really stealing my breath. They feel worse than before." Not glancing at Shylah, the older woman only had worried eyes for the doctor.

Trent's face transformed into one of concern as he moved next to the bed. "I'm sorry to hear that, Mrs. Roberts, I mean Gladys. Could you describe your symptoms for me?"

Nodding vigorously, Gladys touched her hand to her chest. "I started getting pain right here. I decided to give it some time, see if it went away, but when I was eating my eggs, it just kept getting worse. I was going to leave it, but then I got this cough." Gladys stopped talking for a moment to demonstrate her cough. Shylah had to stop a smile at how forced it sounded. "And the burning, Doctor O'Neil, the burning in the back of my throat and chest is bad."

Turning on his penlight, Trent shined it in each eye. "Any dizziness or pain that extended from the chest?"

Shaking her head, Gladys watched Trent as he took out his stethoscope and listened to her heart. "Not so much. It was all chest pain."

After a few more moments of listening, Trent put his stethoscope back around his head. "Now, Gladys, have you been taking that medication I prescribed you?"

Eyes diverting, Gladys gave herself away before she answered.

"Gladys, we need you to take it. This sounds like heartburn, but we'll give you some medication and keep you here for an hour of observation. How does that sound?"

Closing her eyes, relief washed over Gladys's face. "Thank the Lord. I really thought it was it this time." Opening her eyes, Gladys smiled at Trent. "Thank you, Doctor."

"Anytime, Gladys." Turning his head to Shylah, Trent's patience for the older woman shined through his eyes. "Nurse, can you get Gladys an antacid? Gladys, Shylah will take good care of you."

Nodding, Shylah turned, feeling the older lady's eyes swing to her. "Shylah, are you new?"

Turning her head, she smiled. "I am. I haven't been in town long."

"You're a pretty thing. I have a grandson who would be perfect for you." Eyes lighting up, Gladys looked about ready to marry her off then and there.

Walking back over with the medicine and water, Shylah handed them to Gladys. "I appreciate the thought, but I'm not looking to date at the moment."

"Not looking to date?" The older woman looked over at Trent for help before swallowing the pill with the water. "Every beautiful young woman should want a strapping young man by their side."

Trent cleared his throat. "Shylah is already dating Eden Cole."

Swinging her head around to Trent, Shylah's brows pulled together. "I'm n—"

"Oh, Eden Cole from Marble Protection? Those boys are so

lovely." Excitement on her face, Gladys looked about as far from a heart attack victim as she could get. "That is so wonderful. He's so down and gloomy all the time. You're just what he needs. A pretty thing like you will cheer him right up."

"Thank you, but we're not together." Not sure why she was explaining herself to this lady she hardly knew, she glanced over at Trent with questioning eyes. Trent didn't meet her gaze, eyes remaining on Gladys.

Leaning close to the doctor, Gladys put her hand on his arm.

"PTSD can do funny things to a man. My Henry had that from the war." Turning her gaze up to Shylah's, Gladys's held sadness. "They need kindness. Patience. It will be tough for both of you, but a little understanding will get you through."

Deciding that there was no point in disagreeing anymore, Shylah simply nodded. "Thank you, Gladys."

"Six Greenwith Court is my address. Pop over if you need any help with him."

Touched by the older woman's kindness, Shylah smiled. "Thank you."

A moment of silence followed before Trent stood. "We'll head off to the next patient now, but we'll drop by here a few times to check how you're tracking. Press that call button if you feel any pain in the meantime."

As Shylah left the room with Trent, she turned questioning eyes on him.

"I'm not, you know. Dating Eden."

Once they reached the center desk again, Trent reached for a new chart before he spoke. "You're not? I saw you together and just assumed."

Trent saw them together when?

"Eden and I have . . . a history that we're trying to work through, but we're not dating."

Nodding before glancing up at Shylah, Trent's lips curved into a small smile. "Noted."

For the rest of the afternoon, treating the patients went quickly. Things seemed to be back to a professional basis between her and Trent, which was something Shylah was grateful for. At the end of her shift, Shylah quickly got ready to leave. Once changed and ready to go, she stepped out the back door of the hospital and started making her way home.

"Shylah!" Turning at the sound of the voice, it surprised her to see Trent jogging toward her.

"Trent, what do you need?"

Once he was in front of her, Trent held out a phone. Her phone. "You dropped this as you were leaving. Thought you might need it. You know how they're attached to our hips and stuff."

She'd dropped her phone? Jeepers. Just after Eden had replaced it and then she hadn't even heard it hit the ground.

"Lucky you saw it. Thanks, Trent." Taking the phone, she slipped it back into her pocket.

"I wanted to catch you to apologize for suggesting in front of a patient that you were dating Eden. That wasn't my place."

Touched that he attempted to apologize, Shylah smiled. "Thank you, Trent. I appreciate it."

Looking slightly uncertain for a moment, Trent paused a moment before he spoke. "You can talk about it though. If you are dating."

Shylah stumbled slightly over her reply. "I, ah, appreciate it, but we're really not dating. I'm just happy being a singleton right now."

There was sympathy in Trent's eyes. "Eden can be a lot. I have had little to do with him, but I've heard that he's partial to angry outbursts. I hope you're careful around him."

Feeling like she needed to defend Eden, Shylah shook her head. "He's okay. I mean, he would never hurt me."

Stepping closer to Shylah, Trent placed his hand on her arm. "Just be careful. I know we're not dating or anything, but if you ever need a friend to talk to about anything, I'm a good listener."

Eden's eyes narrowed as the doctor moved his hand to touch Shylah's arm.

What the fuck?

He had stood and listened to every word that asshole had said. He was done listening.

Walking up to Shylah, Eden stood so close to her he could feel her body warmth against his. Happy when she didn't pull away, Eden faced Trent.

"Eden, so good to see you," the doctor said, glancing up with a smile. Not seeming fazed by his presence, it's like the doctor had no self-preservation instincts.

Without returning the smile, Eden's eyes narrowed to where his hand still sat on Shylah's arm. Slow to remove his hand, the doctor switched his gaze to look at Shylah.

"Remember what I said, Shylah. See you tomorrow." Giving a nod to Shylah, before briefly glancing at Eden, Trent left.

Asshole.

Turning to face Eden, Shylah's face was masked, making it impossible for him to tell what she was thinking.

There used to be a time Eden could always tell what was going on inside her head.

"You don't seem to take a hint, do you, Eden?" Before he could respond, Shylah turned and started walking.

Keeping pace with her, Eden watched her from his peripheral vision. "The doctor's got a thing for you."

Shrugging, she kept her eyes ahead. "Thanks for the update."

Eden had come looking for Shylah for one reason—to trust her. Hoping, in time, the trust would be returned.

"I wanted to talk to you, Shy. It's been a hard year. Not just for me, but for the whole team." Hearing her breath catch for a moment was the only sign Eden got that she listened to what he was saying. "When we got back from the mission, they herded us into a room with government officials who told us exactly what they had discovered. They said an anonymous source had tipped them off. That the medical staff at Project Arma had injected us with experimental drugs for the whole ten months that we'd been a part of the project. We were the guinea pigs in their off-the-books drug trial. I remember sitting there and feeling like a complete idiot. We were SEALs. Trained to be the best. Yet we couldn't even uncover the truth in our own lives."

Shylah glanced at him out the side of her eye but kept moving.

"You trusted them," she said quietly.

"Exactly. Trust could have gotten me killed. Could have gotten my brothers killed. After my brother died when I was a teenager, and my parents became too distant to care, being a SEAL became my identity. The guys were my brothers, and Commander Hylar was a father figure." At the mention of the commander, Eden's anger intensified, but he pushed it down. Now wasn't the time. "It felt a bit like history repeating itself, except this time, I still had my brothers. And I had you."

Shylah's heart sped up, but her gaze remained straight ahead.

"I asked about you. They said they didn't have any information. They hadn't spoken to you. So, I raced down to the house at the first chance I got. When you weren't there, I didn't know what else to think. If our commander could turn on us when we'd known him for years, what was stopping the woman I'd fallen in love with and only known for a couple of months?"

As they came to stand outside Shylah's apartment building, Eden opened the door, indicating for her to enter and that he would follow. They took the stairs in silence, and Eden waited for Shylah to open her door.

Shylah walked inside her apartment while Eden remained by the doorway. She came to a stop when she realized he wasn't moving any further.

"I've lived for over a year not knowing where you've been, what happened to you, or why you disappeared. I assumed the worst because I lost the ability to trust for a while. It's something I'm working on. I understand that you won't tell me what happened until we can rebuild some kind of connection again. So, I'm going to try. For you."

Stepping closer to Shylah, he pushed her hair behind her ear, skin grazing Shylah's forehead. "I heard what you said, and I know I've been a jerk. I'm sorry. I want to work on us, whatever that may be. We can start as friends and see where that leads. We had something special, and I'm not ready to give up on that right when I've got you back."

Brows pulling together, Shylah placed a hand on Eden's chest. "And you came to discover all this in the last twelve hours?"

"I don't want to lose you again." Eden's voice was hard. Firm.

Now Shylah's heart raced, and there was a hint of uncertainty in her eyes.

"I came back for you, Eden. For us. I don't want to lose that either."

Nodding, Eden's eyes remained on Shylah's. "Good. Friends then."

"Friends," Shylah replied quietly.

"Great. I programmed my number on your phone when I replaced it. Use it."

Frowning, Shylah didn't answer immediately. "Why would I need to use it?"

"If we're friends, we might need to contact each other. Plus, I heard you're not a huge fan of me breaking into your apartment unexpectedly. This way, I can give you a heads-up before I break in again."

A hint of a smile showed on Shylah's face. "A call to give me a heads-up would be good. And I can let you inside."

Shrugging his shoulder, Eden took a small step closer to Shylah. "Whatever you prefer."

Cupping her cheek, Eden lowered his head and pressed his lips to her cheek. "Friends."

For now.

Then he left, feeling a bit lighter than he had in a long time.

14

The sound of rattling from the entrance of her apartment pulled Shylah from her sleep.

Pushing up onto her elbows, it took her a moment to figure out what the noise was. When she did, her entire body froze in fear.

Someone was at her front door, trying to get in. Remaining as still as possible below the covers, Shylah closed her eyes. Eden had put new locks on her door. They wouldn't be able to get in, he'd seen to that.

As the rattling continued, Shylah became increasingly fearful. Even if they couldn't jimmy the lock, there were other ways criminals made their way into apartments, weren't there? Maybe it was the people from Project Arma finally coming to exact their revenge for getting them shutdown?

Eyes darting to the window next to her bed, Shylah suddenly didn't feel safe under the covers anymore.

She grabbed her phone from the bedside table, then moved as quickly as possible toward the bathroom. Once inside, she quietly closed the door and locked it before sitting on the floor of the shower stall. For some reason, the small, enclosed space made her feel safer.

Pulling out her phone, Shylah debated over who to call. She could call the police, but they would likely take a long time to get to her. She could call Eden, but he also lived far away. Were there any other options?

Scrolling down to Eden's number, Shylah's eye caught the name right below his.

Evie.

She would be with Luca, and Luca was just as fast and strong as Eden, and he was closer.

Her finger hovered over the names for a moment, before clicking on Evie's. The phone rang a couple of times before a groggy sounding Evie picked up. "Hello."

"Evie, it's Shylah." Speaking as quietly as possible, Shylah could hear the shaking in her voice.

"Shylah?" Evie questioned, sounding confused. Luca's voice sounded in the background before Evie spoke again asking, "Is everything okay?"

"Um, not really. I think someone's trying to break into my apartment, and I was wondering if Luca could come over and scare them away. I was going to call the police, but—"

"Shylah?" Luca interrupted, and at the sound of his voice, some of Shylah's terror faded. "Are you okay?"

Wrapping her free arm around her middle, Shylah nodded even though she knew Luca couldn't see her. "I'm hiding in the bathroom, but I've been able to hear them outside my front door since they woke me up. I'm scared that it won't take long before they find a way in."

"I'll be there in a few minutes. Don't move and don't make a sound, got it?"

"Okay."

Hanging up the phone, Shylah pushed herself further into

the corner of the shower. If she could make herself disappear into the wall, she would. Closing her eyes, Shylah tuned in to every small sound around her.

The rattling continued for a while. Then there were a couple of loud thumps that made her jump. Maybe a shoe connecting with the door? Followed by silence.

Did the silence mean the thief had left?

A few minutes passed, where Shylah wondered if she was safe. She wanted to look, but her body refused to move. The sound of her front door opening made Shylah go still again. Wrapping her arms tighter around herself, her breaths shortened.

They were inside. Or someone was. If they could break into a locked front door, it wouldn't be long before they made it through the bathroom door.

Her body felt ice-cold as she scrunched her eyes shut and dropped her head onto her knees. She prayed Luca would turn up at any moment.

"Shylah?" Startling at the sound of the familiar voice, Shylah's head shot up.

Eden?

Unable to make her voice work, Shylah sat silent.

"I'm coming in, okay?"

The lock of the bathroom door popped as Eden turned the nob. In any other situation, she would probably be amazed at his strength in being able to break the lock so easily. But at this moment, her fear prevented her from any reaction.

The glass shower door slowly opened, and Eden's shoes came into view. Her gaze slowly rose to his face, and some of the fear leached from her body.

Eden's powerful form lowered until he was almost eye level with her.

"Hey, Shy, you doing okay?" His voice was gentle. Soft.

Nodding, Shylah remained where she was, taking a moment before speaking. "Someone was trying to get in."

Eden's eyes hardened. "I heard. You're safe now."

She always felt safe with Eden.

Frowning, something dawned on her. "I called Evie and Luca."

A disapproving look washed over Eden's face as he reached out his hand and caressed her cheek. "You should have called me. I was with Mason when Luca called, and I was closer than him. He'll be here in a moment. Mason's checking out the front. How about we get you out of the shower?"

Before Shylah moved, Eden reached out and lifted her into his arms. By resting her head on his chest, her body relaxed. "I'm glad you came."

"Me too, Shy."

As they reached the living room, Eden placed Shylah on the couch just as Luca came in with Evie closely behind. Evie slowly walked over to Shylah. She paused before sitting next to her and placing a hand on her back.

"Are you okay?" Evie asked, her voice soft and her hand only lightly touched her back.

"I'm okay. I'm just so glad they didn't get in. Thank you for answering and calling in the guys."

"I think Eden nearly lost his mind when Luca called. We're all glad you're okay."

Evie's calm nature went a long way in putting Shylah at ease. She was easy to like. A bit quiet and reserved, but sweet.

Glancing back over to Eden and Luca, Mason then entered the room. The three men seemed to take up all the space in the small apartment. They made an intimidating group, all huge, and all looked ready for action should it be necessary.

"There were some fresh tracks outside that led to the street. Looked to be male, maybe two hundred pounds," Mason said.

"Just one?" Eden questioned.

"Just the one set of tracks," Mason confirmed.

Turning their gazes to Shylah, Eden came closer, kneeling in front of her. Even hunched down, he looked huge. "Is there anything you heard that might help us?"

Thinking for a moment, Shylah shook her head. "I'm sorry, I just heard the rattling and ran to the bathroom. I called straightaway and didn't take notice of anything. It was stupid. I should have been more observant."

"It was smart. You survive first, Shylah. Always. We'll figure it out." Eden's hand squeezed Shylah's knee before standing.

"I'll see if there are any prints on the door before we go," Mason said, turning toward the door.

As Eden started talking to Luca and Mason, Shylah turned to Evie beside her. Evie's eyes were gentle, as was her voice when she asked, "Are you sure you're okay?"

"I'm okay, just grateful that I had someone I could call to help me." Glancing over at the guys once more, Shylah started feeling her normal self again. "It's hard not to feel safe with those three in the same room."

"Well, Luca and I were supposed to follow a gray pickup truck that was out front, but by the time we got here, it was gone."

Shylah's eyes flew back to Evie's as her heart rate picked up again.

"Gray pickup? There was a gray pickup truck out front?"

A small frown marred Evie's forehead. "Yeah, Eden and Mason saw it when they arrived, but they wanted to get to you first. Why? Does that mean something to you?"

Noticing the room had gone quiet, Shylah turned her head to see Eden studying her.

"What is it, Shylah?" Eden asked, taking a step closer to her.

Nibbling her lip, Shylah took a breath before she spoke. "A

few months ago, the government officials who I was in contact with to get Project Arma shut down approached me. They asked me to come out of hiding and work in a hospital in Georgetown to draw out some people. The idea being, they would search for me, seeing as I was the one who got the facility shut down."

Eden immediately stilled before asking, "You used yourself as bait?"

Shylah cringed at the anger in Eden's voice.

"I did what I thought was best." Shylah took a breath before she continued, "A couple of months passed, and nothing happened, except that every so often, I would get the feeling I was being watched. One day, when I left the hospital, a pickup truck stopped in front of me. A gray one." A shiver ran up Shylah's spine at the memory.

"It was a distraction for two other guys to grab me, tie a cloth over my eyes, and drag me into the back of a van." Glancing up, Eden looked about ready to explode. Shylah took her eyes off him and focused on the other people in the room. "They, um, spoke about you guys while I was in the van. They referred to you as SEAL team six and said that they had located you in Marble Falls."

"Son of a bitch," Eden muttered.

"Things happened really quickly after that. There were gunshots which came from the detectives who were my protection—"

"They shot at the van while you were in it?" Eden interrupted in a murderous tone. "And what the hell kind of protection lets you get taken in the first place?"

Shylah ignored Eden's anger and continued, "I think they hit a tire because the van started swerving before it stopped. Then I was dumped from the back, and it sped off. One of the detectives got out to stay with me while the other went after the van. They never caught it."

Glancing up, she looked Eden in the eye. "The next day, I got out of Georgetown and went back into hiding. The incident really shook me, and I didn't want them to find me. I wanted to come to see you, Eden, and I was thinking about leaving anyway. I just needed your location. Once I had a name, I used that time to research Marble Falls. I found the business, Marble Protection. The timeline of when it was opened matched up with Project Arma being shut down. That was the main give-away, and what your company did—specialize in security and self-defense. Didn't take a genius to figure out it was you guys. Once I felt safe enough to move again, I came here for you, Eden."

Shylah knew that still brought up the question of where she'd been before Georgetown. She hoped he didn't ask her tonight. It felt like all her energy had drained from her body with the drop in adrenaline.

Braving a glance his way, the rage was etched through Eden's features. It was only the feel of Evie's soft touch stroking her back that kept her calm.

"I think it's been a big night for Shylah, and we should let her rest," Evie spoke gently.

"That's a good idea, sweetheart," Luca agreed, walking over to her and pulling her off the couch.

Eden stepped forward, reaching for Shylah.

"Let's go, Shy." His gentleness pulling her to her feet was at odds with the hardness in his voice.

"Go where?" Shylah asked as she came to stand next to him.

"You're not staying here by yourself. You can stay with me at my place. That's not negotiable, Shy."

A wave of relief washed through Shylah. She would never have voiced that she didn't want to remain here alone. Eden's offer took some of the anxiety away.

"I'll pack a bag."

"Make sure that what you bring will last a couple of weeks. We don't know how long you'll be with me."

Nodding, she continued to the bedroom. She wasn't going to argue. If she was honest with herself, she was too exhausted. Exhausted by running and hiding. Exhausted from doing it all alone. She wanted to lean on Eden. She needed him.

Quickly packing a bag, she shoved in as much as she could. There were likely a dozen things that she'd forgotten, but at the moment, getting out was her priority.

Walking back into the living room, Shylah noticed only Eden remained.

"The others went home," he murmured, walking up to Shylah and taking the bag from her fingers.

Nodding, Shylah followed Eden, not quite able to work out what he was feeling. There was fire and anger in his eyes, but his tone was even as he spoke.

As they made their way out, a thought came to her when she locked the fully intact front door.

"How did you get in?"

"I kept a copy of your key when I changed the lock."

Shylah turned to look at Eden. He didn't even dare to look guilty about it. She shouldn't be surprised.

Too tired to fight, she let it slide as she followed him to his truck. Once they were driving, Shylah rested her head back and closed her eyes.

The car smelled like Eden. Musky. With the heater on high, the warmth lulled her body. Too soon, she felt the car come to a stop. Glancing up at the two-story wooden home, Shylah frowned.

"You live here?"

Unbuckling his seat, Eden nodded. "Yeah, why do you sound surprised?"

Because it was a huge damn house and he was one person. "It's just a lot of house for a single man."

A strange look came over his face before he quickly masked it. "Come on, let's get inside."

Shylah followed him up to the door. Once she stepped inside, her breath caught. It was beautiful.

The ceilings were high with striking black pendant lighting. The entrance led to an open floor plan with a huge modern kitchen and living room to the left. Then there was a big grand staircase in the middle.

"Wow, your home is beautiful, Eden."

Eyes softening for a moment, Eden quickly looked away.

"Bedrooms are upstairs," Eden said gently, already heading toward the stairs.

Following behind him, Shylah moved up the staircase and stepped into a masculine room. "Is this your room?"

Not looking her way, Eden nodded. "You'll sleep in here. It's safer that way. It will take me less time to get to you if something happens. I have good security, but having me close will be the safest." Shylah's eyes darted to the bed. The huge-ass bed that she would share with Eden. "It's a big bed. We should be able to keep to our own sides."

Swallowing her disappointment, Shylah nodded. "Sure."

"I'll leave you to get ready." Moving in the direction of the door, Eden stopped before he walked through it. "Next time, call me, Shylah, no matter how long you think it might take me to get to you. Call me."

Taking a small breath, Shylah nodded before Eden disappeared out of the room.

15

Shylah snuggled further into the warmth that surrounded her. It felt like being wrapped in a big electric blanket. But a blanket with arms and legs and a hard, muscular chest pushed against her back.

Eden's breath brushed against her neck, causing a shiver to run down her spine. She was wearing sleep shorts and a shirt, but her top had ridden up under the sheet, and his bare stomach was flat against her back.

With Eden's arms wrapped around her middle, escape would be impossible even if she'd wanted to—not that she did.

With her eyes remaining shut, a slight smile curved across Shylah's lips.

After months of recovery, uncertainty, hiding, and loneliness, this is where she had been trying to make her way back to—the safety of Eden's arms.

If she could pause time and remain in one place indefinitely, that is exactly what she would choose.

Wiggling her butt into Eden, he hardened behind her. One large hand moved from her stomach to below her shirt. Holding still, Shylah didn't dare to breathe. Wrapping his long fingers around her bare breast, the hand engulfed her.

Shylah's breath stuttered as Eden's thumb rubbed against her rock-hard nipple. Subconsciously pushing her chest further into his hand, fire raced down her body.

Eden's mouth clamped onto her neck, exploring and tasting. His breath searing hot on her skin. Eden's other hand trailed down her body before slipping inside her sleep shorts.

Holding her breath, the anticipation of having his hand on her was excruciating.

As his warm fingers found her clit, Shylah arched her back, a moan escaping her lips. Slowly running his finger along her core, while his other hand still tormented her breast, Shylah's arm lifted behind her, fingers running through Eden's hair.

Whole body on fire with need, her breaths shortened, coming out in gasps. If he stopped, she was afraid she might beg him to continue.

Eden's erection pushed harder against her back, begging for attention. Opening her mouth to speak, Eden's finger slipped inside her, immediately halting any rational thought.

Shylah lost herself in the passion between them. Writhing at the torture. Eden's finger entered and withdrew from her as his thumb pushed and rubbed against her clit.

"Eden." His name was a whisper, gasped from her lips.

"You drive me crazy, Shy." Eden's voice was guttural. Deep.

As his teeth bit down slightly into Shylah's neck, she lost the last bit of control she had. Her throbbing body fell over the edge as she cried out at the intensity of her orgasm.

As the throbbing continued, Eden flipped Shylah onto her back and climbed on top, quickly ridding her of her sleep shorts and shirt.

Eyes still shut, it took Shylah a moment to come down from

her high. When she did, she realized how still Eden's body was above her.

Eyes fluttering open, Shylah's brain finally caught up to the fact that she was naked under Eden.

His eyes were firmly fixed on her body. Her naked body. Etched with scars.

Immediately grabbing at the sheet, she went to cover herself but was stopped by Eden's hand on her wrist.

"What is this?" All passion had left his voice, and thunderous anger now replaced it.

Taking a breath, Shylah swallowed before she answered, "Scars." Voice small, Shylah knew exactly where this conversation would now lead.

"Scars from what?"

Eden knew the answer to that. He was a SEAL. He'd seen bullet wounds before.

"They shot me, Eden." Eden's eyes continued to stare at her scars, the silence between them lengthened. "Twice. I was shot twice."

Finally, his gaze rose to her face

"When?" Eden asked, voice hard and deadly. "When were you shot, Shylah?"

Pausing for a moment, Shylah mustered her courage and told Eden, "While you were on your last mission."

There was no change in Eden's expression, but the intensity of his stare made Shylah want to squirm and cover herself.

"You need to explain this to me, and you need to explain now."

The muscles across his chest rippled with anger. Shylah pushed at his huge chest but the man didn't move an inch. "I'll explain, Eden, but at least let me cover myself first."

Processing her request for a moment, Eden's powerful body rolled to the side. Pulling the sheet up to cover her chest, Shylah took a breath before turning to Eden. His eyes remained hard, tension radiating from his body.

Eden fought to still his rage.

All thoughts of making love to Shylah vanished as his brain struggled to comprehend what he'd just learned.

They shot Shylah. Not just once. Shylah was shot twice while she was supposed to be at his house. Safe.

Rolling to the side, Eden watched as Shylah pulled the sheet over her chest. It covered the scarring on her lower abdomen, but it was etched in his mind. The scar on her shoulder remained uncovered, a mark against her otherwise perfect skin.

"Explain." When Shylah didn't speak immediately, Eden thought he might lose his mind. "I'm not fucking around, Shylah, I want to know exactly who shot you and why."

Eyes lowering to the sheet over her chest, Shylah took another moment before she spoke.

"The day after I got to your house, I received a call from the people I'd been working with to get the project shut down. They'd tapped some of the office phones at Project Arma so they could listen in before the raid. That morning there was a communication from another SEAL team."

Eden's body stilled. He knew part of this story. What he didn't know was Shylah's place in it.

When she hesitated, Eden's body tensed. "Tell me."

"They confirmed that they were on track to complete their mission."

"To kill us," Eden muttered, more to himself than to Shylah.

Eden knew their mission had been to kill Eden and his team. Troy, a member of the other SEAL team, had told Evie this when he'd taken her hostage.

Eden's team was sent on a mission to extract people from a building in Peru when they'd received a directive to abort the mission. The building had blown up at the very time Eden's team was supposed to be inside.

"How did you get involved in this?" Eden dreaded the answer before she spoke.

"They called to tell me because they knew you and I were involved. I knew I could stop it. I had the commander's login details, and I knew how he communicated with you. So, I went to the base, and I sent your team an email pretending to be him."

Eden's head spun. "That email directing us to abort the mission was from you?"

"Yes." Shylah's eyes darted down to her hands. A sinking feeling came over Eden about what she would say next. "After I sent the email, but before I could leave the room, Doctor Hoskin and your commander came in." Swallowing, Shylah looked as nervous as Eden felt. "The commander killed the doctor in front of me." A shiver rocked Shylah's body. "Commander Hylar was angry because he didn't know they'd tried to take out your team. Then he turned and shot me. I dropped behind a bed but still got hit in the shoulder and then in the stomach. We could hear people raiding the building, so he left. Otherwise, I'm sure he would have stuck around to ensure I died."

An overwhelming urge to hit something grabbed at Eden.

His woman had been hurt. Shot. Saving him. That wasn't her responsibility, damn it.

Knowing that it was his commander who had shot her, a man he'd looked up to and cared about, was a bitter pill to swallow.

"Tell me what happened after that, Shylah."

Fidgeting with the blanket in front of her, Shylah's gaze darted around the room before she continued, "I spent the first couple of months in the hospital. I suffered significant blood loss. I also needed several surgeries after what happened."

"What kind of surgeries?" Eden's gaze zoomed in on her shoulder before trailing down to her left hand. "That's why your left hand shakes. Why you couldn't swim out of the water in the lake."

Pieces were fitting together in Eden's mind.

"Yes. I have some nerve damage in my left arm, affecting my wrist and hand. There was nothing they could do about that. I had to do months of rehabilitation to get it to where it is right now. I still need to keep up with my exercises. It will never be as strong as it used to be." Eden opened his mouth to comment, but Shylah's placement of her hand on his leg stopped him. "There's more. The worst injury was the bullet wound to my abdomen. I mentioned the blood loss. I stayed in the hospital for a while so that they could perform a number of different surgeries."

When Shylah paused, Eden's anxiety grew. "What are you not telling me, Shy?"

"I can't have babies." Shylah said the words quickly, almost choked them out. "The doctors told me there's too much scar tissue in my uterus, and they don't think I can get pregnant."

At the pain on Shylah's face, Eden felt raw. She couldn't have babies. She couldn't have Eden's babies.

Eden knew there were other ways they could have kids if they wanted, but what cut him the deepest was the agony in Shylah's voice.

Shrugging, Shylah's hands smoothed the sheet in front of her, a slight shake in both hands. "I was in the hospital and then rehab for my hand for months. After that, I spent a couple of months in a government safe house. The government thought it was best. Then they asked me to come out of hiding and work at the hospital in Georgetown to see if they could catch the bad guys. They told me about how almost everyone who'd worked on Project Arma had gotten away. You guys weren't safe. So, I agreed. You know what happened after that."

Raising her head, Shylah looked Eden in the eye. "I didn't want to tell you right away. I know I probably should have, but we never spoke about kids, and I think a part of me was scared you wouldn't want me if you knew. I didn't feel safe for a long time, but I couldn't stay away any longer. When I heard my kidnapper in the van mention you were in Marble Falls, I knew I had to find you. I asked the government not to tell you my location or about what happened to me because I wanted to recover first. Both mentally and physically. I know you don't think that was the right thing to do, and I'm sorry. I intended to tell you when I first got here, but you thought I was a part of the cover-up."

Eden struggled to take in everything that Shylah had said. After spending over a year wondering if she was a part of Project Arma and trying to make himself forget about her, it turns out she not only was exactly who she said she was, but she was hurt because of him.

The room suddenly felt too small. He needed to get out. He needed space.

"I need some time to think, Shylah."

Shylah nodded, her face a mixture of vulnerability and hurt. "Oh, of course. I mean, I've had a while to come to terms with everything. Do you want me to leave?"

"No. It's not safe." Climbing out of bed, Eden threw on some clothes. He didn't know what the hell he put on, he just knew that he needed air. Now. "I'll send Mason over."

Shooting a text to Mason, Eden dropped the phone in his pocket before leaving the room. He waited at the back door until he heard Mason pull up, then left.

16

Shylah pushed down the hurt at Eden's abrupt exit. He'd looked at her like . . . like she was damaged.

Was she damaged? She looked at her scars in the mirror every damn day and often asked herself that question.

Seeing it in Eden's eyes seemed worse somehow. The idea that this could be it for her and Eden was gut-wrenching. Shylah had always maintained the hope that they would find their way back to each other, even when Eden had accused her of such awful things.

Not being able to bring herself to cry, Shylah could only feel hollow.

Climbing out of bed, she moved to the shower. She didn't know what the day held, but she sure as hell wouldn't wait around in bed naked for a man that may or may not want her.

Avoiding the mirror, Shylah stepped into the shower, closing her eyes as the warm water droplets hit her shoulders.

Fourteen months. Fourteen months of not seeing him but all the while believing that they would end up together. This was the first time she'd truly questioned it.

Once Shylah finished her shower, she made quick work of

getting dressed before leaving the room in search of Mason. At the sight of Bodie standing by the kitchen island eating cereal, Shylah stopped.

Turning to face her, his smile went some way in lifting Shylah's spirits.

"Hey," Bodie said, mouth full of food.

"Hey, Bodie, I thought Mason would be here." Proud of herself that she could sound semi-okay, Shylah stepped further into the kitchen.

She was glad it was Bodie. He was less intense than the other guys, and he often put Shylah at ease.

His shaggy brown hair set him apart and gave him a laid-back appearance that suited his personality.

Every other guy on the team had maintained their military cuts. That, combined with his dimples when he smiled and friendly personality, made him easy company.

"Mason? Nah, he's not as good with the ladies." Raising his brows, Bodie smiled before his expression turned thoughtful. "He is good with Eden, though, so he's out there searching for the giant idiot."

Giant idiot sounded about right.

Pushing her sleeves up, Shylah went to Eden's pantry, searching to see what he had. Pulling out jars, she was pleasantly surprised by what she found.

"I didn't think he would have baking ingredients." Ducking her head back in, she pulled out everything she saw that could be turned into some sort of baked good. "He even has chocolate chips."

Plonking them down onto the kitchen island, she went in search of baking utensils.

Shoving some more cereal in his mouth, the corner of Bodie's lips pulled up. "Maybe the guy remembered how much you love to bake and wanted to be ready."

Pausing where she was, she felt a moment of flutters at the possibility but quickly pulled herself back to reality.

"I doubt that's the case. Eden was about ready to have me shipped off to the closest cell when he first saw me in town. I doubt he was prepping his kitchen for me to bake him a cake."

Sitting his bowl on the island, Bodie tossed a bunch of bananas into Shylah's pile. "Maybe he only told himself that you were one of the bad guys because he was trying to protect himself. Sometimes it's easier to believe the worst in someone than to leave yourself open to hurt."

Grabbing milk and eggs from the fridge, Shylah pursed her lips. "If situations had been reversed, I would have believed in him."

Bodie shrugged his huge shoulders. "Did I mention he's a giant idiot?"

A hint of a smile touched Shylah's lips as she started pouring ingredients into the bowl.

"You did, but feel free to repeat it."

Grabbing the milk by her left hand, her wrist gave out. Closing her eyes, she waited for it to hit the ground. When the sound never came, she opened them to find Bodie standing there holding the bottle.

Jeez, he must have been quick. He'd just been on the other side of the island when she grabbed it.

Cursing her damn wrist, Shylah gave a tense smile. "Thanks. I didn't realize it was full."

As lame excuses went, that one was right up there. Unfortunately, it was all her tired brain could come up with.

Without saying anything, Bodie placed the bottle on the island before turning to wash his hands. "Let me help. Maybe you can teach me. I hear baking gets the ladies."

Appreciating his attempt to lighten the mood, Shylah held a measuring cup in front of him. "Measure out two cups of milk and pour them into the bowl. You can do the wet ingredients." Turning to meet his gaze, Shylah gave Bodie a skeptical look. "Also, I don't think enticing a woman with baked goods is the best plan."

"No?" Bodie frowned like it was crazy that she might question his plan. "What about my hulk-like muscles and witty charm?"

Scanning his ridiculously big forearms and biceps, Shylah nodded. "That would work."

"Good. Now I just need to find where all the ladies are at."

This time Shylah did laugh. "I wouldn't be so quick to find one, Bodie. I hear they can be more trouble than they're worth." *Just ask Eden,* Shylah thought. Pointing to the carton of eggs, Shylah gave the next direction, "It needs two eggs then a dash of vanilla extract."

Cracking the eggs like a pro, Shylah gave Bodie a suspicious look. That was no beginner egg cracking. "Don't look so surprised. Scrambled eggs are the Bodie specialty."

"Yeah, I don't think you need any help getting the ladies, Bodie."

"Damn straight."

Laughing again, Shylah felt more relaxed as they started prepping the food.

Working in silence for a few minutes before Bodie spoke again, keeping his eyes set on the bowl in front of him. "For the record, Shylah, the guys and I always believed in you. And we always believed in you and Eden. I'm sure that Eden always believed in you too. He just needed some way to survive while he couldn't find you. You'll find your way back to each other."

Gut clenching, she turned her gaze to look at Bodie. "You didn't see Eden this morning. The way he looked at me. I finally told him everything and he just . . . left."

Shaking his head, Bodie didn't seem deterred. "The man's had nothing on his mind but you for over a year. He'll be back."

He would be back. But would he still want her?

Eden stopped running when he reached the tree line. He'd just sprinted about five miles in a quarter of the time it would take an average man, and he wasn't even out of breath.

He wanted to push himself to exhaustion. Make himself so tired he couldn't think or feel, but his damn body didn't have an off switch.

The scars that marked Shylah's perfect skin were on replay in his mind. So too was the sadness that shined through her eyes when she'd said she couldn't have kids.

It shouldn't have happened. None of it should have happened. Shylah should have been safe.

At the sound of footsteps behind him, Eden turned to find Mason a few feet away.

Walking up to the other man, Eden grabbed a fistful of his shirt. "What the fuck, Eagle. You're supposed to be with Shylah."

Hands in the air, Mason spoke in an even tone, "Red's with her, Hunter. She's safe."

Letting go of his friend's shirt, Eden took a step back and ran his hands through his hair.

"GODDAMN IT." The angry words left Eden's chest in a shout. Frustration swelled inside him, but he had no way to expel it.

"Talk to me, Hunter, what's going on?"

Eden spared his friend a glance before looking away. "She was shot." The words didn't even make sense when he said them out loud. "She was shot saving us."

"I don't understand."

Neither did Eden.

Taking a breath, Eden turned and looked his friend in the eye. "You know that last message we got from Commander Hylar. The one that told us to abort the mission in Peru?"

"The message that saved our lives? I remember."

"That wasn't from him. It was from Shylah. Then after she sent it, he found her and shot her. Damn near killed her. *Tried* to kill her."

The muscles in Mason's arms bunched as he clenched his fists. "The commander shot Shylah?"

"He shot her twice. And now . . ." Eden looked away, trying to hide some of the rage within him. "She was injured pretty bad. She has nerve damage in her left arm, affecting her wrist and hand. She also can't get pregnant."

"Shit," Mason muttered after a moment of silence.

Was that all his friend had to say? Eden looked back at Mason, close to a snapping point, but at the sight of sympathy and anger on his face, Eden pulled himself up.

"She just told you this?"

"Yes."

Eyes narrowing, Mason stepped forward. "What the fuck are you doing out here then? She probably needs you right now."

"She doesn't need me, Eagle. She was in the hospital for months, and she didn't even try to search me out." Kicking a rock beneath his foot, Eden angled his body back to Mason. "Who the hell asked her to take a bullet for me?"

"Who asked her?" Shrugging, Mason stuffed his hands in his pockets. "I'm no expert on the matter, but I'd say that's what people do when they're in love. No request needed."

"No, she should have protected herself. She could have died." *Jesus*, Eden couldn't even consider that.

"But she didn't. She's here. Alive. In your home, waiting for you. The bigger question is, why are you out here instead of with her."

Because he'd had to get out. Away. "I'm so angry at her for making those decisions for both of us. I could have helped her through her recovery. I could have protected her from being shot and kidnapped and fucking frightened and in hiding."

"But you still love her."

Hell, the woman could have been a part of the damn project, and he'd still love her. "I can't live without the woman."

He couldn't damn well breathe without the woman. But he was angry. So damn angry. Every decision she had made had been wrong.

"What else is eating at you? I know there's more."

Shaking his head, Eden took a breath. "You should have heard her voice when she told me, Eagle. Like her heart had been torn in two." Pausing, he looked up at the gray clouds. "We never spoke about whether we'd have a family together, but I could see the longing in her eyes. She sacrificed having kids for me. I don't see how she won't grow to resent me in the long run. Hate me, even."

"So, you're scared."

"No, I'm fucking terrified. I just got her back. There's no way I can lose her again."

"Then, don't push her away, Hunter." Walking closer to Eden, Mason placed his hand on his friend's shoulder. "I know it's been a rough year. Finding out we were all used and betrayed by those we trusted was the toughest damn thing we've been through. We're all trying to learn to trust again. You had the added stress of Shylah going missing. You haven't been the same since."

Hell, he'd been a stranger to everyone these past fourteen months, including himself.

"Since she got back, we've seen glimpses of the old Hunter.

Trust it. Trust your feelings for her and that she's here to stay. Tell her how important she is to you and that you can't lose her again. Otherwise, what the hell was the point of getting our freedom back if we were just going to choose to be unhappy."

Was that true? Was Eden choosing to be unhappy to avoid the pain of losing her again?

"What if she leaves?"

"Then, we hunt her down this time, and we don't stop." Mason took a step back. "And she won't grow to resent you, Hunter. That woman loves you. Every fool but you can see that."

17

As Eden neared his back door, he slowed at the sound of Shylah's laugher. She sounded relaxed. Happy. He hadn't heard that in too long.

Eden hesitated for a moment.

"Stop over-thinking everything and get your ass inside." Mason ordered.

Moving to the door, Eden followed Mason in. His eyes immediately narrowed.

There were ingredients, bowls, and spoons scattered everywhere. The kitchen was a mess. But it was Bodie and Shylah that drew his attention.

They were standing close. Too damn close for his liking. Bodie's arm just about brushed Shylah's.

When Shylah's eyes lifted and met Eden's, they widened for a moment before shifting away.

Damn. He wanted to kick his own ass.

He'd hurt her. He shouldn't have been a jerk and up and left after she'd told him something so personal and painful. He was an idiot.

Drawing his eyes across to Bodie, he could see the disapproval in his friend's expression. "Thanks, Red, I got it from here."

Turning, Bodie washed his hands as Shylah collected two containers. Popping what looked like cookies and muffins inside, she handed one to Bodie and one to Mason.

Lifting the container, Mason inspected the bottom.

"Jesus, Shylah, these look amazing. I need to come over and talk to this meathead more often."

Giving a small shrug, Shylah turned, smiling at Bodie. "I can't take all the credit. Bodie's better in the kitchen than he lets on."

Mason darted his gaze to Bodie. "We should start calling you Betty Crocker."

Walking around the kitchen island, Bodie rolled his eyes. "Dude, don't be jealous that I've got a strong cooking game, and you don't."

Following Bodie to the front door, Mason frowned. "Who said I don't have a strong cooking game? I cook a mean bowl of instant noodles."

Both men turned and nodded a goodbye before walking through the door and pulling it closed behind them.

Once it was just him and Shylah, Eden turned to face her only to find she wasn't looking at him. Her gaze was on the island in front of her. The specks of flour seemed to be the most interesting things she'd seen.

"I shouldn't have left," Eden voiced quietly.

Shylah's head popped up, mouth opening and closing before she spoke.

"That's okay, you needed time."

Striding around the island, Eden walked right up to Shylah so that they were almost touching.

When Shylah dipped her head, Eden placed his fingers

under her chin to raise her eyes back up to his. So damn beautiful, but a sadness lingered. He'd done that.

"It's not okay. It was an asshole move, and I'm sorry. I fucked up."

Shylah attempted a half-smile that didn't reach her eyes. "I get it. Me not being able to have kids is something you need time to consider."

"I don't give a damn about that, Shylah. If we choose to have kids down the road, there are ways we can do that. I care about you. I hate that you got hurt saving me, and I hate that it's still hurting you. It kills me you spent months recovering from injuries, and I wasn't there to help and support you. I hate that you then made yourself vulnerable by acting as bait in Georgetown. And I hate that we lost time that we should have been together."

A tear glistened in Shylah's hazel eyes. "I hate all that too. There were so many times I wanted to find you, but I was a mess."

"It's not just your fault, Shy. I should have searched harder. Project Arma messed with my head. I won't let anything get between us again." Eden's hand went to Shylah's cheek. "I want to be there no matter how hard it is. I want to be by your side in the worst times and the best ones. You are the single most important thing in my life, Shy. You've been my everything since the moment I met you."

Eyes widening, Shylah was quiet for a moment before she spoke. "I never stopped loving you, Eden."

Releasing a growl, Eden lowered his hands and lifted Shylah into his arms. Those were the words he'd been craving to hear for too damn long. "I don't know how not to love you, Shy." Pushing his face into her hair, Eden inhaled her scent. "God, I've missed you."

Wrapping her arms around Eden's neck, Shylah nuzzled her face into his chest. "I missed you every day."

"Never again," Eden said as he pulled his head up to look at Shylah. "Promise me, Shy, that we never separate if we can help it, ever again."

"Never again," Shylah whispered.

Shylah smoothed the material on her red dress.

Standing in front of the mirror looking at her reflection, she couldn't help but wonder what it was Eden saw in her. She had plain brown hair that hung around her face and hazel eyes that were nothing to write home about.

Most men looked straight through her.

Except Eden.

After Eden had returned that afternoon and dropped the bombshell that he still loved her, he'd suggested they go out to eat. On a date.

Shylah's stomach had been doing somersaults ever since. They'd done little more than fight since she got to Marble Falls. She didn't know if she could flick back to the old Shylah. The Shylah and Eden Shylah.

One thing was still the same at least, she still thought Eden was miles out of her league. Whenever she'd gone out with him in the past, she'd always been hypersensitive about what others thought.

Were they wondering why someone as good looking as him was dating someone as plain as her?

"Stop it."

Shylah startled at Eden's voice.

Turning her head, she saw him leaning on the doorframe,

arms crossed over his massive chest. The stance made the muscles in his arms appear even bigger.

Like he needed that.

"Stop what?"

"Judging yourself. Putting yourself down. Whatever critical, untrue thoughts you have running through your head. You're beautiful." Pushing off the frame, Eden walked to the bed and picked up her jacket. Helping her into it, a shiver cursed down Shylah's spine as his hands brushed against her sensitive skin. Dropping a kiss on her shoulder before straightening, Eden put a hand on the small of Shylah's back. "Ready to go?"

No. "Yes."

Shylah didn't know why she was so nervous. She was being ridiculous. She'd dated the guy for months a little over a year ago.

They'd already had sex since she'd been back. There was no reason to be shy. She needed to snap out of it.

Following Eden to his truck, they started heading into town.

Recognizing for the first time how far out he lived, she turned her head to ask Eden about it. "What made you want to live so far from town?"

"The peace and quiet," Eden said without hesitation. "No one close by to just pop over for no good reason. If I see people, it's because I choose to."

Cocking her head sideways, she studied his profile. "You make it sound like you hate people."

"I don't hate people. The world has just shown me time and again that people are assholes." There was no anger in Eden's voice as he spoke.

Not able to hold back the laugh, Shylah couldn't quite work out if Eden was joking. "Not everyone's an asshole, Eden."

Taking his eyes off the road for a moment to look at Shylah, she could see there was no humor in his expression. "Remember what I told you about my brother?"

"I remember you telling me he died in a robbery."

"And then my parents became distant, so I effectively lost them too. I was pretty much on my own for a while there. A few years later, I met you and had a great team around me. I was genuinely happy for the first time in a long time. But in one day, one conversation, I lost you, I lost my commander, and I found out everything I put my faith in was corrupt. I lost faith in people that day. So, when I came here, I didn't want to be around people."

Shylah placed her hand on Eden's leg. "I'm so sorry, Eden." And she was. She hated hearing the pain in his voice.

"My team, my brothers, they were the only thing that got me through. They didn't give up on me no matter how much of a jerk I was. And trust me when I say, I haven't been the best company these last few months."

Fidgeting with a piece of cotton that had loosened from her dress, guilt hit Shylah hard. "I'm really sorry I didn't come find you sooner. I really felt like it was the right thing to do. Like I couldn't bear to have you find out everything. I needed to recover first. I think it came back to me feeling undeserving of you. If I didn't think I was good enough whole, why would you want me damaged."

"You're not damaged, Shy. You're the only thing I want in this world, injured or not," Eden growled. Reaching his hand over, he gave her thigh a squeeze. "And you're here now, Shy. That's what matters."

Placing her hand on top of his, Shylah smiled, feeling like the luckiest woman to have found Eden.

When they arrived at the restaurant, Shylah was glad to see it wasn't the same one she'd gone to with Trent. Being a small town, it occurred to her it was a possibility. Now she felt dumb for even thinking it.

Instead, Eden led Shylah into a small Chinese restaurant. When they got to the table, Eden pulled out her chair for her before she sat down.

"Mm, the smell of Chinese food always makes me ten times hungrier."

"I remember," Eden said, the menu sitting in front of him, but eyes only for Shylah. "Still have an obsession with pork buns?"

"God, I haven't had one of those in months. Let's order ten." Just the mention of her favorite food had her stomach growling.

"Done."

"And some dumplings. Oh, and some basil chicken," Shylah continued, hungrier by the second.

The smile that stretched across Eden's face caused Shylah's stomach to flip.

"With fried ice cream for dessert," he continued for her.

Shylah wouldn't be surprised if saliva dribbled from her mouth right then and there. "I've missed you."

The smile dropped from Eden's face. "You have no idea."

After they placed their order, the food didn't take long to arrive. Shylah was quick to dig in, not caring if she came across like a starved homeless person.

The pork buns were just as good as she remembered. Halfway through their meal, Eden's phone started ringing. Turning it over, he ignored the first few rings. On the third, he picked it up.

"Eagle, what is it?" Falling silent as he listened to Mason, Shylah noticed Eden's muscles tense before his gaze lifted to hers. "We'll be there in ten."

As he hung up his phone, a nervous tension crept into Shylah's shoulders. "What is it?"

"Someone attacked Kye while he was locking up at Marble."

Shylah didn't move or say anything for a moment. Who would be dumb enough to attack one of the guys? They were lethal, even on their worst day.

Eden stood and reached for Shylah's chair, placing a hand on her elbow as he helped her stand. "What's Kye going to do with the guy?"

"He got away."

"He got away?" Shylah repeated, louder than she'd intended. Someone attacked Kye and was fast and strong enough to get away? Jeepers.

Eden made quick work of the trip to Marble. It felt strange walking into the building at night. The street was too dark and too quiet.

Walking inside, all seven other men stood in the large front area, Evie under Luca's arm.

"What happened?" Eden asked as he walked up to the group, holding Shylah's hand in his.

Kye had a scratch on his forehead, but other than that, no one would guess anything had happened. "I was closing up the front door when I heard footsteps. I didn't think anything of it until they got closer. Too close. When I turned, a guy was standing there."

"Did you recognize him?" Oliver asked.

"Never seen him before. He wasn't wearing a shirt, and he was scruffy and dirty. Sort of looked homeless, but strong." Kye hesitated for a moment before adding, "He also had red bruises around his wrists."

Shylah looked around the group to see the men sharing a look that she didn't quite understand.

"What did he want?" Wyatt questioned.

"He kept saying he needed help, but then he'd grab his head. He seemed to struggle on a psychological level. Kept pulling his hair, scratching his skin. He was agitated. When he banged his head with his fists, I tried to grab his arms, but he shoved me. Hard. That's how I hit my head."

"He shoved you hard enough that you fell backward?" Eden asked, his hand tightening a fraction on Shylah's.

"He was strong," Kye said, holding Eden's gaze.

"Any track marks?" Luca asked from where he stood with Evie.

"Not that I could see. If he's like us though, his skin will heal quickly."

They healed quickly? That was a surprise to Shylah.

"Then he left," Kye continued. "He was damn quick. I thought about going after him, but I didn't know where he would lead me."

"Smart. He could have led you back to them," Bodie said, a serious look on his face for once.

Asher shoved his hands into his pockets as he spoke. "So what now?"

"A couple of us should try to track him, see if he left a trail," Wyatt said in a commanding voice. "Evie and I can hack the nearby cameras, see if we find anything. We can catch up tomorrow and see if we have anything."

"I'll see if I can track him," Oliver said.

"I'll go too. I'll recognize him on the off chance we find something," Kye replied firmly.

The men looked around at each other, determination in their eyes.

One thing was clear, there was more going on here than Shylah knew.

18

Eden's fingers slid over the scarring on Shylah's stomach. It was clear the scar was fading, but red discoloration still tinged the wound. The scar was only small. Visible where the bullet had hit, but also where the surgery had been performed.

Eden had seen a lot worse, but seeing the scars on Shylah's body made his blood boil. The knowledge that it was due to his commander's actions, a man Eden had cared about and trusted, killed him.

Shylah's eyes slowly fluttered open, and it took her a moment to become conscious. When she was, her hand immediately reached for the blanket to cover herself.

Lightly taking hold of her wrist, Eden halted her for a moment. "Please, Shylah, I want to see."

Loosening his grip, Shylah could have pulled her hand away if she'd wanted. Instead, she relaxed, but worry stilled glazed her eyes.

"I hate it. It's all I see when I look at myself."

Shaking his head, Eden disagreed, "It's the mark of survival. A reminder of your strength."

Because this woman had strength in spades.

Raising her hand, Shylah placed it on Eden's cheek. "I was so nervous that it would bother you."

Dragging his gaze from the scarring to Shylah's face, he studied her hazel eyes. "Would I love to watch you carry my baby one day? Yes. Does the fact that you probably can't make me question whether I should be with you? Hell, no. If you want to try to get pregnant, we'll go to every specialist in the country to seek help. If it turns out you can't carry a baby, there are other ways to have children. Surrogacy. Adoption. None of that affects how I feel about you."

Shylah's hand stroked Eden's cheek. "It's surreal to me that a couple of weeks ago you hated me, and now we're talking about babies."

"I never hated you, Shylah. I don't even think I could. Even in my anger-fueled craze when I stupidly thought you might have been part of Project Arma, I was so damn mad at you, but hate never came into it."

Shylah's eyes reflected the sadness that Eden had felt. "I'll try to never hide any secrets from you again."

A laugh escaped Eden's chest. "Shy, if I suspect you're hiding a secret from me, I'm gonna lock you in a room and seduce the truth out of you."

Furrowing her brows, Shylah crossed her arms over the sheets. "Maybe I'm hiding a secret right now."

"You're not."

"How do you know?"

"Because when you lie to me, I hear your heart skip a beat and speed up," Eden said, placing his hand over her chest. "Your pupils dilate, and your eyes widen slightly. You breathe slightly faster than normal."

"That's not fair. You have abilities to tell when I'm lying, but I can't do the same for you."

"I would never lie to you, Shylah."

He sure as hell wouldn't ever lie. Lies and secrets are what got them into this mess. No fucking way was Eden going to risk history repeating itself.

Leaning down, Eden placed a kiss on Shylah's lips. "You and me, no secrets, got it?"

Face curving into a smile, Shylah nodded. "Done." Her hand ran down Eden's chest, causing him to harden. "Now, what's the plan for today."

At the mention of the day ahead, Eden's mind went back to the attack on Kye, which happened less than twenty-four hours ago.

Climbing out of bed, Eden didn't show an ounce of care that he was naked. "I was thinking we could have everyone from Marble over for a barbecue. The guys and I try to have a family social gathering at least once a month, and I haven't hosted one. It would give me a chance to talk to the guys about last night and you a chance to get to know Evie and Lexie a bit better."

Sitting up, Shylah drew the sheet up with her. "That sounds nice. I really like Evie and Lexie." Shylah cocked her head to the side. "They're quite the opposite of each other. Evie seems shy and reserved while Lexie just tends to say whatever pops into her head. I'm surprised they're friends."

Eden scoffed, "Lexie could make friends with a terrorist. Evie never stood a chance."

Giggling, Shylah stepped out of bed, dropping the sheet in the process. Eden's eyes drew to her body. She didn't realize how irresistible she was.

"Ooh, I can make my apple strudel. And custard tart." Shylah beamed, oblivious to Eden's heated gaze.

Walking around the bed, Eden pulled Shylah's naked body into his and placed a long intimate kiss on her lips. "Then we'd better get moving before I throw you back on the bed and keep you captive all day."

A flush tinged Shylah's cheeks. "That doesn't sound so terrible."

A rumble vibrated through Eden's chest before he lowered his head. Touching his lips to Shylah's, Eden deepened the kiss immediately. Shylah tasted sweet as his tongue touched hers.

She leaned her body into his, her hard nipples scraping against Eden's chest. Growling, Eden reluctantly pulled away, Shylah's disappointed groan doing nothing to calm the fire inside him.

"We need to prepare for today. I'll make the wait worth your while."

Eyes shooting up to his face, Shylah pouted her lips. "I'm gonna hold you to that, buddy."

Eden was counting on it.

After he calmed down and got dressed, Eden let everyone from Marble know the plan. He and Shylah then spent the day getting ready for that evening.

It felt very domesticated to Eden. Something he'd wanted a little over a year ago but refused to let himself think about when she disappeared.

Now, standing with his team in his backyard, Eden felt content for the first time in months.

"You look happy, man."

Turning to look at Luca beside him, Eden nodded. "Right back at you."

Laughing, Luca nodded. "Yeah, those women got us good, didn't they?"

"Prefer that to the alternative," Eden muttered, lifting a beer to his lips.

Slapping his hand on Eden's shoulder, the smile left Luca's face. "Seriously though, I'm glad you got her back. It means that we got you back. We were worried about you for a while there."

"Yeah, I was an asshole. I still feel like a dick for how I treated you and Evie."

Dick was an understatement.

"You made good, that's what counts."

Eden was lucky his friend was willing to forgive him. If roles had been reversed and someone had treated Shylah like that, he didn't know what he would have done.

"Should we talk business for a minute?" Wyatt asked, coming to stand with Eden and Luca.

Hearing Wyatt's words from their various places around the yard, the rest of the guys made their way over to stand with Wyatt, Eden, and Luca.

"Let's get business out the way so I can spend some time with my woman."

At Luca's words, Eden's eyes tracked Shylah across the lawn. She was standing with Evie and Lexie, laughing at something they said. As she turned her gaze to his, Eden winked and watched Shylah's lips curve into a shy smile.

Damn, she was stunning. And she was his.

"Evie and I hacked the local security cameras," Wyatt said, pulling Eden's attention back to the conversation at hand. "We didn't get much but were able to trace the guy to the edge of town. Then we lost him. From what we could make out, the guy looked scared out of his mind."

"Cage and I tried to track where he came from and where he might have gone," Oliver jumped in. "Didn't find much of anything, but he broke into a drugstore on the way to Marble and raided the pain med cabinet."

"The guy was desperate," Kye muttered. "He wanted help last night but was battling something going on in his head."

"If we're connecting this guy to the deserted warehouse, we're assuming he may have spent some of his time in those cages," Bodie said.

"So, he was likely being held prisoner, getting the next batch of the Project Arma drug forced into his body," Mason said in rage.

Eden couldn't imagine what hell that would be like. His team was lucky to receive a good version of the drug, but to be forcibly injected with something that messes with your mind?

"I'll contact the government and see if they have any more leads we can track."

"Fuck." Eden couldn't hold in the curse. "I'm going to kill those responsible when I find them."

"When *we* find them," Asher pointed out. "And you won't be alone in that."

Shylah picked at the food on her plate, her gaze kept drawing back to Eden.

Standing with the other guys across the lawn, she noted that they all wore intense looks on their faces. Like they were ready to battle at any moment.

They looked fierce. Lethal.

"I am in awe of you, woman. What the heck did you do to that man? He is not the same Eden of a month ago."

Shylah turned back to Lexie and Evie. Evie shook her head before she spoke, "Leave her alone, Lex. She's happy."

"Well, since she landed the great white shark, she should be happy," Lexie said, stuffing a chip in her mouth.

With a cringe, the guilt hit Shylah hard. "I hate that he was angry for so long and that you both knew him like that. That's not who he is."

"No, that's who he is with no Shylah in his life," Lexie said gently. "Your breakup did a number on him because he's been one angry nutcracker."

Evie winced. "It's true. But that's okay because you're back now."

Lexie's gaze darted to Eden then back to Shylah. "But if you even think about leaving us with Tyrannosaurus Eden again, Evie and I will personally hunt you down and drag you back here using whatever means necessary."

Lexie was tall but too slender to pose much of a threat. But the promise in her eyes made Shylah believe she would keep her word.

"Don't worry, I'm not going anywhere," Shylah said, eyes flicking back to Eden. "I shouldn't have stayed away so long as it was."

She was just starting to realize the gravity her actions had on Eden. She'd spent so much time over the last few months thinking about her own physical and mental recovery, and the fear that Eden wouldn't want her anymore, that she hadn't considered Eden enough.

She'd underestimated how much she'd meant to him, something she never intended to do again.

"So, why did you?" Lexie asked, curiosity in her eyes.

"Lexie!" Evie hit Lexie's arm lightly. "You don't have to answer that, Shylah. It's no one's business but your own."

When Lexie rolled her eyes, Shylah had a feeling the other woman didn't agree. "Or, you could share the gossip and get a girl's opinion on it all."

When Lexie just stared at Shylah expectantly, she squirmed under the scrutiny.

She knew that Evie was aware of Project Arma and everything the guys had been through, but Eden hadn't mentioned anything about Lexie. Shylah didn't want to give away any secrets that weren't hers to give.

"I got into an accident. It left me with some injuries. One of the injuries caused nerve damage in my hand, among other things. It was a long road to recovery, and I didn't want to pull Eden into that mess."

Empathy shined in Lexie's eyes. "I'm sorry, Shylah. What kind of accident?"

A huff came from Evie's direction.

"Someone attacked me," Shylah responded, keeping her answer brief.

Eyes widening slightly, Lexie popped her hand on Shylah's arm. "Someone attacked you? A man, I'm guessing? God, what is it with men these days? Do they suck or what?"

The feel of Lexie's hand on Shylah's arm was comforting. Maybe these ladies would turn into friends.

Before Shylah could think any further into it, Eden's arm snaked around her waist. Craning her neck back to look at him, Shylah couldn't stop the giddy excitement she felt at his closeness.

"Hey," she said quietly, not able to hold back the smile that curved her lips.

"Hey, yourself."

Being close to Eden gave her the same feeling as when she consumed too much sugar when she was younger. High on life and ridiculously happy.

When Shylah eventually dragged her eyes from Eden, she noticed Lexie's gaze flick between her and Eden as well as Evie and Luca with longing.

Feeling self-conscious about making Lexie feel like the fifth wheel, Shylah shimmied herself out of Eden's arms.

"I'm going to go grab some more drinks for the fridge." Dashing away before Eden could stop her, Shylah made her way inside.

In the kitchen, she reached down and grabbed a couple of

beers in each hand. Turning around, she almost jumped out of her skin when Mason stood right behind her.

Two beers slipped from her left hand, but Mason easily caught them before they hit the ground.

"Jeez, Mason, you scared the heck out of me." Heart still racing, she took a calming breath.

"Sorry, we tend to walk quietly. A habit from our time as SEALs."

"I know. Eden never makes a sound when he moves. I can't get used to it." When Mason continued to stand in front of her, Shylah started to feel awkward. "Was there something you wanted to chat about?"

"Actually, yes, I saw you walk in here and thought we could talk one-on-one. We haven't had a chance since you got back."

Shylah's chest tightened at the sudden nervous tension that crept into her shoulders. "Sure."

"I can hear your heart just about beating from your chest, Shylah. You don't need to stress."

Then why did it feel like she was about to face the firing line?

Giving a tight smile, Shylah placed the beers on the counter. "What's up, Mason?"

"Are you here to stay, Shylah?"

Was she here to stay? Forever?

"I plan to stay with Eden for as long as he'll have me." Whether or not that was the right answer, it was the truth.

Mason studied Shylah's eyes. He looked like he was a human lie detector. Eden sure was so she wouldn't be surprised if they all were.

"That man loves you. It damn near destroyed him when you up and disappeared."

The guilt in Shylah's chest intensified. "I know. I regret my decision, but I wasn't ready to lean on him for support, and I didn't want to unload my shit on him."

"It was his shit that got you into that mess, and he had a right to know. By leaving him with no answers, you left his life in limbo. You seriously underestimated how much he loved you."

There was no accusation in Mason's voice. He spoke like he was citing facts.

Shylah still felt the words like they were a direct hit on her, though.

"If I had to do it again, I would try to choose differently."

Again, Mason's piercing gaze held her captive, seeing much more than she likely wanted him to. "I hope you mean that, Shylah, and I hope you understand that if you leave, it won't just be Eden tracking you down."

So now Eden, the women, and the guys would look for Shylah if she left. Jesus, she was almost tempted to do it to see who caught her first.

"I understand, Mason, but I hope you understand that I don't intend to go anywhere. I love Eden. I've always loved him. It was hard enough being apart before. I don't think I would survive it again."

"Good. I'm glad to hear it."

With a quick nod, Mason grabbed the beer bottles from the counter and headed back outside.

Once Shylah was alone in the kitchen, she sagged against the counter.

She knew she'd brought pain to Eden's life, but being reminded of it every five minutes was wearing on her.

After a moment, Shylah headed back outside, walking straight to Eden's side. His arm immediately wrapped around her waist, and Shylah leaned into him.

"Everything okay, Shy?"

Glancing up into Eden's worried eyes, Shylah forced a smile she didn't feel. "Of course."

Arm tightening slightly, Eden lowered his mouth to place a

kiss on her head. She didn't deserve him, but she sure as hell would hang onto him for as long as he'd have her.

19

"Gladys, good news, nothing in your test results shows anything serious."

Shylah picked up the chart and made her final notes.

"Thank you, dear, that makes me so relieved," Gladys said with a sigh. "Is it okay if I just rest here for a while? In case the tightness in my chest comes back?"

"Of course, we aren't busy now, so feel free to take your time. I can get one of the nurses to check on you before you leave."

Trent hadn't been wrong when he'd said Gladys came in a lot. This was the third time in less than a week. In all honesty, Shylah didn't mind. She would rather see the sweet older lady than a dumb drunk.

"It won't be you to check on me?"

Glancing up, Shylah gave the older lady a kind smile. "I finish in a few minutes, so unfortunately not. Linda is on tonight, and she's fantastic."

"Oh, yes, Linda is nice," Gladys exclaimed, just as an excited gleam entered her eyes. "So, how is it going with Eden? Word around town is that the boy is a lot happier."

"Word around town? Normally I would say not to listen to gossip, but in this case, Eden is happy, as am I."

"Goodness, what a relief. He needed a sweet girl to take care of him."

"I think, if anything, he's taking care of me." Placing the chart back in the folder, Shylah turned to leave. "It was nice seeing you again, Gladys. Just ring the bell if you need anything."

Giving her a final smile, Shylah moved into the hall and pulled her phone out of her pocket. She quickly sent a message to Eden.

I just saw my last patient. Be about ten.

The reply was almost instant.

I'm out front. Don't take too long, or I'm coming in to get your sweet ass.

Not able to contain the smile that spread across her face, Shylah was sliding the phone back into her pocket, when she heard her name called from behind.

"Shylah." Turning around, she caught Trent walking up to her from the front desk. "I'm sorry to ask, but could you see one last patient before you finish?"

Glancing at the time on her phone, it was already five minutes after she was supposed to leave.

Trent must have seen the hesitation in her eyes. "I hate asking. It's just that Linda's caught up with another patient, and Janet called in sick."

Shaking her head, Shylah smiled. "Of course." She wanted nothing more than to be in Eden's arms at that very moment, but that would come.

"Great, he's in room eight and just needs the flu shot. We've recently moved it to the top draw to the left."

"Got it," Shylah said with a quick nod.

"Thanks, Shylah." Trent smiled before heading back down the hall.

Whipping out her phone again, she sent off another message to Eden.

Will be a few minutes later, seeing one last patient.

Again, the response was instant.

Don't take too long. Same rules apply.

Almost laughing out loud, Shylah popped the phone back into her pocket as she opened the door to room eight. Grabbing the chart on her way in, she looked up to see her patient was a young man with dark hair.

His dark eyes darted to Shylah as soon as she entered the room. Something about him made her hesitate.

A nauseating smell seemed to emanate from him, causing Shylah to want to gag, and his fingers were tapping the chair almost rhythmically.

Pushing aside the uneasy feeling in her gut, Shylah forced a smile.

"Hi, I'm Shylah. I'll be giving you your flu shot today."

"Shylah. I'm Ben."

Ben's eyes trailed down her body, and Shylah had to restrain herself from crossing her arms over her chest when his gaze lingered there.

Moving straight to the drawer Trent had directed her to, she made quick work of getting the shot ready. The faster she got this done, the faster she'd be out.

Turning back to Ben, she had to stop herself from pulling back at his stench. It was like the guy hadn't showered in weeks.

"If you could lean back in the chair and roll your sleeve up to the shoulder, Ben, that would be great."

Leaning back, Ben seemed to study her as he went. "You're too pretty to be a nurse."

Giving a tight smile, Shylah wiped his upper arm. "Thank you, but I assure you I am a nurse, and I'm very good at what I do."

"I bet you are."

Not sure what he was getting at with that comment, Shylah refrained from responding.

Taking the cap off the syringe, she injected the shot into Ben's arm, throwing the empty syringe in the sharps container when she finished. Shylah removed her gloves and picked up the chart.

"Remain seated for a moment, then once I'm done, I can let you go."

Scribbling down the notes, it took Shylah a moment to notice that Ben hadn't responded. Turning her head, she saw that his eyes were shut and body still. Too still.

Panic hit Shylah.

"Ben?" Quickly moving to his side, Shylah lifted his wrist to check his pulse. "Ben, can you hear me?"

Hands turning clammy, Shylah noticed his heart rate was much too fast.

Suddenly, Ben's body jerked, causing Shylah to jump. Then another. It was almost like he was about to have a seizure.

Shylah reached for the emergency button.

Before she could press it, the hand she had been touching reached out and grasped her wrist. The grip dug into Shylah's skin, causing her to cry out in pain.

When Ben's eyes popped open, they were glazed over. Almost like when a person was high on drugs, and they didn't really see what was in front of them.

When his head cocked to the side, his eyes narrowed. Shylah's body chilled. Ben's eyes appeared darker, almost black, and full of unconcealed rage.

Terror stabbed at her, and her heart felt like it would pound from her chest.

Ben's hand tightened around her wrist further, the pain brought tears to her eyes. Then he flung her toward the wall.

Hitting it with a bang, Shylah dropped to the ground. Trying to push herself up, her left hand, the one that Ben had just gripped, gave out on her as pain radiated up her shoulder.

Cradling her arm to her chest, Shylah used her right hand to try to crawl toward the door.

Before she could make it a few steps, Ben grabbed onto her ankle, dragging Shylah toward him again. Strong arms flipped her onto her back.

Scream, a voice in the back of Shylah's mind urged. She needed to scream now before it was too late.

Opening her mouth, Shylah cried out as loud as possible before a foot stomped down on her stomach, stealing the breath from her body. Dropping to his knees, Ben climbed on top of her and reeled his fist back.

The punch hit Shylah in the temple. The shock of the hit prevented any pain for a moment before her vision fuzzed. She could just make out the hand reeling back again.

She prepared herself as best she could for another hit, but it never came. Something big collided with him, pulling the weight off her body.

What the hell was taking her so long?

Deciding he'd had enough waiting in the car, Eden pushed the car door open and headed for the hospital foyer.

Damn, he hated hospitals. They reminded him of all his worst memories.

It was in a hospital foyer he'd been told that his brother hadn't made it. Since he'd lost Shylah, every nurse had reminded him of her.

The smell of alcohol and bleach thickened the air. Glancing

around the foyer, there was still no Shylah. Checking his phone, he frowned when there was no message.

Eden's head shot up when a scream echoed through the hall. To some, it would have been barely audible. To Eden, it was loud and piercing.

Shylah.

Moving his feet quickly, Eden sprinted down the hall, not caring who witnessed him moving so fast. At the sound of a fist colliding with flesh, Eden barreled through the door the noise came from.

The sight of a man raising his fist while sitting on top of Shylah sent him into a blind rage.

Reaching the man in under a second, Eden pulled his body off Shylah before his fist could swing. Throwing the man against the far wall, a loud thud of body hitting wall ricocheted through the room.

About to reach down and check Shylah, Eden stopped when the man grunted loudly before standing.

There was an indent where his body had hit the wall showing how hard the impact had been. The man should be unconscious. Instead, he stood with ease, eyeing Shylah on the ground.

A whimper sounded from where Shylah lay.

Not daring to take his mind off the man in front of him, Eden stepped around Shylah, guarding her with his body. If the man wanted her, he'd have to go through him.

The moment the stranger came to that realization, his eyes shifted to Eden, and a growl tore from his chest.

He sounded like a damn animal.

Only barely aware that an audience was forming outside the door, Eden took a threatening step forward. The man's eyes again darted to Shylah before flicking back to Eden, his chest rising and falling, clearly agitated that he couldn't reach her.

"You will not get to her, asshole."

Eyes turning black with fury, the only warning he received was a snarl before the man leaped toward Eden.

Bracing forward, Eden took the impact of his assailant, ensuring they didn't land on Shylah. Instead of attacking Eden, as he'd suspected, the man was attempting to push him aside to reach Shylah.

Fuck no. There was no way in hell Eden was allowing that to happen.

When the man tried to climb around him again, Eden lifted his leg and kicked out hard so that the man fell backward again.

Before the man could push forward, Eden was on him. Wrestling him to the ground, holding him in a lock grip.

The snarls from the man beneath Eden got louder, and his movements more aggressive. The man was damn strong, but his obsession with keeping Shylah in his sights was leaving him distracted.

Heavy footsteps sounded down the hall. Eden looked up to see Mason and Asher enter the room.

The man below Eden took advantage of his moment of distraction. Pushing Eden's body to the side, he leaped toward Shylah, who was now sitting against the wall.

At the same time, Mason lunged at the man, intercepting him moments before he got to her. With Asher's help, the two detained him.

Trusting that Asher and Mason had the man contained, Eden moved to Shylah's side. Bruising was already visible on her temple, and she was clutching her left wrist.

"How you doing, Shy?"

Shylah's eyes were wide as they glanced up at him, and her pulse was pounding. She was in shock.

Reaching toward her injured hand, Shylah flinched as he

lightly touched the skin, avoiding the worst of the bruising. Gently lifting her arm, Eden inspected the injury.

"I think . . . I think he re-injured the nerves in my wrist." Angry bruising in the shape of fingers was visible, and her wrist seemed to hang at an odd angle. "I'll need a CT scan or an MRI."

Looking back up at Shylah's pale face, he pushed the hair out of her eyes. "That's okay. We'll get that done." As Shylah moved to stand, Eden placed a hand on her shoulder. "Shylah, I think you're in shock. I'll sit with you for a bit, okay?"

"When someone's in shock, they should lie down and elevate their feet," Shylah said as if reciting words from a textbook.

"Would you like to lie down and elevate your feet?" Eden asked gently.

"No."

Shrugging, Eden turned so that his body blocked the commotion behind him. "I'm happy to break the rules and sit with you if you are."

Shylah's eyes were still wide, pupils dilated. "He, um, he attacked me after I gave him the flu shot."

Taking Shylah's good hand in his, he noticed it was ice cold. "He was fine before you gave him the shot?"

"Yes. I mean, he gave me the creeps, and he smelled really bad, but he wasn't attacking me." Eden looked up to see Mason's subtle head nod as his friend went to retrieve the syringe. "If you hadn't come in, Eden, I think he would have killed me."

Giving her hand a soft squeeze, Eden shook his head. "Never would have happened, Shy. There was no way in hell I wasn't getting here in time."

"Shylah!"

Both Eden and Shylah looked up to see Doctor O'Neil run into the room.

Goddamn it, was there no other doctor at this hospital?

"I just heard. Are you okay?"

Crouching down in front of Shylah, the doctor took out his penlight and shined it in her eyes. She didn't react at all.

"My wrist hurts."

"Left or right."

Eden thought that was damn obvious.

"Left. I have some nerve damage there. I'm supposed to be careful with it. I do exercises for it every day. I'm not sure if further damage has been done." Shylah was looking at the doctor, but it wouldn't surprise him if she wasn't really seeing him.

"No need to worry until we have some definitive answers. I'll organize a scan."

The doctor reached down to help Shylah, but Eden scooped her up in his arms before he could touch her.

"I'm staying with her."

"Now, Eden, when it's time for the scan—"

"I'm staying with her." The tone of Eden's voice brooked no argument.

It was clear the doctor wasn't happy, but this time he said nothing.

Good, because Eden wasn't about to let Shylah leave his sight for a second.

20

Eden stood in his living room with his team.

It was early, and Shylah still slept. She would probably be asleep for a while after what happened yesterday.

Eden hadn't slept more than a couple hours. His SEAL training in combination with his body's newer abilities meant he could function on less than most.

With fists clenched at his sides, Eden couldn't shake the rage he felt over yesterday's attack. If he had been five minutes later . . . the thought of what could have happened turned the blood in Eden's veins to ice.

"How's Shylah doing, Hunter?" Oliver asked from his place on the couch.

Attempting to unclench his fists, Eden turned his gaze to Oliver. "She's damn tough. Only woke a couple of times last night. She got an MRI on her wrist straight after it happened—bruised nerves, which was the best-case scenario. She's also got a bruise on her temple that makes me want to hunt down that son of a bitch and kill him."

Mason turned, appearing just as angry. "He's in the county

jail. I spoke to Sheriff Peters, who said we could question him." He paused for a moment before adding, "Off the record."

Worked for Eden. "Good. I'm going."

He would get the answers he needed from that asshole one way or another.

"I'm going with you," Mason said. Giving his friend a nod, he knew it was necessary to have Mason there, particularly if Eden didn't like what the fucker said.

"Do we have any information on what was in the syringe?" Luca asked from across the room.

Wyatt's face gave him away before he spoke. "Nothing. The contents of the syringe were all used up, so we have nothing to test. It's frustrating."

"No shit," Asher muttered.

"I'm thinking whatever was in that syringe is the same shit that the guy who attacked me was on. Probably also the same stuff being given to whoever was kept in those empty cages we found," Kye said.

If that were true, Eden wondered if the guy who attacked Shylah knew what would happen. Had he walked into that room knowing what he would be injected with and how he would react to the drug?

"How would Shylah have gotten her hands on the drug to inject him?" Bodie asked, frowning.

"She said she thought she was injecting him with a flu shot. Someone must have set it up and switched the drug," Eden voiced gruffly.

"Why Shylah though? And why did he want her so badly that he didn't even try to fight you? Surely his first priority should have been to fight the bigger threat. He only had eyes for her," Mason said, crossing his arms across his chest.

"It was like he was desperate to get to her, and Eden was just in his way," Asher added.

"They're answers that we need from him," Mason said, his voice unyielding.

"And we'll get them," Eden responded with equal determination.

There was no question about it. Eden would get the answers he needed. Screw the law and screw ethics. No way was he walking away without finding out why the fucker had targeted Shylah.

Eden paused at the slight shuffling he heard from the bedroom. Shylah was awake.

"Looks like the government is close to locating another possible set up. They said they'd let me know once they have confirmation," Wyatt said.

Asher scoffed, "You mean once they get intel that we know so they can clear out."

"No shit," Oliver said, rolling his eyes.

"We don't really have any other options at the moment," Wyatt said, running his hands through his hair in frustration. "Evie and I have been working around the clock searching for the people we found in the files we hacked. It's like they all disappeared off the damn planet."

Luca shrugged. "Troy said Project Arma is bigger than we can imagine. What if they have people everywhere? Their reach could be more extensive than we think."

Troy had said that when he'd taken Evie. The team had hoped he had been exaggerating, but so far, it wasn't looking like that at all.

Eden kept an ear on what was going on in the bedroom. He heard Shylah in the shower and hoped she was coping okay with her wrist. If he heard even an ounce of discomfort, he would be in there in an instant.

Pushing off the wall, Eden turned to Luca. "Is it okay if I

bring Shylah to you and Evie when I go visit our friend in prison?"

"Not a problem, Hunter. Evie likes Shylah a lot. I think it's been nice for her to have another girlfriend in town."

"Yeah, it's been good for Shy, too, having both Evie and Lexie around."

"Lexie might even be there. Those girls seem to be stuck at the hip these days."

"No, Lex boxes at the boxing and Pilates studio on Tuesday afternoons," Asher jumped in casually. Seven pairs of eyes fell on him once he'd spoken. "What?"

"Are you guys dating or what?" Luca asked with a chuckle.

Frowning like it was a ridiculous assumption, Asher shook his head. "Not that it's any of your business, asshole, but no, we're not dating."

"Why the hell not? You spend enough time together," Bodie said and dug his elbow into Asher's ribs.

"Why do people always need to put labels on everything? We like each other, but that doesn't mean we need to be 'official.'" Asher used his fingers to show air quotes when he said the last word.

Whatever Asher's aversion to commitment was, was his own business, Eden thought. Anyone with two eyes could see that they were obsessed with each other. But only they could sort out their own shit.

Upon hearing the shower turn off, Eden took a step forward. "Okay, time for me to check on my woman." Eden darted his eyes across to Mason. "Once I see how Shylah's doing, I'll message for a time for us to visit the county prison."

"Got it."

Then they filtered out, leaving his home silent.

Walking up to his bedroom, Eden opened the door, and his eyes zoomed in on Shylah struggling to hook the clasp on her bra. Walking straight over to her, Eden's fingers went to the clasp to help her.

"You should have stayed in bed and waited. I could have helped you."

"I'm okay. I need to keep using my wrist anyway. The less I use it, the stiffer it gets."

Growling, Eden turned Shylah in his arms. "You need to rest."

"I'm fine, Eden," Shylah said, placing her hands on his chest. "I know what exercises I need to do, and I'm feeling surprisingly okay today."

Eden's eyes shifted to the purple bruise on her temple, anger boiling inside him. Screw information, he would murder the fucker that had hurt her.

"How's your head feel?" Eden asked, brushing a piece of hair off her face.

"Honestly, if I don't look at myself in the mirror, I forget it's there."

"No headache?" Eden questioned. Shylah hesitated, and Eden's eyes narrowed. "I'll get you some pain meds after you're dressed."

Shylah just nodded as she went in search of her clothes. She had brought most of her things over from her apartment, bit by bit. It helped that she didn't have much.

Eden made a mental note to take her shopping.

Pulling a dress over her head, Shylah turned and gave Eden a tight smile. He could see that she was hiding her discomfort.

"Let's go get you those pain meds," Eden grumbled, taking Shylah's right hand. He would have carried her if she'd let him, but he already knew what the result of trying would be.

Once in the kitchen, Eden took out two pills, poured a cup of water, and placed them in front of Shylah as she sat. Next, he turned and took out some eggs and bread.

"I'm not that hungry, Eden," Shylah said softly.

"You need to eat," Eden grumbled. "Especially if you intend to keep down those pain meds."

While he prepared breakfast, Eden tried to keep the conversation light with no discussion of what happened last night. He knew she was distracted. He couldn't blame her. Her eyes kept flickering back to the bruises on her wrist, making Eden's muscles clench.

Placing their plates down on the table, Eden broached the topic of this afternoon. "I've got to go take care of some work stuff with Eagle. I thought I'd drop you at Rocket's so you can hang out with Evie for a bit."

Shylah glanced up from her plate, a look of contemplation on her face. "You're going to go question the guy who attacked me, aren't you?"

Damn, she was too perceptive.

Not wanting to lie, Eden nodded. "Yes."

"I want to go too."

Eden started at Shylah's unexpected response.

"No." *Hell, no.* No way would he be placing Shylah in the same room as that animal.

"Eden," Shylah leaned forward as she said his name, pleading. "I have questions of my own for him. I'd like to ask them in person."

"No," Eden repeated firmly. "Any questions you have, I can get answers for you."

Sitting back, Shylah cocked her head to the side, a frown on her face. "Won't you and Mason both be there? How much safer could I be?"

"Not being in the same room as the guy who tried to kill you is a hell of a lot safer." Eden couldn't believe she wanted to see the asshole again. He thought even being in the same town would be too close. It sure as hell was for him.

"Eden, please. A guy I don't know, attacks me at my place of work, for seemingly no reason. I need to see him, see that I'm safe when he's not been injected with some mysterious drug. I need closure." Gaze lowering, Shylah picked at the food in front of her with trembling fingers. "Plus, I don't feel safe with anyone but you. I want to stick close to you."

Eden fought for calm as turmoil boiled inside him. "Rocket is just as capable of protecting you as I am."

"I know that makes sense logically, but I don't have the same faith in him as I do you." Eyes lifting again, they were pleading with Eden and, damn it, it was working. "You're my safe place, Eden."

Pressing his lips together, Eden released a low growl before speaking. "Fine, you can come." Eyes widening slightly, Shylah seemed just as surprised as Eden by his words. "But you stay behind me and Mason the whole time, and if for one moment I suspect you're not safe, we're out. Got it?"

Nodding vigorously, Shylah nibbled her lip.

Rising from her seat, Shylah circled the table to stand in front of Eden.

Arms immediately wrapping around her body, he pulled her into him.

"Thank you," Shylah murmured against his chest.

"I already almost lost you once, Shy, I will not lose you again."

Raising her head to look at Eden, her hand pressed against his chest. "You won't. When I'm with you, I'm the safest I could be."

"Damn straight."

21

Shylah didn't have to look down at her hands to know that they were shaking.

Glancing to the side, she noticed the tension in Eden's features as he drove them to the county jail. He hadn't said a word the whole car ride. He may as well be her Uber driver for all the interaction they were having.

Casting her eyes back to the road, the trees thinned as they neared town. The closer she and Eden got to the prison, the more sick with nerves she felt.

It wasn't that she feared Ben. She knew that Eden and Mason would guard her with their lives. There was no way he would get past them.

But Ben's black eyes were on constant replay in her head. The hate and anger had been so strong, and all aimed at her. She hadn't been able to get more than a couple of hours of sleep last night.

Even though the fear was strong, Shylah had to be brave. There were too many questions in her head, the main one being, why her? She didn't know him, had never seen him in her life.

Was he working for someone else? Project Arma? And if he was, was she a target for them?

Shylah's palms got sweaty at that thought. From what she'd heard, they were powerful and had a far reach. Eden was strong, but there was no way he could protect her forever if people so powerful wanted her dead.

When the truck came to a stop, Shylah took a steadying breath before stepping outside. The cool breeze went some way in soothing her.

She could do this. She had to. She needed to hear from his mouth why he'd attacked her and why the fury in his eyes had been directed her way.

Eden came around the car. Taking Shylah's hand in his, they started walking toward the building.

Eden's continual silence made Shylah want to back out and agree to go to Luca and Evie's just so she would get the old Eden back. But she couldn't do it. Shylah needed to do this for her.

"Remember what I said, Shy, you remain behind Eagle and me at all times."

"Got it," Shylah said quietly, in a voice with a slight shake in it.

Of course, Eden heard and stopped immediately.

"Nope, your heart sounds like it's going to beat out of your damn chest. You're scared shitless, Shy. No way are you going in there." Turning, Eden pulled at Shylah's arm only to have her dig her heels into the ground.

"No, Eden, I'm okay."

"You're not." Eden's voice was hard as he attempted to pull Shylah once again.

Stumbling slightly as she refused to move her feet, Eden stopped immediately and turned to look at her.

"Yes, I am, Eden. I'm scared. Who wouldn't be? The guy attacked me, and I'm about to stand in the same room as him.

But there's no way in hell I'm going to let that stop me. I want to see him, talk to him. I need to." Shylah's eyes pleaded with Eden, knowing that if he said no, she would never get her closure.

"Fine," Eden growled after a moment. "But don't for one second think I won't drag you out of there at the sight of danger. Answers or not."

Nodding, Shylah turned back toward the prison, Eden's angry energy bouncing off him.

Stepping inside the building, they caught sight of Mason standing in the foyer. There was no smile on his face. He was all business. "Ready?"

"Let's get this over with," Eden muttered.

Mason started walking down the hall, Eden and Shylah trailing close behind. "They've left him in the back room. No cameras and soundproof walls. We have an hour."

Soundproof walls? Shylah swallowed, sparing the two men a quick glance. What the hell did they have planned for this guy?

Shooting another nervous glance at Eden, his jaw was clenched, and the veins on his arms stood out. She had a feeling she didn't want to know.

"That will be enough time," Eden said, voice devoid of emotion.

At the end of a long hall, they came to a stop outside a closed door. A uniformed officer stood in front of it and gave Mason a nod.

Without a word, the officer handed Mason a key before walking back down the hall.

The sound of Mason inserting the key and turning the lock echoed through the otherwise quiet hallway. As he pushed the door open, Shylah's heart jumped into her throat.

Tightening her clasp on Eden's hand slightly, he pulled her into the room.

Once inside, Eden pushed Shylah behind his big body as Mason locked the door behind them.

Taking a deep breath, Shylah glanced around Eden. Her heart lurched. Ben sat on a bench at the back of the room, an evil smile on his face.

"I knew you'd come. I didn't expect you to bring the nurse. What a nice surprise for an otherwise mundane day."

Shylah took a step to the side so she could get a better look at him. Ben's eyes slid down Shylah's body just as they had yesterday, sending a sick feeling to her stomach.

"Get your eyes off her, asshole. If you knew we were coming, you know this isn't a friendly visit," Eden said, his voice cold as ice.

Ben's brows pulled together, feigning confusion. "You mean you didn't bring me any cookies? What about donuts? They don't provide much in terms of baked goods for the prisoners here." Face splitting into a smile that made Shylah's blood cool, Ben leaned forward. "That's okay, you brought me her. That's much better."

Eden took an angry step forward, only to be stopped by Mason's hand on his arm. Stepping in front of Eden, Mason's voice was angry but controlled. "We want information, and if you work with us, you'll find this will be a lot more pleasant for you."

Lifting his brows, Ben kept his smile in place.

How had she missed the deranged look in this man's eyes yesterday when she'd entered that room?

"Well, I wouldn't want this to be an *unpleasant* experience. What information do I possess that you would like?"

Taking another step closer to Ben, Mason crossed his arms. "How about we start with how you got involved in this."

Ben leaned back again, looking far too relaxed for someone at the mercy of a pair of lethal former SEALs. "Got kicked out of the military. Son of a bitch didn't like some of my methods or ethics. A week later got a call from these guys offering me money to take part in a drug trial. Promised me I'd be stronger, faster. Hell yeah, I agreed to that."

Shylah's eyes widened. They were recruiting soldiers with little to no ethics and giving them increased abilities?

That these sorts of men were being created was a terrifying thought.

"How long have you been part of the project?" Mason continued, not showing an ounce of emotion.

"Maybe half a year. Best six months of my life. I'm a machine. They really delivered the goods." His eyes swung over to Eden. "You were both part of it too, weren't you? Strong. Fast. I could have taken you. Both of you. If it was a fair one-on-one fight."

"Have they been keeping you in a cage?" Eden asked, voice low and guttural.

Ben's laugh made Shylah's toes curl. "They don't need to keep me in a cage. They keep the ones who want out in a cage. The ones that try to leave." Pausing for a moment, Ben then continued, "And anyone who loses their mind after receiving the drugs."

Hairs standing on end, Shylah recalled how Project Arma was going to test a new version of the drug on Eden. If something had happened to him, like him losing his mind and being locked in a cage, she didn't know what she would have done.

"You don't seem very concerned about being locked up here," Eden said gruffly.

"You think they'll leave me here? You have no clue how powerful these people are, do you? I'll be out by morning."

The confidence Ben had in that made Shylah stiffen. He attacks and tries to kill her, and the people who put him up to it are just going to get him out?

"Why me?" Shylah asked, stepping forward.

Eden's hand immediately went to Shylah's shoulder, firmly pulling her back.

Ben's eyes scanned Shylah's face, making her regret her moment of fortitude. Straightening her spine, she refused to back down.

"You're trying to look tough, but I can hear your pulse beating from your chest. Your hands are shaking, your eyes so fucking wide. It's probably taking everything in you not to hide behind your tough SEAL, isn't it?" Leaning forward, Ben lowered his voice. "I caused that terror. Fear is bleeding from you."

"Answer the damn question, asshole," Eden growled.

Eyes not wavering from Shylah's, Ben continued, "It would seem you've made an enemy, honey. Don't know what you did or who you pissed off, but the purpose of you giving me the drug was to test that it worked."

"What's that supposed to mean?" Mason demanded.

Ben's eyes finally released Shylah and moved to Mason. She took a long breath the moment she was free of his stare.

"They gave me a scent in the form of a piece of clothing. I became familiar with it just before I went in. I was told once they gave me the drug, I would know who to go after." Eyes sliding back to Shylah, the smile returned to his face. "Guess it worked. Killing you was an all-consuming thought. It was like a physical pain to not be hurting you."

Shylah's hair stood on end. "But you don't feel like that now?"

Ben stood suddenly, causing Shylah to jump. Eden stepped further in front of her, hand on her biceps.

Excitement lit up Ben's eyes, his gaze fixed on her. "Do I feel that same all-consuming need to kill you? Tear you apart with my bare hands? No, not right now. But don't for one minute think that makes you safe." Pausing, Ben cocked his head to the side. "Imagine if someone else could control what was in these guys' heads. Imagine the chaos and destruction that could be caused."

As Ben took a step forward, Eden's grip tightened on her arm while Mason visibly tensed. "You think you're safe with him?" Ben glanced at Eden before turning back to Shylah. "He's every bit the killer Project Arma turned him into, and once the people who made him control his actions, you'll be dead before you can blink."

Ben's voice dripped with hostility now. Any smile that had once been on his face gone.

Blood running cold, fear shot through Shylah at Ben's words. At the same moment, Eden took a large step toward Ben, his body vibrating with rage. She had no doubt that if she wasn't in the room, this conversation would not be so peaceful.

"Listen to that, the pitter-patter of your pulse just increased," Ben continued. "Scared? You should be."

"Enough," Eden barked. "Mason, take Shylah back to the entrance, I've got a couple more questions I want answered. Alone."

"Eden . . ." Shylah tried to calm him.

"Shylah, go." Eden's tone left no room for discussion.

Swallowing, Shylah spared Ben one last look before following Mason out of the room.

Once in the foyer, Mason sat, waiting for Shylah to join him. Glancing around, she felt like she had too much pent-up energy to sit, but one look at Mason and her butt hit the seat.

Sitting and not speaking for a few moments, Shylah's leg started a nervous bounce. Turning her head to look at Mason, she saw he was staring at a spot on the wall, a look of concentration on his face.

Then it hit her. Mason was listening to whatever was going on in that room. Probably ready to jump to Eden's aid if needed.

Guess the room wasn't soundproof from everyone, Shylah thought, crossing her arms.

Sitting back, she let Ben's words replay in her head. Someone wanted her dead. Likely one of the people who worked for Project Arma. They all probably knew she was the one who uncovered what was really going on and forced them into hiding.

Not only were they still using drugs to turn soldiers into weapons, but they were using lawless, ex-military men, and creating a drug to control their minds.

The possibility that they could control Eden and the others from Marble made her stomach churn. It was a terrifying concept.

"It won't happen, Shylah." Jolting at Mason's voice, Shylah glanced at him.

"What?"

"Eden would never hurt you, even if they did somehow get the drug into his system. You're safe with him."

Shaking her head, she fiddled with the material of her pants. "We don't know what drug they've created or what the effect could be."

"No, but we know Eden."

As if Mason had summoned him, Eden walked into the hall at that very moment. Standing alongside Mason as he approached, Eden's eyes immediately pinned Shylah.

It was impossible for Shylah not to notice the specks of blood on Eden's shirt and the scuffing on his knuckles.

"Let's go," Eden said as he took Shylah's hand, kissing the top of her head lightly before heading out to his truck.

Gripping his hand tighter, Shylah pushed down her fear. There was no way this man would hurt her or any innocent. No drug could cause that kind of shift in who he was.

22

Eden's eyes tracked Shylah as she moved around his kitchen. They'd been home for an hour, and she'd barely said two words to him. Any time she had spoken, her words had been stilted. Short.

Shylah's gaze would catch his for short moments then quickly dart away.

Did she fear him now? Did she actually believe he could hurt her?

Eden understood that they had no information on this drug. What he knew was that if someone wanted her dead, the safest place for her to be was here with him.

Once Eden had been alone with Ben, he'd wiped the smile off the asshole's face damn quick.

Unfortunately for Eden, it had turned out Ben had no idea who was running the project now. Vague descriptions of some scientists and doctors had been the best Eden had gotten.

Ben was clearly too low on the pay scale to know anything of importance. He hadn't even known where the damn facility was located, just that they moved every few months.

The only semi-valuable piece of information that Ben had

shared was that he'd seen a Woodcreek sign when they drove him to Marble Falls. That was only an hour away.

Wyatt and Evie were currently looking into it and would hopefully be able to use their resources to find something useful.

Wiping her hands on a tea towel, Shylah turned and gave Eden a tight smile. "Dinner will be ready in half an hour, I'm just going to take a quick shower before we eat," she told him, then Shylah left the room, not waiting for a response.

Frustration built inside as he sat and listened to her move upstairs to the bathroom, and the water start running. What the hell was he supposed to do now? Sit here while Shylah stood in the shower and decided Eden was too dangerous to be around?

Fuck no.

There was no way in hell Eden was letting an asshole like Ben put ideas into his woman's head. Pushing away from the kitchen table, Eden stood and walked to the bathroom. Stepping inside the room, the outline of Shylah's body through the glass made Eden's blood rush from his head.

Her back was to him, but he could make out every inch of her wet skin from behind.

Removing his clothes, Eden opened the shower door and stepped inside. Wrapping his arms around Shylah's middle as the warm spray of water hit his shoulders.

Shylah startled before going rigid in his arms.

Pushing her wet hair behind her shoulder, Eden lowered his head to her neck. Lips locking with her shoulder, Eden sucked and nibbled on the damp skin.

"I love you, Shylah. Have always loved you." Eden's voice was raspy, only taking his mouth off her for the moments to speak.

"I love you too, Eden," Shylah said quietly, her body loosening slightly in his arms.

"Then, don't ever fear me." Hand trailing up to her breast, his thumb slid over her hard nipple. A gasp escaped Shylah's lips as her head pushed back onto his shoulder. "I would never hurt you, no matter what drug was or wasn't flowing through my blood."

Shylah's breaths quickened as Eden's mouth trailed kisses up her shoulder, stopping and suckling her open neck. "We don't know how you would react to the drug, Eden. If someone worked out a way to control you . . ." Shylah gasped as a shudder rippled through her.

Swapping his hand to the other breast, Eden lightly pinched the nipple before brushing his thumb over it, enjoying Shylah's soft moans. Pushing his feet between hers, Eden nudged her legs apart, spreading her thighs.

"It would be impossible for me to bring your body anything but pleasure. I would never use my strength against you, Shy. Ever."

Eden's other hand lowered to the *V* between her legs. His fingers swiping across her clit, causing a jolt from Shylah at the touch.

Her entire back pressed against Eden's front, pushing against his hardness as the warm water continued to fall on them.

Hand rising from Shylah's breast to her cheek, Eden turned her head and lowered his mouth. Shylah's lips parted already, in eager anticipation of the kiss.

Mouths locking, Eden wasted no time in pushing his tongue inside, deepening the kiss immediately. Her lips were soft, and she tasted sweet.

Shylah's good hand reached up and latched onto his forearm. Her heart thumped so loud he doubted he needed enhanced abilities to hear it.

Knowing he did this to Shylah, caused this reaction from her, intensified Eden's primal need to be inside her. Too many months had passed without touching her skin, hearing her moans. Too damn long of thinking he would never be with her again.

Pulling her body tighter against his, Eden lowered his fingers to her entrance and pushed inside. She was so wet and ready for him, Eden could groan.

Shylah's nails dug into his skin. Her back arching and moans sounding louder.

Spinning Shylah around, Eden lifted her and pushed her back against the shower wall, being careful of her wrist. Thighs spread around his hips, Shylah's ankles locked together behind him.

Pausing at her entrance, every fiber of Eden's being urged him to slide inside, but he waited.

"Tell me you want this, Shy."

Lust glazed her hazel eyes. "I want this, Eden. I want you."

A primal growl tore from Eden's chest at the mixture of trust and love he saw in her eyes. Returning his mouth to hers, Eden pushed his hips forward until he was seated entirely inside Shylah.

Another moan, this time mixed with a sigh, escaped her lips but was quietened by his mouth.

Easing out of her, Eden waited a moment before pushing back in.

"Faster," Shylah gasped, clenching her walls around his penis.

The moment her heat tightened against him, Eden was lost. Increasing his pace, Eden withdrew and pushed back in. Every thrust brought them back together, the sound of body hitting body filling the room.

This woman was everything he'd ever want or need.

Locking his eyes on hers, he needed to see her when she came. Eden continued his deep, hard thrusts, knowing he would not last much longer.

Reaching his hand between their bodies, Eden's finger circled her clit, causing her to squeeze around his penis instantly.

"Eden," she moaned, her voice was breathless, desperation thick in the air.

Then Shylah's body clenched before her head flung back. Crying out his name, the wave of pleasure consumed her. It was the most beautiful fucking sight Eden had ever seen.

Growling, Eden's grip on her hips tightened as he thrust a few more times before his own body jerked, and he came inside her.

Arms bracketing her to the wall, Eden stood there for a moment, not wanting to separate their entwined bodies. The closeness and intimacy, something he wasn't ready to part with yet.

He was never fucking letting this woman out of his sight. He couldn't lose her again. He wouldn't survive it.

When their breaths had slowed enough, Eden reached over to turn the shower off. Shylah loosened her legs, but Eden held her firmly against him.

Stepping out, he took two towels and headed into the bedroom.

Unlatching his hands, Shylah slid down his body onto the bedroom floor. Drying herself with a towel, Eden watched as she struggled to do it one-handed.

"I'll help."

"No, I got it," Shylah said, stepping to the side, eyes not reaching his.

Eden's eyes narrowed. "I meant every word that I said to you in there, Shy."

Head popping up, Shylah nodded. "I know."

"Then why aren't you looking at me?"

Ducking her head, Shylah went to the closet. Grabbing a baggy shirt, his shirt, she pulled it over her head.

"I'm just scared for us, Eden." Her words were spoken softly.

Brows furrowing, Eden took a step closer to her. "I told you, I would never hurt you, Shylah."

"I'm not scared of you, Eden, I'm scared for you. For us. For our relationship. We were torn apart once because one of us tried to save the other. Eden, I really thought I was doing the right thing. What if that happens again? What if we're torn apart because one of us tries to save the other? What if they pull us apart?"

Marching straight up to Shylah, Eden tugged her warm body against his. "Nothing that tears us apart is saving us, Shylah. We learned that the hard way. We work together, always. We're a team. You and me."

Placing her hands against his chest, Shylah glanced up at Eden. "You're not scared? I feel like everywhere we turn, people are reminding us how powerful Project Arma is and how far their reach is."

"I don't give a damn how powerful Project Arma is. What I feel for you is pretty powerful too, Shy. That's something I know for a fact. You and me, we're not breakable."

Eden spoke with all the conviction that he felt.

Some of the fear leached from Shylah's eyes. Lowering her head to his chest, Eden was relieved that she initiated the contact this time.

They stood in that embrace for Eden didn't know how long. He only knew that neither of them wanted to break their closeness.

When Shylah eventually pulled away, her head suddenly popped up.

"Dinner! Oh my gosh, has it been over half an hour?"

Rushing out the door, Eden followed at a slower pace,

painfully aware that Shylah was still naked under his shirt. If she stayed like that all night, there was no way Eden wouldn't be inside her again.

Moving into the kitchen, he watched as Shylah turned the stove off and sighed in relief.

"I think it's okay." Flashing a smile at Eden, he too breathed his own sigh of relief. Shylah's smile finally reached her eyes, and for the moment, at least, there were no shadows there.

The rest of the night was relatively normal. Well, the new normal for Eden, the normal which had Shylah in his home and in his bed.

As they sat on the couch to watch TV, Eden's phone rang.

Giving Shylah a kiss on the head, Eden left the room to answer it.

"Jobs, what's happening? Find anything around Woodcreek?"

"Actually, yes." Eden paused where he stood in the hall.

So that jerk had been useful for something.

"We searched for any large warehouse-type sites and found an old gin distillery in the town. Evie investigated it, and a guy bought it by the name of Adam Brown. Thing is, the guy doesn't exist. Fake background, fake name. The whole cover was poorly done. I'm surprised the government hasn't discovered it and let us know."

"They probably have," Eden muttered bitterly. Eden's faith in the people who should keep civilians safe was waning. "Seems like there must be someone working on the inside."

"My thoughts exactly," Wyatt agreed.

"So, when's the raid?" Eden hoped Wyatt didn't say tonight. As much as he'd love to get right on top of this, he needed time with Shylah.

"We can sort out the details in the morning and go in tomorrow night. Luca has agreed to sit it out and stay with the women."

"Gotcha. I'll talk to Shylah about it tonight."

About to hang up, Wyatt's voice stopped Eden. "There's something else. They found Ben dead in his cell this evening, not even an hour after you visited."

Stopping in his tracks, Eden cursed, "How the hell did that happen?"

"Report says he fell and hit his head. No evidence of anyone being there."

Bullshit. "So much for them getting him out like he thought."

"He was a liability," Wyatt said dismissively. "These guys play by their own rules. We got in there first. That's the important thing."

Damn lucky they did. Otherwise, they wouldn't have the warehouse location that they had. "Thanks, Jobs."

Hanging up, Eden stood in the doorway and watched Shylah on the couch for a moment before going back in.

Turning her head to look at him, a smile curved her lips. Peaceful. That's how she looked. And Eden intended to keep it that way.

There wasn't a damn thing he wouldn't do to keep his woman safe. The people at Project Arma better believe it.

23

Shylah eyed the last custard filled donut. It sat there in the middle of Luca and Evie's coffee table, staring at her. Daring her to reach out and take it.

Glancing up at Evie and Lexie sitting across from her, she wondered if they'd hate her if she took it. They did introduce her to Mrs. Potter's Bakehouse donuts and knew how good they were. They should really be expecting her to take the last one.

They had described the baked goods as cake that melts in your mouth, and holy hell, they weren't lying. They were the best damn donuts she'd ever tasted. Like circles of heaven.

In an hour, the three women had polished off a plate that should have been enough to last the whole night plus another group of women.

"Take it, girl." Lexie laughed from across the living room. "Evie and I have binged on Mrs. Potter's donuts too many times to count. You're a virgin. It's the least we can do."

Looking over at Evie and seeing the other woman's nod of approval, Shylah couldn't wipe the smile from her face. Reaching over, she wrapped her fingers around the donut.

After the first bite, Shylah's eyes shuttered closed, and a

groan escaped her throat. This was almost as good as the orgasm Eden had given her that morning.

When Evie's giggle cut through the silence, Shylah's eyes popped open to find both women staring at her.

"Told you they were as good as an orgasm," Lexie said, reading Shylah's thoughts with scary accuracy.

Evie took another sip of her wine as she pet a golden cat that lay on her lap. "I don't know how she makes them so good. Next, you need to try her apple strudel. Or maybe don't, you'll be as hooked as I am."

Lexie's eyes flicked to Evie's body. "Evie, you're hot. Eat all the apple strudel your heart desires."

Dropping the half-eaten donut on the plate, Shylah picked up her water. "I think I should stop. I'm in sugar overload."

Leaning forward, Lexie picked up Shylah's empty wineglass and started filling it with wine. Shylah's eyes widened when Lexie didn't stop pouring until the glass was nearly overflowing. "That's because you haven't had any wine to wash it down."

"Lex makes up her own rules when it comes to alcohol. I would just go with it," Evie said with a shrug.

The cat purred as Evie continued to stroke its head. The animal clearly enjoying the attention.

Smiling, Shylah reached over and took the glass from Lexie's fingers. "Donuts and wine. I could get used to these girls' nights."

She really could. Lexie and Evie were great company and had so far taken her mind off worrying about Eden almost completely. Almost.

"You have an open invitation to every girls' night. The only rule is no boys allowed. Period." Eyes darting to Evie, Lexie continued, "Tell me again why Luca had to be here tonight?"

Evie's face looked pinched for a moment. Shylah felt bad for the other woman, knowing she looked uncomfortable because she would have to lie to her friend. "You know how the guys go away to work for the military every so often. One person had to stay for Marble Protection."

Frowning, Lexie's face read anything but trusting. "What could happen to the gym in the middle of the night?"

Squirming in her seat, Evie opened her mouth to speak before shutting it again.

"It's because of me," Shylah jumped in, both women turning to stare at her. "You know how I told you I tripped, and that's how I got this bruise on my face and hurt my arm? I lied. A patient attacked me at the hospital the other day. Eden had to go on the mission, but I said I didn't feel safe without one of the guys around. Luca offered to stay behind."

Evie's expression looked grateful while Lexie's eyes widened. "A patient attacked you?"

Nodding, Shylah looked down at her left arm. "He was on something and just went a bit crazy. Hit me and threw me against the wall. I was lucky Eden had come inside the hospital and heard me scream. Otherwise, it could have been a lot worse." Looking up, Shylah gave Lexie a tight smile. "The guy was arrested, but having Eden or one of his friends around right now just makes me more comfortable."

Shylah left off the part that the guy is now dead. Something told her that would raise more questions than it was worth.

"Holy jam on a cracker, Shylah. I'm so glad you're okay," Lexie gushed, worry on her face. "I always hear stories about the mistreatment and abuse of nurses and doctors, but I never thought it could be that bad."

"It usually isn't," Shylah said, to try to reassure her.

"How's the wrist today?" Evie asked.

"Better. I have exercises that I need to do, but it's just bruised, so as long as I rest, it will be okay."

"You can barely see the bruise on your head," Lexie said, squinting.

"The wonders of foundation," Shylah joked before she took another sip of wine.

The wine tasted great. Did everything in Marble Falls just taste better than everywhere else?

Sitting forward, Evie put the cat on the ground before placing her hand on Shylah's leg. "How are you doing with everything, Shylah? Have you been sleeping okay?"

Swallowing another gulp of wine, this time burning her throat, Shylah didn't know how to respond. She sure as hell couldn't get Ben's enraged eyes out of her head.

When Shylah took a moment too long to answer, Evie's eyes turned sympathetic.

"I was in an abusive relationship before Luca. He would hurt me." Shylah's stomach dropped at the idea of any man hurting Evie. She had an air of fragility about her. "I ran away. Luckily, I ran here to Marble Falls and met Luca. When my ex found me, Luca saved my life. My ex is out of the picture now, but even though I'm safe physically, it's not as easy to convince myself of that mentally and emotionally."

Suddenly it made much more sense to Shylah why Evie was the way she was. Also why Luca was so protective of her, hovering over and watching Evie. Not to mention it explained the bruised ribs she examined and stitches she removed not long ago.

"I'm really sorry that happened, Evie."

A small smile touched her lips. "I'm a lot better now. I wanted to tell you because I know what it's like to still feel scared of someone even once you're safe. I just want to make sure you're talking about it to someone. Unpacking what happened."

Shylah's eyes got misty. "I was only attacked one time—"

"Doesn't matter," Evie interrupted. "When someone violates your circle of safety, it's hard to recover from."

Nibbling on her bottom lip, Shylah stared at the other woman. "Sleeping the last couple of nights has been tough. I see his eyes a lot in my dreams. Hear his voice. It helps that Eden sleeps right next to me. He makes me feel safe. Protected."

"Luca does that for me too," Evie responded gently.

"The men at Marble are the ones you want around when shit hits the fan," Lexie said, pouring herself another glass of wine. Shylah was sure the bottle was almost empty, and she and Evie had only had a glass each. "And Eden's a scary dude. Definitely good to have him in your corner."

Sitting back, Evie picked up her wineglass again. "They can all be scary when the time calls for it."

Lexie scoffed, "Yeah, right. Asher might have the body of a warrior, but the only thing he's good at scaring off is a committed relationship."

Lexie's voice was bitter as she drained half her wineglass. Shylah wanted to ask what she meant by that but didn't want to seem nosy.

Lucky for her, Lexie wanted to share.

"Asher and I have been having sex. I would say I've been seeing the guy, but you would assume we've been in a relationship, which would not be at all accurate." There was hurt behind Lexie's bravado.

"Lex, I'm sure with some time he'll come around."

Lexie was already shaking her head before Evie had finished speaking.

"I've given it time. I don't expect him to know he loves me at first sight like Luca did you. But I deserve someone who wants to take me on a date and hold my hand at the movies. Not someone who sneaks out before the sun comes up."

"You do deserve that, Lex."

"Every woman deserves a man who treats them right," Shylah added.

"I've decided I'm going to give him an ultimatum. Either commit to a relationship with me with no secrets, or we're done —no more late-night Lexie time for Asher."

"Lexie . . ."

"Don't want to hear it, Evie, I've decided."

Shylah could tell Evie wasn't all for this decision. She could understand Lexie's anger, though. No woman wanted to feel like she was only wanted for her body.

"Be really firm when you say it," Shylah said, sipping some more wine. "Don't leave him any room to weasel his way out of what you're asking."

Evie shook her head while Lexie nodded. "See, this is the support I need. He'll either be my boyfriend or some guy I used to sleep with before the conversation is over."

"Just be careful, Lex," Evie said firmly, looking concerned for her friend.

"When am I not careful? I just want what you and Luca have. What Shylah and Eden have." Dropping her eyes, Lexie shrugged. "I think I love him. Stupid, isn't it."

Shylah's heart hurt for the other woman. Pain clouded Lexie's eyes.

"If there's anything I've learned, Lexie, it's that we can't help who we fall in love with," Shylah responded as she placed her glass on the table.

"That's true," Evie agreed.

Suddenly sitting up straight, Lexie's face cleared. "Nope, I'm not going to waste my girl time thinking about that manwhore." After picking up the bottle of wine again, Lexie's brows pulled together. "This is almost empty. We need more wine!"

Shylah had to hold in a laugh at how quickly Lexie's whole demeanor seemed to change. She was tempted to tell Lexie that she was the one who nearly drank the whole bottle but decided against it.

"Luca!" Lexie called. Evie put her hand over her eyes, but Shylah could see a smile.

Two seconds later, Luca answered, "Yes, Lexie."

He appeared genuinely interested to hear what she wanted, even though he had likely heard every word they had said.

"Seeing as you're here and all, could you make yourself useful and get us some more wine and donuts?"

Shylah perked up at the sound of donuts. Hell, let's put the man to work.

Luca leaned his shoulder against the doorframe, arms crossed against his chest.

"First of all, I highly doubt Mrs. Potter's is open right now. Second, I stay with you guys, period."

Rummaging through her bag, Lexie pulled out her phone. Her fingers started flying across the screen before anyone knew what she was doing.

"Mrs. Potter, it's Lexie," Lexie said into the phone. "Yes, from Marble. I have a gigantic favor to ask. Evie and I have a friend who hasn't tried your donuts." Lexie winked at Shylah as she lied. "We were wondering if you might have any with you tonight?"

"And some apple strudel," Evie cut in, Luca's eyes narrowing in her direction.

"And some apple strudel." Pausing while she listened, Lexie's eyes lit up. "Perfect, we can pop by right now if that suits . . . Great. See you soon."

Hanging up, Lexie turned to grin at Luca, who looked less than pleased. "Mrs. Potter has donuts and apple strudel. *And* she lives close to Twins Liquors. Road trip?"

Turning his head to Evie, his eyes softened. "Really? You had to get involved in this?"

Giving a small shrug, Evie tried to appear innocent. "Her apple strudel really is the best. Plus, Shylah hasn't tried it."

Shaking his head, Luca headed to the front door. "Let's go. The sooner we leave, the sooner we'll be back."

Lexie squealed as she jumped out of her seat with Evie and Shylah trailing closely behind. She could get used to these girls' nights. Sugar and alcohol almost made up for Eden being absent.

24

Adrenaline poured through Eden's body as he crept through the shrubs and bushes. His muscles were tense as the quiet night surrounded him. His team was scattered around the building, each with their own entry point.

They moved silently. It would be impossible for even people with the keenest hearing to know they were coming.

Taking a step behind a tree, Eden looked out and examined the building. Deserted. At least made to look deserted. And the perfect location for illegal activity.

The building sat far enough off the road that it wouldn't be seen by passersby, and could only be accessed through a long, unkempt gravel driveway. Most would drive right past.

With boarded up windows, by all intents and purposes, the place looked empty.

On foot, the team had negotiated their way through trees and shrubbery. They'd dressed to blend into the dark night.

Eden stood and waited. Mason would speak through the earpiece when it was go time.

"Fuck, anyone else getting an eerie feeling from this place?" Asher's voice came through the earpiece.

"No shit, it's like a fucking graveyard," Kye responded gruffly.

Glancing at the building again, Eden's gut clenched. They were right. Something felt off. His gut was telling him that something wasn't right with this op. "Be ready, moving in five," Mason sounded.

Eden, Mason, and Oliver were moving through the front while Kye and Bodie were at the back entrance. Asher and Wyatt were placed on either side of the building.

Each man could take down a handful of untrained doctors and scientists easily. The trouble would be if there were soldiers with advanced abilities.

They had brought plenty of rope and intended to detain them rather than kill. Every one of them was eager to get their answers. Then and only then, they would contact the US military to come to take it from there.

Eden's team would not share any information until they had what they needed first. All the people he trusted with information were right here. About to raid the building.

"Three minutes," Mason said quietly.

Eden readied his body. Blood pumped through his veins. Even though the plan was to capture and hold, he could kill in seconds if needed.

"I hear movement," Oliver muttered.

Eden's body went still as footsteps sounded.

Any normal person would not hear the steps, but for them, the sound echoed through the silent night. Not a couple of footsteps. Many. Too many.

Blood rushing faster, Eden's eyes cut through the dark night.

The door at the front opened, and men filtered out. Sprinted out. It could have been anywhere between twenty to thirty men.

Each man looked enraged. Their anger causing them to look more animal than human. Just like Ben.

"Shoot," Mason yelled, no longer attempting to be quiet.

Pulling out his revolver, Eden took aim.

By shooting the men in the shoulders and legs, Eden's goal was to injure, not to kill. He wanted them down, not dead.

Blocking out the sound of gunshots around him, Eden focused on the men moving toward him. It became apparent quickly that there were too many of them to defend himself this way.

They were going to reach him, and they were going to reach him fast.

"There are too many. I'm going in," Eden shouted, shoving the gun back in the holster.

Moving forward, the men dove at him. Eden grunted when at least three men hit his body. They were strong, but they were reckless. Wild.

Refusing to fall back, Eden leaned his body forward and braced for the hit. Shoving them off with a grunt, Eden didn't have time to recover. Another man came at Eden's left, eyes storming with fury.

Stepping into the man, Eden head-butted him, before thrusting his arm into the guy's neck.

About to step forward, a weight on his back made Eden stumble before an arm came around his neck.

Flipping the man onto the ground, Eden thrust his foot into him, until he lay motionless.

In his peripheral vision, Eden could just make out similar actions and knew his team was fighting for their lives as he was. He didn't have time to stop and assess. His brothers were deadly.

A man who was easily the same size as Eden launched himself straight into Eden's body. This time Eden fell back onto the ground. Lifting his foot, the large man went to kick him in the gut, but Eden flipped onto all fours before grabbing and twisted the big man's leg.

As the man hit the ground, Eden kept twisting, a shout of pain coming from the other man before Eden snapped the bone.

The sound of engines pulled Eden's attention. Eyes darting across the field, he caught sight of men rushing boxes into a vehicle.

Hell no.

Rising, Eden went to move to the car but was stopped by something hitting him in the head and sending him back to the ground. His eyes narrowed at the man looking down at him.

Carter. The leader of the other SEAL team. The SEAL team that was also part of Project Arma. Only they lacked any form of morals or ethics.

Jumping to his feet, Eden ignored the pounding in his head.

An evil smile slid across Carter's face. "Hey, buddy, long time no see."

Kicking his leg out before Carter could anticipate his actions, Eden sent the other man to his back. Diving on top of him, Eden's hands clenched Carter's throat.

"What the hell is going on here," Eden snarled the words.

Not appearing fazed by Eden's grip on his neck, Carter's smile remained in place. "This is the new look Project Arma, Hunter. What do you think?"

"I wouldn't know," Eden growled, tightening his fingers. "I haven't been able to get inside while you guys are at work. How did you know we were coming?"

A searing pain hit Eden's gut as he dropped to the side. Eyes dropping to his torso, blood had already soaked through his clothes. Even though the blood was flowing, Eden knew the cut was superficial. A flesh wound.

Pushing up into a crouch position, Eden glared at the man in front of him as he spoke.

"This time, we didn't know. But we can pick up and leave any location in less than ten minutes, Eden." Pausing, Carter cocked his head to the side. "What? You think we don't expect you at every location we set up at? You have proven that you can't stay away. Project Arma knows what they created."

"They didn't create us, Carter. They just enhanced us." Not making any move toward the other man, Eden remained where he was, surprised that Carter didn't advance on him. "What do you intend to do about us?"

Carter lifted a single shoulder, not fazed by any of this in the least. "That's not my area, Hunter. I'm the muscle—the front line of defense. I've heard whispers, though. Your time is running out."

"Check your fucking crystal ball, asshole. These guys you're working for will kill you in a second if they need to."

"Why would they need to kill me?" Carter asked, looking genuinely perplexed. "I'm loyal and valuable. You're only half of that."

Yeah, loyal to a bunch of money-hungry, homicidal, assholes.

"Let's cut through the bullshit. What's the new drug you're testing?"

Even though neither man advanced on the other, their eyes remained pinned.

"We actually have you and your team to thank for that. You made everyone realize that just because someone gives you such powerful abilities, doesn't mean you're going to be loyal. Hence, the creation of the new drug. Toved." Turning his head, Carter looked at the retreating vehicle before turning back to Eden. "Time to go."

Pulling out a gun, Carter went to shoot, but Eden dove into him before he could pull the trigger. Wrestling the weapon away, Eden grabbed it just as an elbow landed in his wounded gut. Falling back, Carter took that moment to flee.

Rising to his feet, Eden went to chase after him but was too late. Instead, he watched as the car sped down the driveway.

Turning, he realized for the first time that every man Eden and his team had injured was gone.

"Goddamn it!" Eden shouted in frustration, running his hands through his hair.

"Everyone okay?" Mason's voice sounded through the earpiece.

About to head toward the building, Eden stopped at Kye's words. "Striker's been given something. We're struggling to control him."

Swinging his head around, Eden took off in the direction of his team.

Rounding the corner of the building, Eden stopped short.

Crouched into a fighting position, Asher grunted and growled at Kye and Oliver. Gone was his normal grin and care-free spirit. His eyes were black and ferocious growls emanated from his chest.

"He's a fucking demon," Oliver called as he stood ready to defend himself.

Then Asher dropped his head into his hands and started shaking it. It was like he was at war with himself. Trying to fight whatever drugs were in his system.

When Asher lifted his head, his eyes zoned in on Oliver. In the next moment, he took off toward him.

Before Asher could hit his target, Eden moved quickly, clashing with Asher's body.

It was like hitting a freight train. Both men went flying. As Eden struggled to hold him, Wyatt appeared, grabbing Asher's arms while Bodie took his legs. At the same time, Mason approached with rope. It took all six of them to tie him down. Once he was secured, Asher continued to writhe and fight the rope.

"Jesus. What the hell is this stuff?" Bodie hissed, taking a step back from their friend.

Anger spiked in Eden that the assholes who did this to Asher had gotten away.

"Carter called the drug Toved," Eden muttered.

"Carter?" Oliver reeled, rising to his feet.

"As in Carter from Project Arma? The asshole who was on the same SEAL team as Troy?" Kye questioned.

"Yes. He was here. He left with the rest of them."

Bodie's fists clenched. "Damn it." That didn't even come close to what Eden was feeling. Eyes trailing down Eden's body, Bodie frowned. "You hurt?"

"Flesh wound," Eden said, already feeling it starting to heal, grateful that they healed quicker than most.

Mason stepped forward. "Hunter, Red, and Jobs, come with me. We need to search inside. Cage and Ax, watch Striker and call us if you need help."

Following Bodie, Wyatt, and Mason, Eden moved toward the door, pushing down the anger that was rising. He noticed that everyone had cuts and bruises but had clearly won their battles.

The assholes probably didn't have any new SEALs to test their drugs on. Meaning their new army wasn't as strong as if they had Eden and his team.

Making it to the front door, the entrance of the old gin distillery stood open. All four men took out their weapons. Entering the building in a single file, they covered each other as they went.

Once inside, Eden immediately noticed how similar the set up was to the last warehouse they raided.

"Fuck, more cages," Wyatt glowered.

Turning, Eden saw the similar cage set up on the sidewall. This time, the metal so bent, a man could surely fit through.

Nearing the metal railing, a pungent smell wafted through the room. It was the stench of death.

As SEALs, they had been around death more than most. Since getting their advanced abilities, they realized that death had a smell. It was a musty, metallic smell, similar to blood mixed with bile.

Eyes dropping to the ground, three dead bodies lay in different cages. Each with a bullet wound between their eyes.

"Shit," Mason muttered.

Bodie stepped forward, frowning. "Why shoot some and get the others out?"

Eden had an idea. "They're handcuffed to the railing. They probably put up a fight. When everyone needed to get out, they couldn't take them or leave them for us."

"So, they killed them," Wyatt growled.

"Let's split up and search the place," Mason snarled, voice hard. Flat. "Move quickly. We need to get a sample of Striker's blood before the drug leaves his system. Grab any evidence you see. I want these assholes caught."

25

Shylah grunted as murmurs roused her from her sleep.

What the heck? Did people not know how to be quiet? It was the middle of the damn night.

It *was* the middle of the night, wasn't it?

Cracking one eye open from her spot on the sofa, Shylah glanced around Luca's living room. She had let Lexie take the spare bed while she'd offered to take the couch.

No light shined from behind the curtains. Yep, she might be slightly drunk, but she knew when it was sleep time.

About to drift back to sleep, the voices moved closer.

Damn it to hell, who did she have to kill around here to get some rest?

Glancing up, she saw Eden walking in her direction with Luca trailing close behind. Well, maybe she would give Eden a free pass.

Scanning his body, Shylah's eyes stopped at a red patch on his shirt. Was that blood?

Shooting up into a sitting position, the room spun. Grabbing her head, her fingers latched onto the side of the couch to stop from toppling off.

Eden's face came into view as he crouched in front of her. Worry lines etched his face, and dark circles colored beneath his eyes.

"Hey, Shy, ready to go home?" Lifting his hand, Eden pushed some hair out of her face.

"It's nighttime, Eden." Her words slurred slightly.

No smile touched his lips. "Sorry, I needed to see you tonight. I hope that's okay?"

Eden needed her? Worry seeped through the drunk haze as she considered what they might have found on the mission.

"Are you okay?" Nodding, Eden took a seat on the couch next to Shylah's legs. The red stain coloring his shirt coming back into her view. "You're hurt."

"Just a graze. I'm fine."

Reaching out, Shylah lifted his shirt. A large bandage covered his lower abdomen. If the size of the bandage was anything to go by, that was no small cut.

Looking up, Shylah glared at Eden. "Liar."

Shylah attempted to push his shoulder as she spoke, almost pushing herself off the couch in the process.

Eden turned his head to Luca, eyes narrowing. "How much did you let them drink?"

Let them?

She wasn't sure if it was the alcohol or her inner feminist, but Shylah took offense to that.

"Eden, I am a grown-ass woman. If I want to drink a bottle of wine with my new friends well, then that's what I'll do."

Expecting some equally snarky response, Shylah was surprised when Eden's lips quirked. "God, I missed you."

Eyes softening, Shylah leaned forward, sliding her head against his chest. "I missed you too." She wasn't sure if they were talking about that night or the last year but, she missed him anytime he wasn't right by her side. "Wanna share the couch with me?"

Shuffling over, Shylah eyed the space she'd created, then Eden's body. It would be a tight squeeze.

A deep chuckle made Eden's chest vibrate. "I think you'll find my bed a bit more comfortable."

"But your bed isn't here." Shylah frowned. "Besides, you're the only thing I need to feel comfortable, Eden."

Wasn't that the truth. How many nights had she woken over the last few months searching for Eden? Too many.

"That's damn beautiful."

Shylah's eyes shot up to glare at Luca's, about to chew him out for his sarcasm. When he looked nothing but serious, she rested her head back on Eden's chest.

"We are beautiful, aren't we, Eden? Let's never separate again."

"Already done," Eden whispered, his lips touching her head.

Wrapping his arms around her body, Eden stood.

"Don't drop me," Shylah muttered. "I ate a few of Mrs. Potter's donuts and strudels. I think I'm double the weight I was when you dropped me off."

Her stomach was a cocktail of cake and wine. And she had zero regrets.

"A few? I think you women about cleared her out for the month," Luca muttered with a chuckle.

Shylah wanted to be offended, but the baked goods were just too dang good to feel bad about. "She should bake more or make them taste less good, then."

"I'm not going to drop you. You weigh nothing," Eden said sternly as he marched to the front door.

That was the support she needed.

"Sorry, Shylah. Someone needs to be honest around here," Luca teased from behind Eden.

Shit, had she said those words out loud?

Entering the dark night, Shylah shut her eyes.

"Thanks for having me, Luca," Shylah sighed the words but knew he would hear.

After securing Shylah in the car, Eden walked around and climbed into the other side. The quietness of the engine, mixed with the musky scent of Eden, began to lull Shylah back to sleep almost immediately.

"Let's have some drunk sex when we get home." Her mind was a bit cloudy but, hell, she didn't think she'd ever had a better idea.

"I like the sound of that," Eden's voice responded, deep and rumbly.

"Yeah, drunk sex is the best." Shylah smiled over at Eden, only to see his face hard and set.

"No. I like that you called it home. Although sex with you always sounds like a good idea."

"Well, it is home for me, for now."

Furrowing his brows, Eden didn't respond for a moment. Shylah had the distinct feeling she'd said the wrong thing.

"Would you do it differently if you had your time again?" Eden asked quietly.

"What?" Shylah questioned, dreading his answer.

"The months we were separated. Not telling me about Project Arma when you found out. Not coming back to me sooner."

Jeez Louise, Shylah was not in the right mindset to answer that question right now.

On second thought, maybe alcohol infused honesty was the best time.

"I know what you want to hear, Eden, but I really don't know. I don't think I would change what I did to get Project Arma shut down." Sparing a glance at Eden, she saw his knuckles turn white as his hands tightened on the steering wheel. "Because I knew that I could do what I needed to do to save you, and I didn't want to put your life at risk."

"But in the process, you put your life at risk, Shylah," Eden pressed, voice hard.

Giving a small shrug, Shylah looked ahead at the dark night. "That's love. It's nothing that you wouldn't do for me."

Eden huffed out a breath. "But I'm trained and can look after myself."

Slightly miffed by that comment, her eyes shot back to Eden. "Untrained females can look after themselves. They just do it differently. We use our brains rather than our muscles. Everything would have worked out exactly like it was supposed to if you hadn't been sent on a damn suicide mission."

Eden stiffened, eyes narrowed on the road ahead of him.

Shit, she could have phrased that in a gentler way.

"After Project Arma. Would you have done that differently?"

"It wasn't supposed to be that long, Eden," Shylah spoke softly. "I woke up in this white room with beeping machines, all alone. I remember scanning the room, having no idea where I was or what was going on but needing you. When you weren't there, it was almost more painful than my injuries.

"The doctor walked in. He was older, and I remember he was wearing a white lab coat. I was relieved to see another person. Someone who would tell me what was going on. Then he started talking in some mumbo jumbo doctor language. I started putting together pieces of what he said. The first thing that became clear was that I'd been in the hospital for a while. My mind automatically went to you, Eden. Did you get out? Were you safe?"

Taking a breath, Shylah continued, "Then he told me about my arm." Shylah glanced down at her hand, remembering the absence of feeling in it. "He told me about the months of rehab that would be required to make it functional again. Told me it would never be like it was. I thought back to you again, and I wondered if that would bother you. Then he started talking about the second bullet wound. I didn't even remember I had a second bullet wound." Closing her eyes, Shylah said the words she hated saying out loud, "He told me I couldn't get pregnant. I didn't know I wanted kids until they told me I couldn't. Suddenly the idea of you being there wasn't so great."

"Why the hell not?" Eden's voice was loud. Angry.

Shrugging, Shylah leaned her head against the chair as the emotions of that day came rushing back to her. "I felt damaged. Like I couldn't give you what you deserved." Eden growled, but Shylah kept speaking. "He said there were surgeries they could perform that would have about a fifty percent chance of success. I got it in my head that that would fix me. My plan was to find you after the surgery. So, I waited, had the surgeries, they didn't work. So, then I told myself that once my hand worked again, I would find you. So, I started my rehab. In my mind, the thought of finding you without the ability to have kids, the scars, and a hand that didn't work seemed too much."

"Too much? What does that mean, Shy?" When she was silent for a moment, Eden spoke again, "I'm trying to understand."

"I just . . . I already felt not good enough for you. So, the thought of returning as even less than I was before . . . I needed to get myself better physically, mentally, and emotionally before I returned."

Eden pulled into his garage and switched off the engine. Not making to move or saying anything, Shylah held her breath as she waited.

"Can you say something, Eden?" *Before I have an aneurysm,* Shylah wanted to add but didn't.

"I wish you trusted me and my feelings for you."

With the alcohol wearing off, a bone-deep tiredness began to creep into her body. "I just see you as this perfect man, while I'm just ordinary Shylah."

Shaking his head, Eden looked straight ahead. "You're anything but ordinary, Shylah. And I'm only perfect for you."

Pushing his door open, Eden stepped out, shutting it harder than normal.

Yep, he was mad.

Opening her own door, Eden was already there, offering her a hand to help her down. Stealing a glance at his face, she noticed he gave nothing away with his expression.

Shylah nibbled her lip as they went up to the bedroom. Damn her and her honesty. She bet Eden had asked her while she was drunk on purpose. Sneaky bastard.

Once in the bedroom, Shylah stripped off her clothes and jumped straight into bed.

"I could sleep for years," she groaned as she sank into the cotton sheets.

"I'm going to take a shower," Eden muttered, exiting the room before Shylah could stop him.

Damn it to hell. She couldn't very well sleep if she knew he was angry at her. Rolling onto her back, Shylah stared at the ceiling.

Would she do it differently if she had the choice? She would have loved to have Eden there with her for her recovery and rehab. Hell, it would have made everything a million times easier.

Shylah had so much self-doubt in her worth, though. She knew it stemmed from growing up with parents who had little faith in her. Moving away from them had been the best thing she ever did. Calling them a couple times a year was the extent of their contact with each other, and she'd never told them what happened. For all they knew, Shylah was still working at a US Navy Base.

Sighing, Shylah's eyes darting back to the bathroom door. She loved Eden, and she needed to trust Eden's love in her.

Shutting her eyes, Shylah tossed and turned until she heard the bathroom door open. After some shuffling sounds, the mattress dipped, but Eden didn't move to embrace her.

Rolling onto her side, Shylah wrapped her arm around Eden's middle.

Mouth next to Eden's ear, she spoke quietly, "I wouldn't change saving you for a second, Eden. But if I had my time again, I would come to you earlier. Trust you to love me even if I didn't feel worthy."

Motionless for a moment, Eden's arm snaked around Shylah and pulled her close. "There won't be a next time, but if for some reason there was, I would hunt you down. There's not a place on this Earth you could hide from me. And you are worthy of so much more than you'll know." Dropping a kiss on her head, Eden pulled her body closer. "I love you too damn much to lose you again, Shylah."

"I love you too, Eden." Too damn much.

26

Eden kept his body low, crouched to the ground so he could move quickly at any moment. Ten sets of eyes sat trained on him, watching. Waiting for his next move.

The key to winning any fight was to not give anything away. As soon as the other person could anticipate your next move, it was game over.

Around him, Eden could hear the ticking of the clock, the sound of a car engine, the chirping of birds. But he would not take his eyes off the man in front of him for a second. No way in hell would he risk it. He knew exactly how deadly his opponent was.

One wrong move would cost Eden more than he was willing to pay.

The man in front of Eden's weight suddenly shifted. It was only slight, but it was enough to give him away.

Asher's leg shot out for Eden's gut, but Eden easily sidestepped the hit. Not fast enough so that the watching eyes would know how quick he was, but quick enough to avoid the grazing of the foot, because there was no way Asher would lighten the kick to save Eden any pain.

Asher's arm then shot out to swipe Eden's head, to which Eden narrowly avoided.

Ducking, Eden threw his leg out, kicking Asher to the floor. Attempting to move straight on top of his body, Asher rolled out just before Eden landed.

Wrapping his body on top of Eden's, Eden was almost done. Almost.

Asher had left one arm un-manacled. Asher's mistake. One arm was all Eden needed. The bastard underestimated him and what he would do to win this fight.

Reaching his arm back, Eden grabbed onto Asher's shirt and flipped his body over onto the ground. Eden was on his friend before Asher blinked, immobilizing every limb.

"Cheater," Asher muttered under his breath so that only Eden would hear.

During defense classes at Marble Protection, they weren't supposed to use their enhanced abilities. Most men would not be strong enough to flip a man with one arm. So technically, Asher was correct, Eden was a cheater.

Glancing up at the eyes that were now wide open in awe, Eden didn't care that he'd broken the rules.

Jumping to his feet, Eden helped Asher up before they turned back to the students.

Luca stepped forward from the side. He was the third man running the class at Marble Protection this morning.

Eden was learning more than anything. He hadn't run a class before, had done more behind-the-scenes support for their business.

Feeling more and more like his old self every day, he'd decided it was about time he took a more active role in the business. Hell, it was past time.

Turning his head, Eden's eyes tracked Shylah standing with Lexie at the front desk. As her head tipped back and she laughed at something Lexie said, Eden felt himself tighten.

So goddamn beautiful.

Grunting at the elbow that pierced his ribs, Eden narrowed his eye at Asher.

"Eyes to the front, Hunter. You have a question." Asher raised a brow as he spoke.

Turning back to the group, all eyes were on Eden.

Luca chuckled before turning to a gangly teenager in the front row.

"Josh, want to ask your question again?"

The kid looked up at Eden with eager eyes. "How do you get to be so strong?"

"Strong my ass," Asher grumbled quietly.

Crossing his arms, Eden looked across at the kid. "You work hard. But being able to defend yourself isn't just about strength. It's about awareness of the other person. It's about strategy and using what's in your head more than your muscles. You only gain those things from training and experience."

As the kids asked the next few questions, Eden and the guys answered them in depth before they finished the class.

Once it was over, they started packing up the few pieces of equipment.

"Great work, Hunter. I think you'll be ready to take the lead on the next few classes," Luca said, looking up from where he was stacking chairs.

"But fight within the rules next time, asshole," Asher said with a grin. "Or I'm gonna show everyone how strong I am."

"Wouldn't be much to show then, would there?" Eden responded with a laugh, dodging the punch that came his way.

Walking up to where Eden stood, Luca put his hand on Eden's shoulder. "In all seriousness, it's good to have you back, Hunter. We missed our friend. Even if he can be an ass."

All three men glanced up when they heard Mason's footsteps moving toward them.

"Your blood test results came back, Striker." Mason held up the piece of paper in his hand.

Eden stiffened. They'd been waiting for these for over a week, ever since the raid at the old gin distillery.

Asher had woken up the next day back to his old self. His memory of how it had made him feel was vivid. Angry and enraged. He'd described the feeling of the drug like losing all control and being consumed by fury.

"There's a plant that only grows in the Congo rainforest called Agrilla. It's a newly discovered species. It was the largest ingredient identified in Asher's blood. The second largest was animal DNA. They're still working on which one. There were also new components that couldn't be identified."

"Son of a bitch," Asher swore.

Eden clenched his fists. The bastards were injecting people with animal DNA.

"Apparently, if a normal person was injected with that same combination of ingredients, it would likely kill them," Mason continued.

"So, what's our next move?" Eden questioned, arms across his chest.

"We cut off the supply," Mason said sternly. "Wyatt's already looking into where it would be coming in from. The CIA is going to work with us on monitoring what's coming into the country."

"I don't trust anyone outside of our team at the moment," Luca muttered, shoving his hands in his pockets.

"I don't either. That's why I'm hoping Wyatt can locate where the drug is coming in first, and we can stop the supply chain," Mason said, eyes darting to the office and back.

All four men eyed each other in agreement. They needed this taken care of and fast.

The idea that Project Arma could be building an army of genetically altered soldiers, drugged with a rage fueling substance, filled Eden with a fear he hadn't felt before.

"He never would have done that a few months ago, you know?"

Dragging her eyes from Eden to Lexie, Shylah lifted her warm mug of coffee. "Done what?"

"Participate in a class," Lexie responded, watching the guys packing up the equipment. "He always hid away. Only ever came out when he needed to growl at someone."

Shylah's eyes flickered back to Eden as he went to stand with Luca, Asher, and Mason. "I'm glad he's back to his old self."

A part of Shylah still hurt that Eden had been so angry for so long. He was healing, though. Just like she was.

"What do you think they talk about in those cozy mother meetings of theirs?" Lexie asked as her eyes narrowed to the men.

Shylah's fingers tightened slightly around the mug. "Probably the business."

In particular, a program that genetically alters men and is now experimenting on a new drug to send them into a blind rage.

Eyes darting to Lexie, Shylah kept her thoughts to herself.

Guilt always swamped her that Lexie didn't know all the facts of Marble Protection. She was such an integral part of the business but was left in the dark much of the time.

Lowering her gaze to her mug, Shylah kept quiet. It was the guys'—Asher's in particular—place to tell her, not Shylah's.

"Well, I, for one, am part of the business and would like to know."

"Know what?" Evie questioned, exiting the office and walking up to the counter.

Lexie leaned her body over the desk so that her face was only inches from Evie's. "Hey, you're chummy with Luca, go find out what they're talking about."

Evie turned her head to look at the guys for a moment before she faced her friend again. "It's probably boring business stuff."

Rolling her eyes, Lexie pushed off the desk again. "Or top-secret, ex-Navy SEAL secrets."

It was scary how perceptive Lexie was.

Evie's eyes widened for a moment before she gave a tight laugh. "You overthink things too much, Lex. When I look over there, all I see are some sexy, god-like men who would make very good-looking babies."

Lexie's body visibly stiffened for a moment. "You're thinking about having babies already?"

Shrugging, Evie glanced back at Luca, flushing when he caught her eye. "I'm not saying I want them right now. Could you picture little Luca's running around, though?"

Lexie was silent for a moment. "You only started dating Luca a few months ago."

Eyes darting back to Lexie, Evie frowned. "I know. One day."

Lexie turned to Shylah, eyes pleading with her. "Back me up here, Shy. You and Eden are going to wait. Yeah?"

Fiddling with the corner of the counter, Shylah hesitated before answering, "I actually can't have kids." Both women's eyes immediately turned from shocked to sympathetic, so she hurried to add, "It's okay. If the time comes where Eden and I want to start a family, there are options for us."

Shylah and Eden had spoken about it a couple more times, and each time it became easier. Eden had assured her they would find a way to have kids together one day if that's what they chose.

The reality of the situation still hurt, but she had Eden, and dealing with it with him by her side was a million times easier than trying to come to terms with it by herself.

"I'm so sorry, Shylah," Evie said quietly.

"Me too," Lexie added gently.

"Thank you," Shylah said with a small smile. "Honestly though, talk about babies anytime you like. It's a bit hard for me, but the more I talk about it, the more I come to terms with it."

Lexie opened her mouth to say something when Eden suddenly appeared next to her. His soft expression told her he'd heard every word. "Ready to go, Shy?"

Reaching up, way up, Shylah kissed her man on his cheek. "Let's get out of here, my fighting superstar."

"Hey!" Asher shouted from across the room. "Do not commend him for that. The asshole cheated."

Lexie snorted. "How could he cheat, Asher?"

Asher's eyes narrowed before he looked away.

Wrapping his arm around Shylah's shoulder, Eden started heading to the door. "I'll see you guys tomorrow for the next class. Get ready to eat mat again, Asher."

Shylah heard cursing coming from Asher's direction as they stepped outside.

"Did you cheat?" Shylah asked suspiciously.

Eden gave nothing away. "Would I do that, Shy?"

Hell yes, he would.

Laughing, Shylah jumped into Eden's truck, and they headed home.

"What time does your shift start?"

Glancing at the clock, she still had plenty of time. "Twelve. I can drive myself. My car battery's going to die if I leave it sitting around."

"Shy—"

"Eden," Shylah interrupted. "What's going to happen to me

on a short drive to work? You can't just babysit me my whole life waiting for something to happen. I'll be okay."

"It's not babysitting, Shylah, it's making sure the woman I love stays alive," Eden said, voice deepening.

"I'm just going to work, and then I'll come straight home." At the clenching of Eden's jaw, Shylah changed the subject. "Asher looked good. Wouldn't even have thought he got drugged a week ago. I still don't understand why they did it."

"To turn him against us," Eden responded, seeming happy to change the subject. "When he had the drug in his system, he wasn't loyal to anyone. Everyone was his enemy. Everyone was a threat."

Jeez, that's one hell of a drug. "Did the blood test results come back?"

"Yes, that's what our mother's meeting was about." Eden's mouth lifted into a lopsided grin causing Shylah to laugh softly.

"You shouldn't listen to conversations you're not a part of. Super hearing or not," Shylah chided. "What did they find?"

"The drug contained a large quantity of a plant called Agrilla," Eden responded, voice lowering.

"What's that?"

"Not really sure. Apparently, it's native to the Congo rainforest."

"Congo rainforest?"

Before she could ask much more about it, Eden continued, "There were also traces of animal DNA in his blood."

Eyes widening, Shylah thought back to the look she saw in Ben's eyes when he had the drug in his system. A tremor ran down Shylah's spine at the memory.

Eden's hand immediately reached out to give Shylah's leg a gentle squeeze. "You have nothing to worry about, Shy."

Glancing over at Eden, Shylah smiled when his eyes met hers. It was a smile she didn't feel.

If they had given that drug to Eden and his team wasn't around to stop him, many people would be in grave danger. Particularly, Shylah.

27

The best part about being a nurse was that Shylah got to help people.

That look on a patient's face when you were able to provide care and support was the stuff Shylah lived for. Sure, not all days were like that. Some were downright tough. But today wasn't one of them.

Walking out of her last patient's room, Shylah couldn't wipe the smile off her face. Her patient, a young boy and his family, had just received the test results that confirmed he didn't have a tumor.

The tears he had shed with his parents had made Shylah get misty herself. The mother had even hugged Shylah. Not a tentative, chests-barely-touching hug. A huge, body pressed against body, make-you-feel-loved hug.

Breathing out a sigh of gratitude that the beautiful family had received the good news they were hoping for, Shylah headed to the break room for lunch.

Just before she stepped into the room, familiar red hair caught her attention. Stopping in her tracks, Shylah glanced up to see Lexie walking down the hall.

At the sight of her friend's pinched face, Shylah's smile dimmed.

As Lexie went to walk past her, Shylah placed a hand on her arm. Lexie startled before turning to look at Shylah with wide eyes.

"Lexie, are you okay?" Shylah felt a moment of worry that the other woman had been so in her own world she hadn't even seen Shylah standing right in front of her.

"Shylah! Ah, I didn't know you would be here," Lexie said, her gaze darting around Shylah's body before returning to her.

"I work here, Lexie." Shylah felt silly having to remind her friend.

A smile suddenly crossed Lexie's face, so bright it was almost comical. "Of course, you do. I'm just here to visit a friend. She's just down the hall. I'll see you later, okay?"

Walking around Shylah, Lexie took off.

Confused, Shylah stood there a moment longer before pushing into the break room. She had never seen Lexie so frazzled. It was none of Shylah's business, but her gut told her there was more to the story than visiting a friend. Maybe Shylah would mention it to Eden. See if he had any idea what was going on.

Taking an apple from the fruit bowl, Shylah sat next to a couple of nurses. She couldn't quite remember their names. Maybe Sophie and Grace? As her butt hit the seat, both women's eyes landed on her.

"Hey, you went on a date with Doctor O'Neil once, didn't you?"

Brows shooting up, Shylah turned to the woman who had spoken. She was fairly sure that one was Grace.

"Just one time. It wasn't really a date. More just friends having dinner because I was new in town." Taking a bite of her apple, Shylah smiled at the women. She hadn't really made any friends at the hospital. Now that she and Eden were in a good place, she could concentrate on settling into the new town and getting to know her colleagues a bit better.

"Gosh, if I got to go to dinner with him, no way would I let him slip through my fingers. Those big blue eyes . . ." The other woman got a dreamy look in her eye as she stared at the wall in front of her as her words trailed off.

"He is very lovely," Shylah said between mouthfuls.

She wanted to add that he'd been a bit self-absorbed and arrogant all night, but why ruin the dream for these ladies.

"Lovely? The man spent his summer in the Congo saving the monkeys. He's an angel and hottie rolled into one."

Almost choking on the food in her mouth, Shylah's eyes flew to the other woman. "Did you say the Congo?"

Nodding vigorously, Grace leaned across the table. "I overheard a conversation he was having with management. They were talking about his travel visa because I think he might be going back for a short period. He doesn't seem to want everyone to know."

"The man's humble too. Gosh, how do I get him to ask me on a date?" Sophie cooed.

Shylah's hands became clammy as the women's voices faded into the background.

Trent had been in the Congo. And Eden had just told her that the drug being used by Project Arma's main ingredient was native to the Congo. That was too big of a coincidence, right?

"Don't get too ahead of yourself, Grace. The man drives a pickup truck. It's not like he's raking in the money."

The blood leached from Shylah's face. "What . . . what color pickup truck?"

Sophie's brows rose. "Um, maybe gray? I've only seen him in it once."

"He might have multiple vehicles," Grace said.

Shylah's hair stood on end as it all started to fit together.

It had been Trent who had sent her to see the last patient that day. Trent, who had told her where to find the drug that had sent Ben into a blind rage. Trent had also made a big deal about her dating Eden.

God, she'd completely pushed those facts to the back of her mind.

Breaths coming out shorter, Shylah's skin chilled.

"Are you okay?" Sophie's voice pulled her back to the present. "You've gone really pale."

"I, um . . ." The room spun for Shylah as she struggled to speak. "I'm not feeling well. I think I'm just going to go home."

Standing abruptly, Shylah ignored whatever the women said next. Rushing out of the room and to her locker, Shylah rummaged through her bag for her phone.

A whimper escaped her lips when she couldn't find it.

Damn it.

Quickly changing out of her scrubs, Shylah grabbed her bag. On the way out, she mumbled something to the nurses at the desk about not feeling well, then rushed to her car.

Whatever the nurses had said, didn't register. Nothing did. Her eyes were too busy darting around to make sure Trent wasn't there.

Getting behind the wheel, Shylah took off for home. Focusing on the road in front of her required effort. Not stomping her foot on the accelerator and exceeding the speed limit did too. It wouldn't do her any good if she crashed the damn car before she got home to tell Eden.

How had this happened? Trent had been right there in front of her the whole time, and no one had suspected him for a second. She'd seen him every day while she'd been at work. Hell, she'd gone to dinner with the guy.

Maybe she was wrong. Maybe everything was a series of

coincidences, and Wyatt and Evie would check it out and confirm.

Nibbling her bottom lip, Shylah prayed that was the case, even though, deep down, she knew it wasn't.

Pulling into Eden's driveway, Shylah jumped out of the car. At the sight of movement in the living room window, Shylah breathed a sigh of relief.

Eden was home.

Running inside, Shylah shut the door before stepping into the living room.

Lifting her head, Shylah stopped in her tracks, bag slipping from her stiff fingers and hitting the ground.

A slow smile crept across Trent's face as he stood next to the living room table. It wasn't the kind smile she was used to seeing. This one resembled a vindictive sneer.

"As soon as I heard the nurses tell you about my pickup truck, I knew this was the first place you'd run."

Shylah's stomach lurched with fear at Trent's words.

"Heard?" she questioned quietly as her eyes searched the room for her phone.

"Looking for this?" Trent asked, holding up her cell. "Swiping this from your bag was the first thing I did before I headed here. And yes, I spend a lot of my day following you, Shylah. Listening to the things you say, watching what you do. You fool everyone into thinking you're an angel, don't you? Hell, if you hadn't killed my brother, you might actually fool me."

Confusion mixed with fear settled like a stone in Shylah's stomach. "Killed your brother?"

Shylah had never killed another person in her life. The very idea made her sick to her stomach.

Opening a black bag on the table, Trent began pulling items out. "You don't have to act innocent with me. When they first came to me and told me what you did to Peter, I was full of rage.

I wanted to go to you and kill you right there and then. But then they told me what my brother was trying to accomplish. What he'd already achieved. I realized I could finish his life's work and get my revenge at the same time."

Peter? The name sounded familiar to Shylah, but she couldn't quite place it.

"We had different fathers, hence the different last names. Other than being doctors, I always thought we were so different. Turns out, not that different at all." Shylah swallowed at the sight of Trent pulling out a syringe from his bag.

As his eyes lifted to meet Shylah's, she suddenly saw it. The slightest resemblance. It was the eyes.

Terror stabbed at her heart. How had she not seen it before?

Because she hadn't been looking.

"Doctor Hoskin from Project Arma is your brother."

All traces of a smile left Trent's face to be replaced by anger. "*Was*. He still would be if you hadn't shot him in the head."

Reeling back, Shylah frowned. Trent thought she shot Doctor Hoskin in the head?

Shaking her head vigorously, she felt a desperate need to make him understand the truth.

"Trent, it wasn't me who shot your brother. It was Commander Hylar."

A hateful laugh escaped Trent's lips. "You're not going to blame him, are you? Why would I believe that Commander Hylar killed my brother? They were on the same team, Shylah."

"I swear, he shot your brother right in front of me when he found out—"

"STOP LYING TO ME." Shylah jumped at the sudden venom in his voice. Pulling out the last bottle, Trent dropped the bag to the ground. Lifting his gaze toward her, he seemed to calm. "They told me where you were right away, you know. Which hospital, right down to the room number. You were never hidden from us."

Shylah struggled to get deep enough breaths in. "Why . . . Why didn't you come for me then?"

Picking up the syringe, Trent studied it in his fingers. "I got people to watch you. I was waiting for you to go to him, or him to come to you. It didn't seem to be happening. Right when I was ready to give up and just kill you, the feds came up with that stupid plan to plant you in the Georgetown hospital." Shrugging, Trent looked up. "So, we used it to our advantage. Took you, revealed Eden's location, knowing you were listening. And I started working here to set it all in motion."

"You were behind the kidnapping, and . . . and you told me that he was in Marble Falls on purpose?"

Trent smiled again. "Of course. Then off you went like a good girl, researched Marble Falls, you applied for a job, and here we are. I knew I wanted to kill you, but it took me a while to figure out how exactly. I wanted the drug my brother spent his life working on to be part of it so that his death wouldn't be in vain. I also wanted Eden to suffer, seeing as my brother is dead to save him."

Trent's face scrunched like it disgusted him. "Such an unworthy substitution." Trent looked out the window. Someone watching might think he was having a casual chat with a friend. "It just took me a while to come up with a plan. At first, I thought Ben was the answer. You may have noticed I tried to break into your apartment to get your scent, but you'd changed the damn locks."

Shylah's eyes widened. "That was you?"

Eyes shooting back to Shylah, full of disdain, he replied, "Ben was supposed to kill you just after you'd reunited with your precious SEAL. Imagine Eden's fucking heart break. Then he came and saved you though, didn't he? I could have shot you both on the spot. But that's when an even better plan hit me. You killed my brother to save Eden. Now I want Eden to kill you while he's on the very drug my brother created. How fucking poetic is that?"

The excitement in Trent's eyes and voice sent chills down Shylah's spine. He was nuts.

"You're crazy," Shylah whispered, unable to keep her thoughts to herself any longer.

"I prefer the term brilliant. Now, I need you to come over here and take a seat so I can take you through what's going to happen." Shylah's gaze darted to the door, then back at Trent. Reaching behind him, Trent pulled out a gun and aimed it directly at her chest. "Let's do this the easy way, Shylah. The hard way ends with you dying right now, and that's no fun for anyone."

Swallowing, Shylah dragged her feet as she moved across the room. Taking a seat across from him, she looked down at the bottles and syringe he'd placed in front of her.

"This is what's going to happen, Shylah. You're going to make Eden dinner and pour some of this into his wine." Trent held up a bottle with a yellow liquid in it. "He'll get a bit lethargic, but only enough that he's not at the top of his game. There's no scent, so he won't detect it."

Lowering the jar, Trent then lifted the other one, this time filled with a clear liquid.

"Then, later in the night, when you go to hug the asshole, you need to inject this into his bloodstream, just like you did Ben."

My god, if she injected Eden with that, he'd be unstoppable. Shylah fought the rising panic.

"And if I refuse?" Shylah asked, even though she dreaded the answer.

Trent's malicious smirk returned. "I shoot him right between the eyes, right in front of you. Your man may be powerful, but he's not bulletproof. See that camera up there?"

Shylah's gaze lifted to where he pointed in the corner of the room. A tiny camera that was barely visible sat there. You would only see it if someone pointed it out like Trent had.

"I'll be watching everything, and there'll be men that work for me surrounding the house, ready to move at my direction. They'll be far enough away that Eden won't hear them, but close enough to get in before either of you can get out."

Shaking her head, Shylah struggled to comprehend what Trent was asking her to do.

"The man you love, the man you killed my brother to protect, will kill you with the drug you stopped my brother from finishing," Trent spoke the words slowly but firmly.

Shylah had to work hard to stop herself from hyperventilating.

"There's always the chance that he won't kill me." A slim chance, but still a chance.

"Yes!" Trent said, his excitement confusing Shylah. "There is that chance. Which is what makes this the greatest experiment of them all. Is the drug strong enough to overpower love?"

Walking toward the door, bag in hand, Trent turned just before leaving. "Cook a roast, it goes well with wine. I've left a bottle on the kitchen island for you. You've got until eight. If you haven't injected him by then, he'll be dead by eight-o-one."

28

The moment Eden stepped inside his home, he knew something wasn't right. Beneath the scent of Shylah and food and wine was a new scent. New to his home, not new to Eden.

Eyes narrowing, he spotted Shylah by the stove. She hadn't turned toward him yet, even though she would have heard him come in. That alone was a reason for Eden to be suspicious.

Closing the door slowly, Eden took his time making his way over to Shylah, eyes inspecting her from behind.

The first thing he noticed was how ramrod straight her spine was. The next was how still she stood. Unnaturally so.

Placing a hand on her shoulder, Shylah flinched. It was subtle, so much so that you couldn't see it, only feel it.

Eden's worry peaked when he saw her face. Shylah's eyes were wide and her face too pale. There were shadows under her eyes that made her appear unwell.

Shylah smiled, but it was all wrong. Panic flared in the depths of her eyes.

"Hi, Eden, dinner's almost ready if you want to get changed." Her voice was formal, stunted like she was reading from a script. When Eden didn't make to move away, Shylah's heart pounded.

Raising her left hand to Eden's chest, he noticed how badly it shook. "Please, Eden. Can you get ready for dinner?"

There was an air of desperation in her words. Placing his hand on hers, Eden noticed her fingers were ice cold.

What the hell was going on?

Studying her face, he tried to read her but saw nothing but panic.

Someone had been here, in his home, and now Shylah was scared out of her mind but couldn't tell him why. The longer Eden stood there, the more the panic in her eyes intensified.

Bending his head, Eden placed a kiss on her cheek. "I'll go get ready for dinner. I love you."

Shylah's brows pulled together slightly. "I-I love you too."

Were those tears Shylah had just blinked away?

Moving away from her, Eden headed in the direction of the bedroom, gaze darting around, searching for anything out of place.

When he found nothing, he went upstairs and closed his bedroom door. Pulling out his phone, Eden shot a quick text to Mason.

Someone's been in my house. Shylah's scared shitless but can't speak. I want you and the team to get ready for a raid. If you don't hear from me at 2000 hours, come prepared.

Mason's response was instant.

I can get the guys to come now.

As much as Eden wanted to agree to that, he needed to figure out what the hell was going on first. He didn't want to put Shylah in any danger. She was his priority.

No. I need to get more information.

Mason's reply was short.

Done.

His friend knew he would do what he could to get any information about what he'd just walked into while simultaneously ensuring Shylah and his safety.

After changing into jeans and a shirt, Eden re-entered the kitchen. Shylah was cutting a roast, but her left hand trembled so badly the knife kept slipping from her fingers. She was damn close to slicing off her finger.

Sidling up next to her, Eden gently put his hand on top of hers. "I'll cut the meat, Shy."

Pausing for a moment, Shylah slid her hand off the knife and went to take the potatoes out of the oven.

"Sorry I wasn't home when you got back. I was training with Cage. I thought you were working until later." Eyes lifting to Shylah, he studied her for her reaction.

Shylah swallowed before she replied, "They, um, weren't terribly busy at the hospital. Sent me home early." Looking up for a moment, Shylah gave Eden a tight smile before going back to the potatoes.

Eden didn't need to pay much attention to know that that was a lie. Something else had made Shylah come home early. Had someone forced her to leave and brought her back here? Her car sat out front. Was she followed?

Eden wanted to kick his own ass for not being home this afternoon. Maybe whatever was going on could have been avoided.

As Shylah started moving food to the table, Eden watched her from his peripheral vision. It wasn't until she moved the pre-poured wine glasses to the table that he noticed the hitch in her breath.

Transferring the meat to the table, Eden eyed the wine for a moment before glancing away.

He had to be smart about how he handled the situation. There was a reason she was hiding whatever it was from him, and he was betting that it was because one or both of their lives had been threatened.

Sitting down at the table, he watched Shylah's stilted movements as she took the final bowl of food to the table. Her gaze flickered to the top corner of the room one too many times.

Rising from his chair, Eden grabbed the table salt. On his way back, his eyes looked up momentarily, then quickly away.

Motherfuckers. There was a goddamn camera in his house. Someone was watching them, and Eden sure as hell would find out who.

Taking his seat opposite Shylah, Eden analyzed every move she made. "The wine looks good," Eden said, taking in the way her body froze for a moment before her eyes met his.

Pure, raw panic shined through. As her breaths came out quicker, Eden reached under the table to give her knee a comforting squeeze.

Eyes shooting up, she met his gaze. Confusion swirled with fear.

That's it, sweetheart, I'm here with you. I know something's going on. You're okay.

Eden wished he could say those words out loud to Shylah, but he hoped that his touch reassured her to some extent.

Opening her mouth, it took Shylah a moment to form words. "I just thought seeing as we're in such a good place in our relationship now, we should celebrate."

Lifting the glass of wine to his lips, Shylah's sharp intake of breath was the last confirmation Eden needed. They laced the wine with something.

Tipping the glass back, he made sure that it would appear to whoever was watching the camera that he drank when the liquid didn't so much as touch his lips.

Placing the untouched wine back on the table, Eden glanced up at Shylah.

"Cage and I were talking about Project Arma. We still have no leads on the drug that they injected Ben with. We don't know the ingredients or where they originated."

Attempting to push the conversation in the direction of the drug, Eden hoped that by saying things she knew weren't true, Shylah could work out a way to tell him something without saying the words.

Shylah's eyes darted up to meet his for a moment before returning to her food.

Pushing her food around her plate, Shylah wet her lips then looked up at him. "It's okay, Eden. I heard you talking to Mason about how the ingredients of the drug originate from the Congo. I also heard you say that you suspect it involves someone with a medical background in Marble Falls. You don't need to hide it."

Pausing for a moment, Eden considered her words. He told Shylah about the origins of the drug, but they had never made suggestions of who was responsible. She was trying to tell him it was someone with a medical background. The only person at the hospital who had attempted to get close to her was . . .

"Doctor O'Neil is the one who approved me to go home early. Encouraged me to have a nice dinner with you." Another tight smile flashed across her face.

Her eyes darted to the wall clock and back. So, Trent had told her to lace the wine and given her a time limit to achieve something.

"Well, I'm glad you're here now. We're stronger together than apart. And I'm glad you overheard my conversation with Eagle about Project Arma. It's important we're both open about everything that's going on."

A tiny flicker of relief flashed through Shylah's eyes. She knew he understood something was happening. Then her eyes flickered back to the clock, and the worry returned.

Silent minutes ticked by in which Eden watched what little

remnant of calm Shylah had when he arrived home slowly deteriorate. Eden's own eyes flickered to the clock.

Almost eight.

His team would be here soon. That was on the proviso they didn't meet with any trouble on their way.

Standing, Eden took Shylah's hand and led her to the couch. Sitting down, he placed her on his lap.

"It's okay," Eden whispered the words into Shylah's ear. "Whatever happens, we'll be okay."

Shylah's eyes were tortured, her hands clammy on his chest. "I love you, Eden. And I'm glad I found you again. You have no idea how happy you've made me."

Fuck. Shylah was talking like she was saying goodbye.

"Not seeing you every day for fourteen months was the hardest thing I've ever had to do in my life." Her eyes flickered over his face. "Most days, I struggled to breathe, knowing I wouldn't see you that day. My goal, through all the pain, surgeries, and rehab, was to get healthy so I could be with you again."

"And you are, Shy. We're together, and that's the way we will stay." His voice was firm.

A tear rolled down Shylah's cheek. "Everything I did, I did to save you. There's nothing in this world that I wouldn't do to save you, Eden. Even if it meant . . ." Shylah took a few quick breaths while Eden stroked her cheek to calm her. "Even if it meant that harm would come to me."

"No fucking harm is coming to you, Shy." There was no way Eden would let that happen.

Not breaking eye contact, Shylah's body was now trembling so violently that Eden firmed his arms around her.

Damn, eight o'clock couldn't come quickly enough.

Starting to regret not telling Mason to come immediately, Eden no longer cared about information. He needed backup, and he needed it now.

Laying her head on his shoulder, Shylah wrapped her arms around him.

"I'm sorry." The two words were faint. Barely a whisper.

Distracted by Shylah's words, Eden felt the prick of the needle in his arm too late. Reaching over, he grabbed the syringe from her fingers, but it was empty.

Eyes going back to Shylah, Eden frowned, his blood running cold. "What did you do?" But Eden knew what Shylah had done. She'd injected him with Toved.

Immediately, his mind clouded.

Pushing Shylah away from his body, confusion swirled through him. All the small sounds of the night that were normally so clear, were suddenly distant.

Clenching the sofa beneath him, the material tore under his grip. A piercing rage built in his gut, and his heart sped to a thundering speed.

"You need to get away from me, Shylah." The fury was consuming him at an alarming rate. His body itching to move. Harm. Kill. "GET THE FUCK AWAY FROM ME," Eden yelled, voice portraying the anger within.

He distantly heard Shylah running up the stairs, followed by the click of a lock. But the waves of fury that were crashing inside of him were blinding him from everything.

Her. He needed her. He could smell her. She was everywhere. Where the fuck was she?

Eden searched for the scent that was all over him. He was fucking covered in it.

Hearing the thundering of another heart, her heart, Eden moved his body through the house, not stopping to think. Pause. Stop.

29

Shylah's knees shook as she raced up the stairs.

Slamming shut the master bedroom door, Shylah frantically searched the room for something to prop against it. Her heart almost beat right out of her chest at the thought of Eden rushing the door before she could secure it.

It had only taken Ben moments to be consumed by the drug. That meant she didn't have much time. Certainly not enough time to run from the house like she would have preferred. Her key was in her bag and her car out the front, there was no way she would have made it. She had to hide. Pray that help was coming.

Eden had hinted to her he knew something was going on. He must have sent for help. She had held off for as long as possible, but as soon as the hour hand had neared eight, she knew she'd run out of time.

Shylah's gaze paused at the dresser. It might be too heavy for her to move, but she'd try. She had to.

Using all her strength, Shylah leaned against the dresser and shifted it to the front of the door. Eden could easily break in, but she hoped the limited space between the dresser and the bed would slow him down.

Sprinting across the room, Shylah slammed the bathroom door shut, clicking the lock. Eden's growl startled Shylah so badly she fell to her knees.

Ignoring the pain of her body slamming against the tiles, she crawled into the bathtub.

The sound of heavy footsteps moving closer to her had Shylah's blood pounding in her ears. Her whole body shook so ferociously that had she not been sitting, Shylah was certain she would have dropped to the ground.

Please have sent for help, Eden, Shylah prayed as she pushed herself into the far corner of the tub.

The sound of wood splintering in the next room confirmed Shylah's thoughts that no door could keep him out. As more bangs followed, it became clear that Eden was tearing the dresser apart.

Wrapping her chilled hands tightly around herself, Shylah's nails dug into her arms.

Eyes shooting up, Eden kicked the bathroom door inward and stood in the doorway. He was almost unrecognizable. Eyes red with fury, fists clenched so hard that his whole body looked solid. Hard.

Huge. That was the only way to describe him. He was huge and looked about ready to kill.

Taking a threatening step toward her, Shylah whimpered and pushed herself into the wall. Her stomach churned as a wave of nausea hit.

Eden's breaths were coming out hard and fast. He was all predator. And she was his prey.

Moving closer again, Eden bent down and grabbed onto the edge of the bathtub. Pausing, the sound of porcelain and brick crumbled beneath his fingers.

Shylah's terror increased at his incredible display of strength. It was like nothing she'd ever seen.

Hanging his head for a moment, Shylah questioned what he was doing. This was not the same reaction as Ben. Ben had blindly attacked her. Consumed with killing.

"Eden," Shylah whispered his name.

"Get . . . away . . . from me," Eden snarled, the words seemingly torn from his chest. When Shylah didn't move, more of the tub crumbled beneath his hands. "GO!"

Jolting at the incredible volume, Shylah forced her legs to move, pushing herself up and sliding beside him. She made sure not to touch him. The heat came off Eden in waves.

Once she was around him, Shylah ran into the bedroom, only making it a few steps before Eden's strong hands grabbed her, throwing her onto the bed.

Before she could rise, Eden was there, on top of her, the flames of anger flashing through his eyes. His weight rested on his forearms, his body not touching hers. Eden's eyes were a mixture of pain and anger.

He was fighting the drug, Shylah realized. But at the moment, he looked like he could go either way.

"Eden." Lifting her shaking hands, she placed them on either side of his face. Every instinct she had told her to keep her distance. But this was Eden. Her Eden. And she needed him to see her. "It's me, Shylah. You don't have to hurt me." Eden's muscles bunched as his arms bracketed her to the bed.

His hand suddenly moved so quickly, it was a blur. Grabbing Shylah's wrist and pushing it to the bed.

It would bruise for sure, but she knew that he contained as much as his strength as he could.

More guttural sounds emanated from Eden's chest. His breathing quickening again.

Swallowing, Shylah took a breath before she continued,

"Remember . . . Remember that time in the shower. When you told me to never be afraid of you. You swore to me you would never hurt me."

A growl rippled from Eden's chest. Lowering his head, Shylah scrunched her eyes shut, preparing for the pain. Instead, his forehead touched hers.

"I feel so much anger," Eden choked the words out, his voice full of torment.

Shylah's heart bled for him.

"I love you," Shylah whispered, trying to soothe some of the turmoil inside Eden. Moving her free hand to the back of his head, her fingers ran through his hair. "You can fight this, Eden. And I'll be right here with you."

There was still fear lurking inside of Shylah, but Eden was stronger than the drug flowing through his veins. He just needed her help remembering that.

Just as calm was starting to enter Shylah, a growl caused Eden's chest to vibrate, sparking a new fear inside of her. But when her gaze lifted, Eden's eyes weren't on her. They were trained on the door.

"Well, isn't this romantic," Trent sounded, as he aimed a gun in Shylah's direction. "Thank you for testing my drug, Eden. I now know that my work is not complete. The drug must be stronger." Glancing her way, Trent's brow furrowed. "What? You didn't think I was going to let you live, did you? After you killed my brother?"

Eden's body tensed for a moment, and then he launched forward. Before he could reach the door, the sound of gunshots echoed through the room.

Jolting upright, Shylah's gaze zoned in on the doctor's neck. Red blood poured from the wound, as his body crumpled to the ground.

Mason then came into view, stepping over the now still body.

Oliver trailed closely behind.

Breathing a sigh of relief, Shylah started pushing off the bed, only to stop in her tracks as Eden turned to face her.

A red patch on his chest had Shylah's world stopping. Eden was shot.

For a moment, her whole body froze as it struggled to comprehend what was happening, then he dropped to his knees, causing Shylah to swing into action.

Kneeling on the floor beside him, Shylah applied pressure.

A snarl tore from Eden's chest. "Get her away from me. I've been . . . drugged."

Strong hands latched onto Shylah's arms, tearing her from the man she loved. "Get off me. I can help him."

"Shylah, we can handle this," Oliver said as he pulled her away. Realizing he was pulling her from the room, Shylah struggled harder.

"No, Oliver, he needs me, please. I'm a nurse. I can help."

Wrapping his strong arms around her middle, Oliver lifted Shylah from the ground and swung her into his arms like she was a rag doll. "We know how to handle a bullet wound. He'll be okay. You here in the room is too much for him."

Shylah squirmed and wriggled her body, but it was futile. Oliver's arms were like bands of steel.

Eden's snarls were the last thing she heard as she was carried downstairs. Feeling a physical pain that she would be away from Eden while he was hurt, Shylah scrunched her eyes shut.

Releasing a sigh of anguish, she stopped moving her body and let the events of the last few hours settle inside her.

She'd drugged Eden. But Eden hadn't killed her.

"It was me," Shylah whispered to no one in particular. "I drugged, Eden."

God, what if he didn't forgive her?

"I'm sure you had your reasons, Shylah," Oliver attempted to reassure gently.

Entering the living room, Shylah opened her eyes to see Eden's team scattered around the space. All bore blood and bruises and looked like they had just left a war zone.

That's when Shylah remembered.

"Oh god, the men outside . . ." Eyes darting to the window, fear entered Shylah's body.

"We got them, Shylah," Bodie spoke from his place a few feet away. For the first time, there was no smile on his face. Or on any of the men's faces. They looked fierce. Lethal. Like they would take on any man who threatened one of their own.

"Eagle needs some more hands," Oliver said, addressing the men. "Hunter took a bullet to the chest. Missed all vital organs though."

"On it," Wyatt said as he left the room with Kye following closely behind.

Swallowing, Shylah turned back to the other men. Exhaustion weighed heavy, but more than that was the need to know that Eden was okay.

"We'll need to know all the details, but that can wait," Luca said as he stepped forward. "For now, how about I take you to my place, and you can stay with Evie for the evening."

Already shaking her head, her gaze darted back in Eden's direction. "No, I need to stay with him."

"Shylah," Oliver said softly, her gaze drawing up to meet his. "Trust us. He'll be okay. He needs time to rest and recover. You here will prolong that process."

Tears prickled her eyes, but they were right. Jesus, she didn't want them to be right, but they were.

"Okay."

It had been two days, and Shylah still hadn't laid her eyes on Eden. It was torture. Agony.

Everyone had assured her that Eden was doing okay. But if that were the case, why hadn't she seen or talked to him? Just hearing his voice would do so much to settle her frayed nerves.

Exiting the room she had been staying in the past couple nights, Shylah couldn't complain about Luca and Evie's hospitality. They had been amazing hosts, especially because she had been beside herself the entire time.

Each day, without fail, they tried to keep the mood light. Luca had been encouraging Shylah to go outside and get some sunlight whenever possible. Even though all she wanted to do was curl up in bed and wait for Eden to come to her.

Evie, on the other hand, had been shadowing Shylah as if waiting for her to break. Shylah appreciated her attention, but she was more likely to go crazy from Eden deprivation than curl up in a ball and cry.

When Shylah had suggested she stay at the apartment she was still renting, Luca muttered something about women not accepting help while Evie looked at her like she was crazy.

Moving into the kitchen, Shylah fixed herself a coffee. Frowning, she paused when it suddenly dawned on her how silent the house seemed. Normally, the chitter-chatter between Luca and Evie pulled her attention before she made it into the kitchen.

The ringing of the doorbell had Shylah's head twisting around. Hesitating, she waited for Evie or Luca to emerge.

When the room remained silent, Shylah slowly made her way to the door.

Glancing through the peephole, Shylah had to do a second take when she saw who it was. She practically fell over her own feet when she tried to open the door quickly. When she did, Shylah looked up at those familiar gray eyes.

"Eden." She was breathless. It had been two long days.

"Hey, Shy," Eden said, a lopsided grin curving his lips.

The moment that smile curved his beautiful mouth, Shylah couldn't wait any longer. Jumping into his arms, Shylah latched on to him, swearing she would never let go. Eden's arms immediately came up to wrap around her. Pulling her even tighter against his body.

This was where she needed to be every minute of every day, in the arms of the man she loved.

"I missed you," Eden muttered into her hair.

"You have no idea," Shylah whispered back.

She had been close to losing it on too many occasions in the last couple of days. Too close.

Suddenly remembering that Eden was shot, Shylah tried to push her body away from Eden's. "Eden, your wound."

"It's fine, Shylah," Eden said, his arms remaining around her, unbreakable. "I heal fast."

Shylah lowered her gaze to his chest, even though his shirt covered any evidence of a wound. "I want to see."

Walking into the house with Shylah securely in his arms, Eden shut the door after them before moving to the couch.

Sitting with Shylah still on his lap, he leaned back. She tentatively lifted the shirt to see a small bandage on his chest. Slowly moving the bandage down, Shylah couldn't believe her eyes. There, where a bullet had hit his chest only a few days ago, sat a small, circular graze.

Moving her fingers over the wound, Shylah skimmed Eden's skin.

"Holy hell, Eden. It's like this is months old."

A smile pulled his lips up. "Like I said, I heal quick."

This wasn't just quick. This was breaking a damn record, Usain Bolt quick.

Pulling the bandage back into position and his shirt down,

Shylah lifted her head back up to Eden's face. A face that had been in her thoughts nonstop for too long.

"I really missed you," she repeated, lifting her hand to Eden's cheek. "I was so scared for you."

"Not coming here and taking you home yesterday was the hardest damn thing."

"Then why didn't you?" Shylah questioned, genuinely confused.

"I'm not taking any chances with your safety, Shy. I wanted to take an extra day to make certain that Toved was completely out of my system. We don't know enough about the drug yet, and you're too important to me."

Running her fingers down his cheek, she wanted to memorize every inch of this man. "You wouldn't have hurt me, Eden. You proved that."

"No. I wouldn't. You're safe with me. Always, Shy. But we're not taking that chance ever again." His voice was stern as he spoke.

Running her fingers over the place that she'd injected him, Shylah cringed. "I'm sorry I injected it into you."

Taking her hand in his, Eden gave it a gentle squeeze. "You don't need to apologize. You were so damn strong. I knew right away something was wrong, and because of that, I could alert the guys."

One side of Shylah's lips quirked up. "So, me being terrible at hiding something from you saved us both."

"Me knowing you and being able to read you saved us." A shadow crossed Eden's face. "I hate that I wasn't home when that asshole threatened you."

"I feel so stupid that I worked with him every day, and I never realized something was wrong." She could have saved them all this trouble if she'd figured it out earlier.

"Some people are good at hiding the truth. They only show

you the side of them that they want you to see." Eden brushed hair off her face. "It kills me that you were afraid of me."

Lowering his eyes to her wrist, Eden lightly skimmed his fingers over the slight bruising.

"Was this me?" Eden's voice was pained.

Glancing down, she saw the imprint of his fingerprints from where Eden had grabbed her wrist.

Eyes shooting back up to Eden's, Shylah's hand caressed his cheek. "Don't. Whatever you're thinking, don't. You fought that drug and saved my life."

"I hurt you."

Shaking her head immediately, Shylah didn't break eye contact. "No. Trent hurt me. Hurt us. Your strength saved us." Shylah's lips found Eden's. Raising her head again, Shylah looked Eden in the eye. "Thank you. For loving me. For protecting me. Always."

This time Eden lowered his head to Shylah's mouth. Deepening the kiss immediately, their tongues met as Shylah's hands flattened on Eden's chest.

"I love you so much, Eden."

Eden's thumb stroked Shylah's cheek. "Not nearly as much as I love you, Shy."

That was debatable. Shylah didn't argue. Instead, she lay her head on the chest of the man who had captured her heart. The man that she had almost lost.

"Let's go home," Shylah murmured against his chest.

"Our home."

Our home. Shylah liked the sound of that.

30

Asher lifted the table from the floor mat. It weighed nothing in his arms.

He should probably act like it was straining his muscles, but he didn't give a rat's ass about appearances now. Not when Lexie Harper stood ten feet from him, pretending he didn't exist.

A rumble emanated from Asher's chest. Well, he sure as hell existed when he was giving her that earth-shattering orgasm last week.

Moving to lift the next table, Asher's mind went back to the feeling of having Lexie's delectable body beneath him. Moaning and writhing as she reached her climax.

Fuck. He needed to get that vision out of his head.

Subtly adjusting himself so that no one noticed, Asher cursed himself for letting his mind go there while at Marble Protection.

Eyes darting back over at Lexie behind the counter, he noticed her gaze cut to his before quickly averting again.

Damn. What the hell was she playing at?

Usually, their eyes would meet and hold at least a dozen times an hour. It was one of the reasons he always volunteered to be out front. Hell, it was the only reason. She was his reason.

For the last week, she'd barely looked at him. Barely touched him. The frustration was building.

"Something caught your eye? Or should I say someone?" Luca asked, coming to stand next to Asher.

Not in the mood for their normal banter, Asher's voice was gruff. "Leave it alone, Rocket. I'm not in the mood."

Luca put his hands on his hips. "Not in the mood for what? Me, or for Lexie to be avoiding you."

Both damn it.

Even though Luca was his closest friend, Asher never spoke about what he and Lexie had. That was because he didn't want to drag her into a relationship with him. His life was far from safe.

Lexie wouldn't stop, though. Her wanting a commitment had reached an all-time high this last month.

He probably had his friends to thank for that. Seeing Luca commit to Evie and now Eden with Shylah. It had seemed to light a fire in Lexie.

He liked her. A lot.

He was infatuated with the woman, but did that mean he wanted to throw her into the world of Project Arma, genetically altered soldiers and drugs that made you want to kill? *Hell no.*

Experiencing the effects of Toved firsthand had just solidified Asher's decision. The drug was a biological weapon, damn it. Eden may have had the capacity to not hurt Shylah, but Asher doubted he had the same willpower.

When Asher didn't respond, Luca took a step closer to his friend. "You know it's okay to let her in. Tell her about us. We all trust her. You're allowed to have a genuine relationship with her, Striker."

Glancing back over at Lexie's bright red hair and serene face,

Asher inwardly winced at the idea. No way was he dumping all that shit on her doorstep.

"No. I can't do that, Rocket."

Silent for a moment, Luca shrugged. "Then, you need to be prepared to possibly lose her."

Shit. Could Asher watch her walk away? That would damn near destroy him. But it might be better than knowing he messed up her perfect life.

"Whatever decision she makes is her own," Asher said dismissively.

"Idiot," Luca muttered.

Luca didn't get it.

Shaking his head, Asher looked back to his friend. "How's Evie?" Asher asked, keen to get off the topic of Lexie.

Raising a brow at the change of subject, Luca shrugged. "That woman never ceases to amaze me with her strength."

Damn straight. After what she'd been through, she was a fucking warrior.

"We visited Hunter and Shylah last night. Everything seems to be back to normal. Well, their new normal."

"I still can't believe Hunter didn't kill Shylah. That drug is brutal. I wanted to kill everyone in sight. Especially you guys because your scent was most familiar to me." Watching as Lexie dropped some envelopes in a drawer, Asher clenched his fists. "I hope I'm never on it around Lex."

Placing his hand on Asher's shoulder, Luca gave it a squeeze. "Don't underestimate yourself, Striker."

Turning away, Luca had only taken a step before he turned his head back to Asher for a moment. "I almost forgot, Shylah mentioned to Evie that Lex was at the hospital the other week. Said she seemed a bit scattered, and when she saw Shylah, she turned to leave."

"What the hell? Why was she there?" Freezing on the spot, Asher's eyes zoomed in on Lexie.

Was she sick? Ice filled Asher's veins at the possibility.

Eyes flashing to Lexie then back to Asher, Luca's brow lifted. "I think that's a question for your woman."

Not bothering to correct Luca on the "his woman" part, Asher went to the desk.

Screw this "ignoring him" shit. He wanted answers, and he wanted them now.

"Lexie."

Lexie's head immediately lifted at the sound of his voice. An emotion that he couldn't identify flashed over her face before it vanished.

Longing maybe? That might have been wishful thinking on Asher's part. Before he could analyze it, she masked all emotion on her face.

"Hello, Asher. How can I help you this morning?"

Asher's blood boiled at the formality in her voice.

"Lex, can I talk to you for a moment? Maybe in the office."

"Sure, we can talk. But I'd prefer to talk out here." Lexie's distant smile did nothing to settle the frustration inside him.

Fine, if that's how she wanted to play it.

"I heard you went to the hospital the other day. Are you okay?"

The blank mask faded, and anger took its place. "Does no one get any privacy in this town? Shylah shouldn't have said anything. I'm fine, like I told her, I was visiting a friend."

Turning back to the envelopes, Lexie all but dismissed him.

Not deterred, Asher rounded the desk and stood close to Lexie. Too close for a friend to stand, but it still felt too damn far for him.

Lexie's wide eyes flashed up at him. Standing this close,

Asher saw new shadows under her eyes. Her skin was also more pale than usual. Her normal glow strangely missing.

Placing his hand on her back, Asher immediately felt the zing of electricity he always felt when he touched her. "I want to be there for you if you need me, Lex."

Lexie's face immediately changed at his words. If he thought she had looked mad before, that was nothing compared to the fire her eyes were spitting at him now.

"Actually, no. What you want from me is sex, Asher." Her voice rose. He wouldn't be surprised if all the guys in the building had heard, no super hearing needed. "That is something you have made abundantly clear. So, if you aren't going to share your personal shit, then get used to me not sharing mine."

Grinding his teeth, Asher ignored the eyes of his brothers on him. "Lex, you know I care about you."

Rolling her eyes, Lexie turned back to the papers. "Was there anything else, Asher?"

Before he could respond, the door to Marble opened, and Evie strolled up to the desk.

"Hey, Lex, I'm here to take over for the last couple of hours."

"Great," Lexie muttered, grabbing her bag from below the counter. Evie's eyes darted between the two of them, but she remained silent.

Pushing past Asher, Lexie didn't spare him so much as a glance. Stopping at Evie's side, Lexie gave her friend a quick hug before walking out of the building.

Hell no. If Lexie thought they would leave it like that, she was dead wrong.

Storming out behind her, Asher reached Lexie before she got to her car. Grabbing her arm, Lexie stopped but didn't turn, forcing Asher to walk around her.

Dropping his hand from her arm and studying her face,

Lexie refused to meet his eye. "What is going on with you, Lexie? You and I work great together, why are you pulling away?"

Lexie's eyes closed for a moment before opening them. When she did, there was a mixture of exhaustion and fear clouding them.

"You don't get it, do you, Asher? I can't do casual with you anymore. We've been doing it for months, but I want more. I need more." Taking a small step closer to Asher, Lexie's voice lowered a fraction. "I care about you. Like 'give you the key to my apartment, plan a future together' care."

Asher had no words. He cared about Lexie too, so damn much. But he didn't know if he could give her what she wanted. He was a tornado of baggage.

When the silence lengthened, the hurt on Lexie's face was like a dagger through Asher's heart.

Before Asher could blink, all sadness on Lexie's face was masked with anger. "We're done. Please don't come to my apartment anymore. Don't call me. I'm the receptionist at your business, and that's it."

Moving to step around Asher, he latched onto her arm again, not able to let her leave like this.

As Lexie turned, her breathing suddenly changed. That was the only warning Asher got before her eyes fluttered closed, and her legs gave out.

Catching Lexie before she hit the ground, she blinked a few times before grabbing onto his shoulders.

"Jesus, Lex, are you okay? Do you need a doctor?"

Taking a few breaths, Lexie seemed to compose herself before pushing off his body. Asher allowed her to put some space between them but kept a firm hold on her arm.

"I'm fine, Asher. I just haven't eaten." Her eyes flickered to his face again, then away.

"Okay, let's eat."

Standing that bit taller, Lexie's voice firmed as she spoke. "Asher, please remove your hand from my arm."

Slowly untangling his fingers, Asher knew he would catch her in time if she fell anyway.

"I respect your decision that you don't want to make a commitment to me, but you need to respect mine as well. If we can't date, we can't be anything."

Asher wanted to argue. God, he was one step away from throwing the woman over his shoulder and making love to her until she took it all back.

One look at her set expression, and he knew he would not get anywhere. He also didn't want her passing out on him again.

Worry about her too pale features set in again.

"At least let me drive you home, Lex. You just about passed out on me."

Swallowing, Lexie took her keys out of her purse. "I've got an apple in my bag, I'll be fine." Eyes darting to her car door before flicking back to Asher, the sadness returned. "I'll see you next shift, Asher."

Asher remained silent as he watched her climb into her car.

What the hell else could he say? She wanted a relationship, he didn't. There was no getting around that.

Lexie backed out of her parking spot, and Asher watched her drive away.

Whenever she wasn't there, Asher felt hollow. He had to figure out what he was going to do and figure it out fast. Because he refused to lose her from his life. She was too damn important.

ALSO BY NYSSA KATHRYN

PROJECT ARMA SERIES

(SERIES ONGOING)

Uncovering Project Arma
Luca
Eden
Asher
Mason

ABOUT THE AUTHOR

Nyssa Kathryn is a romantic suspense author. She lives in South Australia with her daughter and hubby and takes every chance she can to be plotting and writing. Always an avid reader of romance novels, she considers alpha males and happily-ever-afters to be her jam.

Don't forget to follow Nyssa and never miss another release.

Facebook | Instagram | Amazon | Goodreads

CPSIA information can be obtained
at www.ICGtesting.com
Printed in the USA
BVHW080045130122
625993BV00010B/1441